THIS SECOND CHANCE

ANGELS & EVILDWELS SERIES BOOK 1

D. L. FINN

THIS SECOND CHANCE

ANGELS & EVILDWEL SERIES BOOK 1

D. L. Finn

Cover design by Angie of pro_ebookcovers on Fiverr

Book design by Maureen Cutajar

www.gopublished.com & D. L. Finn

Library of Congress number: 2017910203

ISBN Print: 978-0-9977519-0-1

ISBN eBook: 978-0-9977519-1-8

❀ Created with Vellum

ALSO BY D. L. FINN

Evildwel/Angel Series

This Second Chance (Book 1)

The Button: This Only Chance (Book 2)

This Last Chance (Book 3)

Companion Evildwel/Angel Stories

A Long Walk Home: A Christmas Novelette

Red Eyes in the Darkness: A Short Story

I Wouldn't Be Surprised: A Short Story

Paranormal Thriller

A Voice in the Silence

Other Short Stories

Bigfoot: A Short Story

Poetry

Just Her Poetry Seasons of a Soul

No Fairy Tale: The Reality of a Girl Who Wasn't a Princess and Her Poetry
(Memoir)

Children's Books (middle grade)

Elizabeth's War (historical fiction)

An Unusual Island (fantasy)

Things on a Tree (holiday/fantasy)

Dolphin's Cave (fantasy)

Tree Fairies and Their Short Stories (fantasy)

DEDICATED TO

My lifetime friend, Elizabeth McMaster,
who has inspired me to write about survivors.

CHAPTER 1

They hovered over the familiar woman in the wedding dress. She looked terrified, and on the day that she should be at her happiest.

"You are getting a chance most do not get. You understand that, right?" Zelina asked.

He meekly nodded at her. Her brown eyes narrowed, piercing his soul. She clearly didn't like him—not that he blamed her.

"Good. We are clear. You give Rachael her happy ending. Then you can move on and let go of *some of* that bad you did." Zelina pursed her lips tightly together.

Her pale silver gown flowed around her like an ocean wave ebbing in and out. He never understood how angels' clothes did that yet, at the same time, kept their form enough to cover them modestly.

"I understand, and I'm grateful I've been given this second chance. I won't let you, or Rachael, down. I'll do whatever it takes to make it happen," he replied, more confidently than he felt.

Although it confused him that he was being given this chance, he'd never question this angel. He certainly didn't deserve it and hadn't had a moment's peace since his death. Everything he'd done flashed before him—over and over. He was relieved to have a break from it and a chance to finally do some good, but he was merely a ghost—a soul, or a man without a body. What could he do to take away that expression on Rachael's face?

"Yes, it is a break from your much-earned reflections." Zelina crossed her arms, obviously irritated at him.

He felt his face redden as he nodded back at her. In this form he felt all the physical and emotional reactions he had when he was alive, but stronger. He needed to remember that angels always knew what he was thinking. He had no privacy now.

"I had to watch Rachael make some bad mistakes. I will not do this again; this is too important. You must figure out how to fix this and make your atonement. You know the rules. If I see you doing any harm, I will send you back. This is your *only* chance to do some good. I will be watching if you need some guidance, but I think you will figure it out," Zelina finished, suddenly seeming taller to him.

Her black hair glowed as she put her hands on her hips with her wings fully extended. He never tired of seeing the shimmering, feathered wings that reminded him of a peacock tail. They were beautiful. Under all that splendor, he knew, there was a ferociousness akin to a bear protecting her young. Rachael was her cub.

When her wings were tucked behind her, unseen, Zelina seemed perfectly ordinary. She could walk among the humans unnoticed. She turned her gaze on him again and scowled. She oversaw people like him—the tough cases. He sighed. Zelina responded to his sigh with a smirk. On Earth that look would have infuriated him, coming from a woman. Now it scared him.

A sudden chill ran through him. "Is someone else here?" he asked.

"It is not a someone; it is more of a thing, and it is what you are up against. It has no conscience, unlike even someone like you; your conscience peeked out after your reign of terror. This thing has no empathy, no love—only hate. I cannot hear what it thinks. It is the purest form of evil and is called an *evildwel*. This one has consumed its human—even in death. You had one in control of you, but a part of you remained. Death might have saved you, or you might have fought it off someday. I do not know things like that. What I do know is that this evildwel means Rachael harm. Be careful, and do not disappoint me," Zelina warned, and then she vanished.

In the corner of the room, there was no form for him to make out, only thick, dark mist. Did the evildwel know he was there? He suddenly wished Zelina hadn't left him. He was afraid, yet he was going to do what Zelina requested—not because he had no choice, but because he had a lot of things to make up for. It was time to get to work.

CHAPTER 2

*R*achael's detachment from the image in the mirror smoothing the satin, off-white wedding gown puzzled her. After all, this was the same scalloped three-quarter dress, showing off her newly trim waist, that she'd pictured herself in after seeing it on a *Bridal* magazine cover over twenty years ago. Frowning, Rachael adjusted the tiny yellow roses and baby's breath in her Gibson-styled, lightened auburn hair with her set of pink, acrylic nails.

"Not bad for age thirty-seven and three kids," Rachael tried to reassure the pale image in the mirror.

It didn't work. The urge to rip off the dress and fake nails and make a dash out the back door was even stronger now.

"Why?" Rachael asked the woman staring back at her in the mirror, unaware of her unseen visitors.

Rachael couldn't have asked for a more perfect day. The weather, the gazebo Tony had built for their ceremony, the dress that her mother had spent hours making for her—everything in her life had finally fallen into place. It was perfect. Maybe this was just a very delayed reaction to her first wedding. That was when the strong urge to run out the back door would have come in handy. But if she'd done that, her kids wouldn't be here. Besides, Rachael couldn't compare this June morning to that snowy December day nineteen years ago when she'd stood holding a stale bouquet of faded satin flowers at some nameless chapel in Reno.

Rachael sighed and felt a chill shoot through her, even though the room was over 75 degrees. Stress, she concluded. Careful not to wrinkle her satin dress, she sat in the old maple rocking chair and pulled the handmade pink comforter over her. The comforter had been made by Tony's mother, Nora. She raised Tony alone after his father, Wayne Battaglia, died in a horrible car crash when Tony was barely a year old. Tony knew very little about his father, and his mother had never talked about him to her son. Tony was convinced this was due to grief and never pressed for information. Rachael thought his mother's response, not to tell a son about his father, was strange. One thing Rachael was positive about was that Nora had done a fantastic job raising Tony into the man he was.

Unlike her first mother-in-law, who'd raised (well, at least given birth to) Ed. Tammy kept food on the table and a roof over his head by helping make meth in a lab next door to their trailer. When she finally walked away from that addiction, she turned to others: drinking and pain pills. Tammy always had a man in her life. Some of them helped raise Ed; others didn't. Ed hadn't been sure if one of them was his father. He wasn't sure if his mother knew, either.

After Rachael gave birth to their first son, Eddie, Tammy had confided to her in an emotionless tone, "Al, this man I was seeing, fooled around with little Ed, if you know what I mean. I think he was eight or something like that. I didn't stand for that crap. I kicked Al right out on his ass, I did. I'm glad Ed grew up to like women. Never know which way they'll go after that. You keep an eye on little Eddie Jr., here, so you can have grandkids someday too," Tammy added with a nod, as though she had imparted some heavy wisdom to Rachael. Tammy then brushed her frizzy, bottle-blond hair out of her face and took a long drink from her vodka-scented orange juice.

Rachael had been horrified and tried to talk to Ed about it. He'd refused and made sure his mother knew to never bring that subject up again. Rachael understood he had good reason to be angry. What she didn't understand was why it was directed at her and not at the people who'd hurt him. The one good thing Tammy had done for Rachael and her kids was to stay out of their lives after the divorce. Tammy had even left the planning of her only child's funeral in Rachael's hands. Rachael had been shocked when her ex-mother-in-law didn't even attend Ed's funeral because it fell during happy hour.

The motherly rhythm of the rocking chair wasn't easing Rachael's anxiety. The turmoil she had thought she was rid of when she signed the divorce papers still haunted her. After Ed's funeral a couple of years ago, she thought she had *finally* found closure—guess not. Images from those dark days slammed at her like Ed's fist used to do when he drank too much.

The most predominant image was falling snow. Snow was something Rachael had only seen on TV (until her first wedding) because it didn't snow in the Bay Area, where she grew up. There was one exception, of course (because there always is an exception with everything, Rachael learned quickly), when she was in junior high school. It had snowed for five minutes and melted in even less time.

So when her first soon-to-be husband, Ed, suggested, with his best smile, "What do you say to going to Reno, building us a snowman, and tying the knot?" Rachael had quickly agreed. To be a bride *and* see the snow seemed perfect. Neither Rachael nor Ed had much money; they were both freshly out of high school. So Rachael bought her wedding dress off the discount rack at the local department store. She found a light-silver prom dress at 75 percent off that covered her already bulging belly. They got into his old, beat-up, red Chevy pickup and drove. The snow at the summit was beautiful and magical. When they got to the "biggest little city in the world," it started to snow. She had been convinced this meant they would have a long and happy life.

Ed had a fake ID so he could gamble, and he won big. They went out for a steak dinner at a fancy restaurant at the casino to celebrate and got a room that overlooked Reno. She'd watched the snow fall from the eleventh floor with Ed by her side. She was completely at peace. The next morning, they went to the chapel in the hotel and got married.

Things went downhill the moment they returned home. A few years later, Rachael (who had just found out she was pregnant again) grabbed her two small children and escaped when her husband wasn't home. They only had the clothes they were wearing when they found safety at a local women's shelter.

"What am I doing?" Rachael jumped out of the rocking chair. "This is going to be the happiest day of your life, Rachael, whether you like it or not! This just has to be those prewedding jitters they always talk about." The wide-eyed figure in the mirror didn't look convinced. "Besides, all the important people in your life are waiting for you downstairs! Well, not everyone..." Rachael sank heavily back down into the chair.

Eddie wasn't going to be there, all because of a comment Rachael had made to his girlfriend a couple of months ago.

"If you need *anything*, you can always come to me, understand? My door is always open to you. You have a place to go." Rachael hugged Sasha goodbye before going down to bail Eddie out of jail.

He'd gotten into a brawl at a bar where he shouldn't have legally been. She promised herself this would be the last time she'd help him until he helped himself.

Unfortunately, when Eddie finally got released (and later put on probation), Sasha repeated what Rachael had said. Eddie didn't see it as a sweet gesture, like Sasha did. He caught the intended warning. He cut his family out of his and Sasha's lives—just like his dad had done.

Ed had moved Rachael away from her family right after they eloped. Los Angeles was a seven-hour drive from her family and friends. It was a place Rachael had never got used to living in. But Rachael could be wrong about Sasha and Eddie. He certainly didn't move her away from her friends, and she had no family to cut out of their lives after her parents died, although Rachael could see Eddie becoming more like his dad every day, with drugs, drinking, and stealing, which worried her.

Just over two months ago, Rachael still believed Eddie would change his mind and come to the wedding. He hadn't. Rachael's calls were screened by an answering machine, and her messages were never answered. In one final attempt last week, Rachael tried dropping off a birthday gift to Eddie at his apartment. To Rachael's surprise, Sasha opened the door.

"I'm sorry, Rachael. I must honor Eddie's wishes and not let you in or take the present. It's his birthday, and I don't want to upset him. You understand, don't you?" Sasha offered a weak smile.

Sasha looked like she was coming down with the flu. She was as pale as her white-blond hair. Rachael held back her questions on Sasha's health. It wouldn't help the tensions between her and Eddie if he thought Rachael was suggesting more than the flu.

"Yes, Sasha. I understand perfectly. But if you would just tell Eddie —well, maybe don't tell him I came by. I'll try coming back when he's home. Thank you, Sasha."

"You're right. I don't want to spoil his nineteenth birthd—I didn't mean it to come out like that! It's just that Eddie is cleaning himself up. He wanted one more celebration tonight. Eddie's gonna quit drinking. He brought home some catalogs from colleges to go through. Tomorrow we're deciding where he's going to school. Oh, I forgot about Eddie's cake in the oven. I hope you have a wonderful wedding day. Sorry we can't make it. We'll be in touch soon, but maybe you shouldn't drop by anymore unless you talk to him first— sorry." Sasha quickly shut the door.

Hurt, Rachael climbed back into her blue SUV. She prayed Sasha was right about Eddie cleaning up. Rachael had tried to help him, as had her mother, the counselors, and Sasha—but only Eddie could overcome this. What if that therapist at the women's shelter was right? She said that Eddie, at six years old, couldn't be helped—he was too far gone. Rachael thought the woman was not only rude but completely wrong. Eddie had been in therapy for that first year, after she left Ed. It was fine for a while, until Rachael began to see signs that he might be taking after his dad. By that time Eddie was refusing all help. Ed was coming around and playing the victim card with his oldest son.

Rachael finally had to change the child visitation rights. Ed was only allowed to see the kids on supervised visits, twice a month. She always felt Ed found a way around this with Eddie, but she could never prove it. Eddie was as good at lying as his father. More therapy followed Ed's death, with no results, even with the medications. Eddie always slipped back into his bad behavior, until he was kicked out of school in his senior year—then he moved out.

It was painful to have her oldest son push her out of his life. Rachael sighed as a single tear flowed down her cheek. She quickly wiped it away, right as her mother burst into the room.

"I finished Kelly's hair," Mae announced. "She looks like an angel, and so does her mom."

"Thanks-s, Mom." Rachael hopped up from the chair and rushed to check her hair again. *No more bad thoughts. Today marks the wedding I have always dreamt of,* Rachael thought, staring at the bride in the mirror, who returned her look with a phony smile. "Where's Kelly?"

"She's in the bathroom. Probably fixing her hair exactly like you used to do after I styled it. Like all girls do, I guess." Mae grinned.

"Well, I could use some help. Do you think we should put more flowers in my hair, or less? Should I put the back down, or leave it all up?" Rachael was relieved to be back in action.

"I think you look perfect. I wouldn't touch a thing, except for this." Mae held out a box.

"What is it?"

"Open it," Mae encouraged with a smile.

Rachael ripped through the pink paper. It was a ring box. In it was the 1.5-carat, square-cut diamond set in white gold that her father had given to her mother on their thirtieth wedding anniversary. When he died five years ago, her mother had put it away and started wearing her old gold wedding band on a chain around her neck.

"Oh, Mom! I can't take this!"

"You can, and you will. Tony and I had this conversation a long time ago when he asked me for your hand in marriage. Besides, the Lord only blessed me with one daughter and one son. I plan to spoil them both as much as their father spoiled me. So you have your wedding ring, you are wearing the blue garter, which is also new, and your pearl necklace is borrowed and old. You're set. Now all I have to do is deliver you to that gem waiting for you in your gazebo."

Rachael smiled. Her mother had loved Tony the minute she met him. The fact that he was Italian, like Rachael's father, was a big selling point. For the last four years, she had fussed over Tony like he was her long-lost child. It was such a relief to Rachael that she had fallen helplessly in love with Tony—her mother would have been lost without him.

"Is Stevie dressed?" Rachael asked.

"Yes. I already got some wonderful pictures of him and Tony—I mean, Dad, now. They look so handsome. Oh, I forgot. There's a small box that came for you this morning. A note on it said, 'Open Now.' Bet it's something from your husband-to-be. I'd better get it."

Rachael's mother seemed to float out of the room. Rachael grinned when she noticed a similarity between cotton candy at the fair and her mother in her long, pink gown. That shade of pink was Mae's favorite color. Rachael's dad always said that when her mother wore pink, he always had good luck. Rachael hoped this worked for her, too.

Kelly pushed past her exiting grandmother and straight into Rachael's arms. "Mom! You look so beautiful!"

Thank heavens Kelly had her dad's dark looks, but not his dark moods. She was the most even-tempered of her kids, and also the most stubborn. She tugged impatiently at her pink, rose-covered dress cuffs, which were too short. Rachael's mother swore that Kelly had grown an inch just last week, and she couldn't let them out any more before the wedding. Rachael and Kelly knew the dress was too small. Mae thought of Kelly as perpetually ten years old, but she was fourteen.

"Thank you, Kelly. You look good, yourself. I don't know if I should let you out there; you might take away all my attention," Rachael teased.

"No one will be looking at me today." Kelly shook her head.

"I hope you're right." Rachael beamed at her daughter.

"I am. Where'd Grandma go?" Kelly checked her hair one more time.

Rachael glanced at the doorway. "Grandma went to get a package that came for me this morning."

"Here it is." Mae came back with a small box and handed it to Rachael.

"This isn't Tony's handwriting," Rachael commented. No return address, but it had been sent to Tony's house. No—it wasn't going to be Tony's house anymore; it was going to be *her* house now, too. That was what Tony kept telling her over and over. It didn't seem real yet.

"Well, another wedding gift to add to the rest. Kelly, you'd better go downstairs with your brother for a few pictures. It's almost time for you to lead your mom down the aisle." Mae's soft doe eyes teared up.

"Why don't you open the present first?" Kelly insisted.

"No time. Besides, you need to get downstairs and get things ready. You have a bigger job to do as flower girl since the sick twins had to stay home. Those dresses were so cute on them, too! Can you believe that *both* sets of twins have the chickenpox?" Mae paused for a moment, so Rachael shook her head. Satisfied, she continued. "They should have gotten the shots for it. Oh well, at least Kathy, Patrick, and the boys made it, right? Now scoot, Kelly, and don't forget your flower basket," Mae finished breathlessly, making shooing motions with her hands.

"Okay," Kelly replied with a glance at her mom. She rolled her eyes. Yes, she was too old to be a flower girl, but she was playing along for her grandmother. At least she was head flower girl, they'd joked. "See you downstairs!" Kelly dashed out the door.

"Stay clean," Mae warned, but Kelly was, thankfully, long gone. "What else do you need, Rachael?"

"Nothing. I think I'm ready." Rachael's glance kept returning to the package. "I can't wait. I have to open this and see who it's from." She tore through the brown mailing paper and found a beautifully wrapped box underneath. "Isn't this paper pretty? Look! There are

11

tiny gazebos on the paper. It must be from Tony! Maybe someone else addressed it for him."

"That would be like him. What is it?" Mae tried to peek in the box.

"This isn't from Tony," Rachael quietly informed her mother. Her icy hands shook as she took the gift out of the box and handed it to her mother.

"A snow globe? Who'd send you this? Why, it's—"

"Yes, it's the same snow globe Ed gave to me on our wedding day. It was the snowman he promised me. I thought we got rid of this years ago." Rachael shook her head in disbelief as her heart started racing.

"We did. I helped you take it to the charity myself. It must be another one just like it, a coincidence. Who sent it?" Mae put her hand on Rachael's arm.

Rachael quietly shrugged and took back the snow globe, studying it.

"Mom, something is written on the bottom of the globe. 'Remember.'" Rachael dropped the globe onto the hardwood floor. It cracked open on impact and rolled into a small wooden table next to the bed, decapitating the snowman, and the severed head rolled under the bed. Shimmering goo splattered all over the satin mauve comforter.

"Don't walk in it, honey. You could slip. Thank my pink luck this didn't get all over you! I'll clean this up." Mae sprang into action. "Here, you'd better touch up your lipstick. Your brother, Kathy, and the boys just pulled up—late, as usual. It's eight forty-five already. The wedding starts at 9:00 a.m. sharp. We'd better get down there. Hurry."

Rachael numbly did as she was told and spread pink lipstick over her lips. But her feet wouldn't take her out of the feminine room with its lace doilies cradling the mauve lamps. This gift was a bad omen; her mother's "pink luck" wasn't working. Limp, Rachael sank back into the rocking chair. She watched as her mother dabbed up the last of the fake snowflakes on the floor and bundled up the comforter. Her mood had darkened and filled her body with a foreboding that she hadn't felt in years.

"I'll run this comforter through the wash later to make sure it doesn't stain. Now, you put this strange prank out of your mind. Don't let anything ruin *your* day. Please!"

"But Mom, it's as if Ed..." Rachael couldn't say the words she'd been thinking, that Ed was reaching out from the grave.

"Ed's gone. I saw him myself, in that coffin, where he belonged. But you know, little Eddie might have something to do with this."

"No. How could he know about this globe? I put it in the top part of my closet after he was born for safekeeping. I didn't see it again until I got out of the shelter and picked up those boxes that Ed left in the apartment. Then we got rid of everything that Ed hadn't ruined, and the snow globe was in one of them. We only took the kids' clothes when we flew home with you." Rachael felt like her whole world was crashing down on her.

"Yes, we did get rid of all that stuff. Oh, Rachael, if you hadn't been so far away from me, I could have—you—but..." Rachael's mother faltered for an uneasy moment. "But now isn't the time for all of this. Shame on both of us! There must be a good reason for this. Right now, I don't care what the reason is, or who sent it. No one is going to ruin your day! And none of this 'reaching out from the grave' nonsense. Now, give me a hug, and let's go get you married!"

Rachael smiled and held onto her mother, taking in her floral scent. It was soothing. Mae was right; this wasn't the time. And after today, it would *never* be the time for it again. Rachael and her matron of honor, her mother, hurried downstairs. It was a family wedding, including Ava (who was like her sister), whose job was to play the song Tony had written for their wedding on his new Martin acoustic guitar while Rachael walked down the aisle. Ava began playing the song the moment Rachael stepped on the last stair and entered the kitchen to make her grand entrance out the back door.

Rachael's second wedding began with the oldest flower girl on record (that term had become a personal joke between her and Kelly) leading the procession. Rachael walked slowly down the aisle, covered in red rose petals, with her mother at her side. Not proper—the matron of honor should have led Rachael down the aisle—but Rachael wanted to do this *her* way today. Her brother, Patrick, could've taken their father's place at her side, but he was Tony's best man, and his sons, twelve-year-old Paddy and nine-year-old Sammy, were serving as ushers. At least Rachael hoped they were. She hadn't looked up yet. Couldn't. She felt that if she did, everything would be taken away from her.

"Isn't Kelly sweet?" Mae whispered to her as a couple of *oohs* and *ahhs* came from the guests.

"Like her grandma." Rachael forced her eyes to look up.

Kelly didn't disappear as Rachael watched her stroll ahead of them. Each step was perfect as she left a trail of rose petals. Rachael's eyes watered. Now that she had overcome her fear, tears were going to be the new problem. Rachael was *not* going to cry and ruin her makeup, not with all the cameras trained on her!

Mae squeezed her arm, sending a shock down her body. That was just what her father used to do when he was trying to cheer up Rachael or Patrick. She could clearly picture her father beaming down from heaven in approval at his family. He would have an extra twinkle in his eyes for his beloved wife in her pink dress. Rachael was smiling as they came to a stop at the gazebo.

She sent a silent message. *I love you, Daddy.*

It was time for Mae to hand her over to Tony. She tenderly kissed Rachael's cheek and put her cold hand into Tony's outstretched, warm one. Rachael immediately locked eyes with Tony. Everything disappeared but him.

She felt no qualms about doing this; love flowed through the rose-covered gazebo, the twenty guests, family members, and the priest. Her anxiety forgotten, Rachael had never felt safer in her life, except for when she was little and her mother or father could take her into their arms and make all the bad go away. Before Rachael knew it, she was saying "I do" and kneeling before the priest for the final blessing.

After they shared a shy kiss in front of the guests, Father Michael made the introduction: "May I present Mr. and Mrs. Battaglia."

This was met with clapping and whistles. Tony kissed her again, not as shyly as before. Suddenly, they were crushed by hugs, with Rachael's mother leading the way. Ava got the last hug in.

"I'm so happy for you, Rachael. You deserve all the happiness in the world." Ava sniffled.

"It almost seems too good to be true—" Rachael started to say.

"It isn't. You've earned this one many times over. And don't forget me, now that you've inherited an opal mine named Tony."

"I did." Rachael grinned. Opals were Ava's favorite stone; their fiery colors reminded Rachael of her best friend's personality. She added, somberly, "I'd never forget you. Only you and my parents were there for me when I reached out."

Ava shrugged and then added, with a wink, "Well, it looks like you'll be reaching out tonight and doing some mining." She pulled Rachael into another quick hug and then broke away and grabbed Kelly, who grinned at her mom, into her embrace.

"I believe you owe me a dance, Mrs. Battaglia." Tony claimed his bride.

"I believe I do, Mr. Battaglia," Rachael said. Boy, it sure felt good to be called "Mrs. Battaglia."

Tony nodded to Ava, who rushed back to the guitar. She quickly began playing the song Tony and Rachael had shared their first kiss to, *Before You*. Ava's honeyed voice carried over the microphone and silenced the party. Tony held Rachael tightly, making her feel like nothing bad could ever happen if she was with him. They slowly glided over the backyard's freshly cut grass to the rhythm of the guitar. Rachael couldn't wait to get her high heels off, but for her wedding, she could stand it another hour or so. She was almost as tall as Tony at five feet ten inches in her heels (or "hells," as she liked to call them). Ava had run across these shoes, which went with her dress, last week, and they looked perfect—painful or not.

Tony nuzzled her cheek with his strong, Italian nose, and their eyes met. He was the most beautiful man Rachael had ever seen. His sloping, golden-brown eyes rarely flickered with anger; instead, they were creased at the corners as a sign of someone who always had a smile on his face. His wavy hair was under control today, thanks to some hair gel and Ava, even with the slight ocean breeze. Usually, his hair was endearingly tousled. The only imperfection Rachael could find was a small scar above his right eye, a reminder of a trip over the handlebars on his mountain bike on their third date.

"I love you, Rachael Battaglia," Tony whispered.

"I love you too," Rachael choked out.

Suddenly Tony dropped Rachael into a deep dip. The clicking sounds of cameras filled the air. Rachael caught her breath as she came back up and laughed, only to be dipped again. This time, Rachael had time to look around and noted how nice the house looked with its newly painted white trim from their sprucing-up party a few weeks ago. She was about to pull her glance away when she saw a shadow in the window of the bedroom where she'd just gotten dressed. No, it wasn't a shadow. It looked like a bearded man, but his facial features were darkened or perhaps blocked, like he was taking a picture. Unsure of what she was seeing, a sudden chill shot through her just as her husband pulled her upright.

"I think someone is taking pictures from your bedroom." Rachael glanced around the backyard. All the guests seemed to be accounted for.

"That's because we're such a good-looking couple. They want to get all our angles, and it's *our* bedroom now." Tony twirled her around while the photographer snapped picture after picture until their song ended.

The morning was going by fast under a perfect June sun that pleasantly lit up the worn, dark wood of the two-story house that was to be her new home. Tony's mother, Nora, had been fond of mauve and dark brown, while Rachael had always leaned toward yellow and white. Tony had already suggested a redecorating party when they got back from their honeymoon. He didn't care if the whole house was bright pink, like everything in her mom's house, as long as Rachael was in it. She was so lucky.

When Ava finished her set of songs for dancing, the caterers served brunch. It was a huge spread of eggs, bacon, sausages, pancakes, waffles, French toast, potatoes, egg casseroles, and fruit—all of Rachael's and Tony's favorite foods. Soon it would be time to leave, after a delicate exchange of cake (cramming cake into someone's face wasn't the best of ways to start a life together, Rachael and Tony believed).

The wedding was ending, and the honeymoon waited to begin, even if it meant getting on a plane. Rachael's doctor had given her a prescription to help her through the flight. Her last flight had been to come home with her mother and kids after leaving Ed. She would have drunk her way through the trip if she hadn't been pregnant. Even though it was only an hour and a half, she was almost crawling out of her skin by the time they landed in Oakland. This trip out of San Francisco would be different, Rachael hoped.

Patrick made the toast. "May my baby sister and new brother, Tony, live happily ever after."

Kathy, her sister-in-law, piped in. "At least until you get home from the honeymoon and pick up your kids!"

Kelly loved going to her aunt and uncle's house. She and Kathy both had a love for all things paranormal, especially shows about ghosts and hauntings. Rachael knew they'd have a ghost movie marathon this week. Stevie, on the other hand, had bonded with his uncle. They both loved building things, just like Rachael's father. Kathy had assured her that she wouldn't notice either one of them mixed in with their six kids, who ranged in age from three to twelve years old, especially "whatshisname"—Stevie. Kathy loved to tease Stevie, who was the spitting image of Rachael's dad. He always played along.

They were amazingly tireless parents. Rachael didn't know how they did it, and they made it seem easy, too. She hoped it was something that would rub off on her and Tony. At least Rachael wouldn't have to worry about being away from her kids for the first time since she'd had Kelly.

The next toast came from Tony's only living relative in America, his mother's sister, Lee, who lived in San Francisco. Tony had only been around his aunt during the holidays when he was growing up. She was distant but made a point of making it to their wedding. Her blessing was in Italian, so Rachael didn't understand a word of it.

Aunt Lee had two boys around his age. Tony warned Rachael they wouldn't come to the wedding, and they hadn't. Tony hadn't been invited to their weddings years ago—nor had his mother. His aunt's explanation was that they'd had small weddings.

Tony confided once to Rachael that his cousins acted like he and his mother had a contagious disease.

"Jack and Steve were always polite, but they seemed like they wanted to leave the moment they walked in the door," he told Rachael and shrugged. "I haven't seen them since they graduated from high school. But we do exchange Christmas cards."

Well, with a strange mom like Lee, how could anyone expect the kids to be normal? Rachael thought, studying the woman. *Who wears black to a wedding, anyway?* In addition to her style choices, Aunt Lee sat apart and kept glancing at her watch. She would be the first to leave, Rachael determined. What really held the woman's attention, though, were the upstairs windows. Did she see someone up there too? Maybe it was time to introduce herself and ask. Rachael started making her way to her table.

She smiled and nodded as she passed by guests. She wondered if Tony's father's family had been as odd. They were killed in a helicopter crash right after he graduated high school. They were both teachers, like his father. It ran in the family, even though that was all she knew about that side.

Rachael had almost made her way to Aunt Lee when the woman suddenly stood up and rushed into the house. Was she avoiding Rachael, or did she suddenly have to use the restroom? Rachael sighed. It felt like Aunt Lee was avoiding her, and she understood Tony's comment about being treated like they had a contagious disease. Fine.

Rachael spotted her only other family members. Her mother's rich brother and his wife had moved to Arizona from San Diego (where Rachael's family used to spend vacations at the beach, visiting them). Her uncle and aunt were too busy eating, as usual, to join in the toasts. The remaining people were from work, except for Ava and her husband number two, Tim. He turned out to be the husband who had Ava talking about wanting children. Right now, though, Ava sat, surprisingly quiet, next to Mae. Rachael had thought Ava would say something at the toast, at least a quick joke, but instead, she had smiled with tears in her eyes and raised her glass to her. Rachael reciprocated.

Rachael made her final rounds through the rented banquet tables covered with pink flowers that, of course, her mother had helped pick out. Rachael smiled when she saw that Tony was in deep conversation with Patrick. From the way Patrick was demonstrating air fishing, she knew they were discussing their upcoming trip at the end of the summer. Rachael would then be in this house without Tony, the house his mother had bought after inheriting some money from her late aunt, who had left nothing to Aunt Lee. Maybe that was the issue? Nora had moved her seventeen-year-old son from San Francisco to Rachael's hometown, Pacifica. Tony said once that his only regret was leaving all his friends behind, but his mother was happy from the day she moved in, so it was worth it to him—once he got over the move. It was too bad they hadn't met earlier in life. He went off to school, and she got married, but finally they'd found each other.

Tony said he had never been married because he'd never found his soulmate until he met Rachael. At least, that was the story he told her, and Rachael chose to believe it. Luckily for Rachael, Tony had been a very devoted only child to his mother, and now that devotion passed to her.

Rachael knew she was the luckiest girl on Earth, even if she did have to walk through fire to get to this point. Speaking of fire, Rachael finally released her feet from her hells and watched Aunt Lee leave the party. She already didn't like one of her new relatives. She quickly headed back to her table and sat down next to her husband, who had another glass of champagne waiting for her. She didn't drink it; she'd already had two glasses during the toasts.

Ava came up behind Rachael, startling her.

"Time to throw that bouquet, Mrs. Battaglia."

She heard Tim telling Tony the very same thing about the garter. As soon as Kelly caught the yellow roses and Bob, a teacher colleague of Tony's, caught the garter, their morning wedding came to an end.

Rachael and Tony ran to his truck through a steady rain of bird-seed. Tony's truck had been decorated with a "Just Married" sign in the back window and pencils and erasers tied to the back. Rachael was sure she had Ava and Kelly to thank for that.

She had spent the last few years getting her teaching degree at night while she worked in an elementary school office during the day. She'd met Tony in a night class, but he wasn't a student; he was her math teacher. Now there would be two teachers in the house. She had a job waiting for her at the same junior college where Tony worked and would be putting her English degree to use next fall.

Rachael turned to her kids, who were lined up at the door of the old green pickup.

"I love you guys," Rachael said, with tears in her eyes. She gathered Kelly and Stevie (who was way too big to be called Stevie since making quarterback for the varsity football team this year, but old habits were hard to break) and pulled them into a group hug.

"Hey, don't leave Dad out of a hug," Tony protested.

The new Battaglia family clung together until Mae cleared her throat.

"You'd better get going so you don't miss your flight. Don't worry, everything will be just fine. I'll keep an eye on things. Now go have a wonderful honeymoon, you two. I love you."

"We love you too," Tony said. Another hug.

"Hey. Don't forget me!" Ava threw her arms around them.

"We'd never forget you," Tony said.

"Better not, or I may keep Tootie."

"Thanks for watching her."

"What are friends for but watching each other's cats?" Ava laughed.

Tootie had been Ava's cat to begin with, until they found out Tim was allergic; then the little spoiled cat became Rachael's. Ava planned on introducing Tootie to her new house while Rachael and Tony were on the beaches of Hawaii. Patrick's job, while they were gone, was to move Rachael and the kids' stuff out of her apartment and into their new home. Kathy and the kids were going to clean up the apartment for the next occupants. Mae was going to help not only with fixing up the kids' rooms and getting them settled in, but adding Rachael's stuff to Tony's room. No, no—it was *their* room now.

All Rachael knew was that everything was going to be ready for them when they got back. She didn't have a say in this part, and this was one time when she didn't mind.

"Have a great time, and don't worry about anything!"

"Thanks, Kathy. Let us know how the girls are doing," Rachael responded.

"They're almost better. A few more days, I think. The boys had it at their age, and so did your kids. I couldn't bring them here and take the chance of anyone getting it who hadn't had chickenpox. And I couldn't expose the newlyweds before their honeymoon, since you don't know if Tony's had it."

"Yeah, don't worry, sis, we've got this. Just enjoy!" Patrick added.

"Thanks, guys!" Tony waved.

Kathy's attention had shifted to her phone. *Checking on her girls,* Rachael thought.

Rachael looked for her nephews but didn't see them. They were probably playing video games. Rachael couldn't imagine having two three-year-olds, two six-year-olds, plus the boys, too.

Tony grasped Rachael's hand and winked at her. Time to go.

"Goodbye!" Tony and Rachael said together before he helped her into the truck.

"Goodbye, Mom. Goodbye, Dad," Kelly yelled over her brother. They had accepted him as their father, but not Eddie.

Tony pulled away, honking his truck horn, and then slipped in a CD: *Before You.* Settling her head on Tony's shoulder in contentment, Rachael closed her eyes. This was going to be a perfect honeymoon to top off a perfect wedding. There was that word, "perfect"—only now, unlike her first wedding, she knew what it meant, and she dozed off with a smile on her face.

Her dreams should have been peaceful at this point, but they led her back to her first wedding. She saw herself standing in that pale silver dress, so young and hopeful, next to Ed. She'd only known him for six months but thought she had met her Prince Charming. Then her dream took her to opening the package with the snow globe and watching it break. She opened her eyes, but kept her head rested on her new husband's shoulder as they passed the beach she'd always taken her kids to so they could chase the ocean waves.

Thinking of good times didn't rid her of that knot in her stomach. She'd thankfully forgotten about the snow globe during the wedding. She hadn't even told Tony about it yet. Rachael wondered who would send it to her. And why did they write the word "remember" on the bottom? Then there was that face she thought she'd seen in the window when they were dancing.

She was almost positive everyone was watching them dance. How strange—but not as strange as the snow globe. She wasn't going to tell Tony about this until they got back. She didn't want him to worry. Nothing was going to spoil this week for them. She fell back into a fitful sleep as they left Pacifica and headed for the San Francisco airport.

Rachael was woken out of a dreamless slumber with a gentle kiss.

"Naptime's over. Let the honeymoon begin."

"We're here already?" Rachael sat up and ran her fingers through her hair. She pulled it out of the bun and shook it free. She glanced in the truck mirror and smoothed it down so she didn't look like she'd been in a wind tunnel.

"We are, and, might I add, you look amazing." Tony helped her out of the pickup into his arms. Her bad thoughts floated away as he began kissing her; gently at first, then more urgently. His hands began to slide down past the small of her back.

"Careful, Mr. Battaglia. You could get us arrested if you begin our honeymoon too soon." Rachael pulled away with a smile.

"We have a little time before we need to check in." He guided her back into the pickup. They were rolling around on the truck seat like teenagers when a car pulled into the parking space next to them.

"Now, that's enough! There will be plenty of time for that later," Rachael scolded, sitting up and dabbing lipstick off Tony.

The sour older couple looked at them as though they'd never seen people kissing before. Rachael thought it had to have been a while—

like maybe a decade or two—since they'd even held hands. The "Just Married" sign didn't seem to soften them toward Rachael or Tony.

"Maybe we can finish this in the restroom on the plane," Tony said, loud enough for them to hear.

Rachael stifled a laugh and replied in a fake Southern drawl, "It's a long flight, so when the movie starts, so can we. We don't need that cramped bathroom, honey."

The man was as red as his wife as he slammed down his car trunk and hurried away with their luggage. They heard the woman say to him, "I sure hope those two animals aren't on our flight!" The man nodded as they left.

Rachael and Tony burst into laughter, which they ended with one more kiss.

"I bet those two haven't had that much to talk about in a long while. I sure hope we don't get like that." Rachael smoothed her hair down again and grabbed a bag as Tony checked the pickup to make sure they weren't forgetting anything.

"We'll never be like that, I promise. Besides, we're starting out with more sparks than those two have probably ever seen in a lifetime. No man with a hot chick like you would ever turn into such an old sour-puss as that."

"Hot chick, really!" Rachael huffed like the older lady and walked off in a snooty fashion, with Tony closing in behind her.

"That's why I love you so much, Mrs. Battaglia," Tony breathed in Rachael's ear.

"I love you too, Mr. Battaglia, but look at the time. We'd better get moving so we don't have to run through the terminal to our plane. Truck locked?"

Tony nodded.

They hurried to the shuttle, through screening, and to the airplane that was waiting to take them to Hawaii. Unfortunately, they never got their date on the plane. Rachael's nerves got the best of her when she sat down in her seat. She took the anti-anxiety pill the doctor had given her. She was skeptical, but it knocked her right out, and she fell asleep in Tony's arms. She didn't wake up until he nudged her.

"Rach, look, there's the island through the clouds."

They'd made it! Rachael hoped her mother's pink luck would get them safely on the ground. It did.

* * *

ED WAS WATCHING over Rachael like he was supposed to. He could even see her dreams. How he'd treated her was something he had been reliving since the day he died. He knew the day he married her that she was too good for him. Why hadn't he told her that? Tony seemed to be totally in love with her. Ed understood that, or at least he thought he did. Ed truly wanted Rachael to find happiness, but he had a job to do first. What if Tony wasn't what he seemed? *Could he be part of the problem?* Ed observed the dark entity following along behind Rachael and Tony. It kept its distance from them, but it was never far away.

Ed followed the newly married couple from the airport to their hotel. He pondered over who could have sent that snow globe to her. He knew that figuring that out would help him. Would one of their kids do it? Stevie and Kelly had certainly turned out well, thanks to Rachael. That was apparent at the wedding. That only left Eddie, who wasn't there for his mother. Ed's heart ached when he thought of his oldest son. He had not only failed his wife, but his son. Ed wasn't sure how he was going to make this right.

CHAPTER 3

*H*awaiian music filled the elevator as Rachael and Tony went up. They didn't hear Elvis's smooth voice; they were wrapped around each other. The doors opened at their floor, and they hurried to their room. It had an incredible ocean view, as they had been assured at the front desk, but that seemed unimportant at the moment. They were past ready to get this part of their honeymoon started.

Tony dropped their luggage in front of Room 222 and held up their key card. "Here, Mrs. Battaglia. It is traditional to carry the bride over the threshold." He picked her up.

"The threshold at home, silly." Rachael's giggles were soon silenced as they kissed again, more urgently. Their separate breaths merged into one.

"This is our home for the next week." Tony opened the door.

He kicked their luggage into the room and let the door shut behind them. Gently he set Rachael on the green, orange, and white tropical-flowered bedspread. He smiled at Rachael tenderly and brushed her cheek with his lips.

"I will be right back, Mrs. Battaglia." He grabbed a sign from the white bamboo desk.

"I am not going anywhere, Mr. Battaglia."

He grinned, holding up the "Do Not Disturb" sign, and proceeded to put it on their door. *Good warning,* she thought—and grinned too. Rachael quickly took in their room: a TV, microwave, minifridge, a desk with a green-and-white wicker chair, a small floral couch that matched the bed, an unseen bathroom through a mirrored door, and a sliding glass door that went out onto a small balcony. She could see the ocean from the bed. Perfect. Everything they would need for the week.

Rachael smiled at her new husband as he approached her. His gaze was intense as he removed the guitar-covered shirt the kids had gotten him last Christmas. He tossed it on the ground, never taking his eyes off her. She took in his broad shoulders and the strong arms that had only shown her gentleness and kindness. At thirty-nine years old, he had the body of a man in his twenties.

She beamed at him as she removed her yellow-and-orange sundress under his watchful brown eyes. His chest rose and fell in rhythm with the ocean crashing against the shore. She suddenly felt shy. She was glad Ava had bought her the black lace bra and panty set for her bridal shower, because modeling them now for her husband was worth it. Her confidence increased when she observed how his jeans molded tightly to him. It was obvious how much he appreciated her bridal shower gift. Within seconds his jeans were on the green-carpeted floor. She reached out to him.

He gathered her into his arms, engulfing her in the strength of his scent. She loved how his musk mixed with her gardenia. In fact, she loved how perfectly everything blended with them. She'd found her soulmate. As they pushed together, Tony slowly moved his kisses down her neck. Her body was quivering as she dug her pink fingernails into his thick, brown hair. She was ready to fully be his wife.

* * *

"These are times when we give them privacy." Zelina startled Ed.

"I, uh—I was watching the ocean, not them," Ed protested from their balcony.

He wasn't sure what he was supposed to be doing when this was happening. It was uncomfortable, to say the least.

"I am aware. Come out into the hall."

"The evildwel thing isn't in the room." Ed entered the hall.

"Oh, no. It would not be. Too much love for it." Zelina's face reddened.

"Thanks for showing me what to do." Ed tried not to hear the moans coming from the room.

"I know you thought you loved her. You must know that was not love now, correct?" Zelina's gaze that shot through him like a lightning bolt.

Ed nodded, yet in his own way, he had loved her—just not like he should have.

"You will make up for what you did to her. I could not protect her from your dark side. It is too bad you did not have the sense in life to work on that small, redeemable part of you and let go of all that childhood pain; then, your evildwel might have moved on to better grazing or not even bothered you. This does not happen often. But I suppose that is what studying your life is for." Zelina sighed. "See the evildwel over there? I cannot go near it, but you might be able to get close enough to it to maybe find out who it was. Then maybe you can deal with it. When Mr. and Mrs. Battaglia come out of their room, stay with Mrs. Battaglia. There is a lot you are going to see that you are not going to like. I am almost sorry for you—almost. As the humans say, you sucked. Pay attention. Things are going to happen fast. I will be close by. In the future always give them privacy when they share their love. It is my fault I did not mention what you should do under these circumstances. I apologize," Zelina said, and she was gone.

Ed stared blankly at the ocean, not registering the beauty of it. Instead, he was wondering if Zelina had wanted him to see that: how a man treats a woman he loves, like he should have done with Rachael. He flashed back to when he had a family. He'd always thought he would bring his family to Hawaii, but drugs and drinking always came first. He was a lot like his mother, he realized too late. He hoped he wouldn't have to see *that woman* while helping Rachael. He still had a hard time with the idea of forgiving his mother.

Ed frowned and pushed his mother's face out of his mind. He went back to reflecting on what he had done, instead, like "borrowing" things from other people's houses. He never had called it what it was: stealing.

He had no shame then, but now—he shivered. This evildwel presence was bringing back all those memories he thought he had made peace with. He had to stay focused. *But,* Ed wondered, *how bad of a person did you have to be in life to end up like this after you die?* Ed turned his back on the thing. It unnerved him that he felt a strange kinship with it.

He'd never felt as lonely as he did in that moment. He observed the waves hitting the shore over and over, exactly like his memories were doing to him. He wished he could push all his pain away. Finally, the door opened, and the happy couple exited.

* * *

"COME ON, Mrs. Battaglia! I'm starving. And, by the way, you look beautiful!" Tony held the door open.

"Let me brush my hair! Someone made it look like I was in a wind tunnel. And, by the way, I'm hungry too."

"I like the wind tunnel look on you," Tony teased, making Rachael giggle.

They hurried out the door hand in hand. Rachael felt a chill as she stepped into the elevator and trembled. As wonderful as everything was, she couldn't shake the feeling something was about to go wrong. *No,* she told herself. *Not this time.*

* * *

ED WATCHED THEM ORDER, eat, kiss, giggle, kiss, hold hands, and basically do all the things he wished he had done with Rachael when he was fortunate enough to have her. He had been blind to what he had been given and had taken out all his rage from his childhood on her. She paid for what a terrible mother he'd had. He realized that after she divorced him, but he had still been too stupid and proud to at least ask her forgiveness. What did he do instead? Tried to turn their oldest son against her, because that is what one does to the mother of one's children.

"Yeah, I wasn't her knight in shining armor. Although I should've provided her armor from me. I really hope that what I can do for her makes up for at least some of it," Ed mumbled to himself.

He half expected Zelina to respond. She didn't and was nowhere to be seen. At least Zelina was giving him a chance. He hoped the old Ed wouldn't try to creep back. He hated the weak man he'd been. Only a pathetic coward would attack the woman who loved him. He made that realization while watching his life over and over. It gave him more insight than he knew what to do with. If he could do it over, he'd do everything much differently. That wasn't an option, so he was doing the next best thing and dealing with what he could.

He observed Rachael and Tony walking hand in hand on the beach. They cuddled on the sand and took in a beautiful, orange-and-red sunset. Rachael stopped looking at Ed the way she was looking at Tony soon after they were married, thanks to him. He should feel jealous (the old Ed would have), but he was truly happy for her.

So how to help her? He had no clue. It confused him that the evildwel stayed in the hall and didn't follow them like it had been doing. An alarm was going off inside of Ed. He wanted to go and check on it, but listened to Zelina, who insisted he stay with Rachael. Soon they were back at their door, kissing.

"Great, more hall time," Ed sighed.

Tony somehow got the door open without removing his lips from Rachael's. Ed had to admire that, even though it made him uncomfortable at the same time. He glanced around. The evildwel wasn't there. Tony swung the door open, and the evildwel left their room.

"Oh no. What does that mean, Zelina?"

No response. Ed saw Rachael shiver. "You feel the evildwel's presence, Rachael."

Ed watched Tony enter first, with Rachael behind him. Then Tony gently guided Rachael back into the hall, where she stood, motionless. Ed was about to follow Tony into the room when he saw a familiar face peering around the corner in the hall next to the evildwel. That stopped Ed in his tracks. He couldn't believe what he was seeing. Now he had two people to help. How was he going to do that? He needed to talk to Zelina. Tony went back into the room. Rachael sighed and followed, with Ed close behind her.

* * *

"No one is in here now." Tony checked their balcony one more time and relocked the sliding door.

"Why?" Rachael asked with tears in her eyes.

"I honestly don't know. But we're fine, and that's all that matters to me. We can replace all this *stuff*. We need to report this." Tony put his arm around her.

"I don't feel fine." Rachael tried to take it all in.

Someone had opened their unpacked luggage and taken all their clothes out. They had cut up each garment into small pieces. The scissors had been left on their bed, and their clothing covered the room like confetti.

"I know, but it's going to be okay, I promise. I'll get us another room. Unless you'd prefer another hotel?"

Rachael shrugged. She wasn't sure where she'd feel safe. This felt personal, and she felt violated. She couldn't help thinking it was tied to the snow globe. Someone had it in for them—or her. It certainly felt like Ed was back from the grave, but that wasn't possible. She didn't believe in ghosts or hauntings.

Eddie? She didn't want to believe that Eddie was capable of this. Besides, where would he get the money to come here, and how would he get into their room? She would let the police sort it out, for now.

No point in starting off marriage with her new husband by questioning one of her—no, their—kids.

Tony started talking into the hotel phone, startling her back to reality. "Yes, this is Room 222. Right. I'd like to report a break-in. No. While we were at dinner. No. I'm not sure what's gone, but all our clothes are ruined. No, cut up. The scissors are still here. Yes, we'll wait for the police here. You'll send security up now? Great. No, but my wife is extremely upset to have this happen on our honeymoon. No, no. Yes, of course we want a new room. Thank you."

As soon as he hung up, Rachael exclaimed, "All our stuff! It's all ruined. Yet they didn't take my Kindle or your cellphone. What were they after?" Rachael looked around the room in disbelief.

"No idea, but it looks more like a prank than a robbery to me. Someone sees a newlywed couple and wants to mess with them. But we won't let this ruin our trip. They're changing our room, and I'll gladly take my wife shopping," Tony finished, not meeting Rachael's gaze.

"How did they get in here?"

Tap, tap.

"I don't know, but at least hotel security is here." Tony opened the door.

"Mr. Battaglia?" The older man had a full head of gray hair that matched his wide-set eyes. His docile demeanor didn't help Rachael feel any safer.

"Yes." Tony offered his hand.

"I'm Hank Borders, and I'm part of hotel security. I'm sorry this happened to you. We've never had any issues like this, but I personally assure you that we will step up security and find the person who did this. We'll not tolerate this here." Hank let go of Tony's hand.

"I'm glad to hear that."

Hank smiled. "I'll be talking to all the hotel staff in case they saw something or might have more input for us. Once the police leave, I'll make sure you have all you need in your new room. And I'll have someone move the rest of your stuff for you. It's the least we can do. To be on the safe side, we'll have someone patrolling the halls, especially on this floor and your new floor. It will not happen again." Hank frowned as he surveyed the mess quickly and checked their closet, bathroom, and balcony.

"Yes, well, that's good to hear, Mr. Borders." Tony grabbed Rachael's icy hand and squeezed it.

"Why would someone want to cut up all our clothes?" Rachael finally spoke.

"I've never seen this before at a hotel, and I used to be a police officer. I'll call around and see if this has happened at other resorts. Don't worry, I'm going to figure this out, Mrs. Battaglia. And call me Hank. We aren't formal here in Hawaii. Will you both be okay for a few minutes if I check the other rooms around you? I want to make sure everyone is okay." Hank crossed his hands over his chest, and then he wiped them on his pants, as though he couldn't decide what to do with them, but his eyes were hard and observant.

There was more to him than his pleasant persona. Even though he looked like a favorite grandfather who took you fishing while sharing charming stories about his childhood, Rachael realized he wished he had a gun on him as his hands settled on his hips. His first impression must have helped him solve cases when people underestimated him.

"We'll be fine, Hank. Please call me Tony."

"Good. I'll be right back, Tony. Use the chain to secure your door," Hank warned.

"Done."

Rachael wanted to sit, but there wasn't any part of the room that wasn't covered in shredded clothes.

"This is what I came home to one day, when I was married to Ed. He went through my closet and cut up all my clothes because he thought a man at the grocery store was flirting with me. Don't you think it's odd that this isn't the first time this has happened to me?" Rachael burst into tears.

Tony pulled her into a hug and stroked her hair. "I know this brings back bad memories for you, Rach. It's just a coincidence. I don't believe it was personal or directed at you. I'm sorry this happened, but you're safe with me now. No one will ever hurt you like that again. We'll let the authorities deal with this. I trust Hank to keep us safe from here on out. This was one of those random acts by someone who wanted or needed some type of attention. A hotel full of tourists would be a great place for them to start."

"This morning—" Rachael started to tell Tony about the snow globe when Hank knocked.

"I checked the other rooms. It's all clear. The police are on their way up. I'm sure they'll have a few questions. Then we can get you into your new room. I already have housekeeping making sure you have all you need, along with some complimentary items that will make your stay more pleasant. You'll have an account at the hotel gift shop to replace your clothes," Hank said.

"Thank you," Rachael numbly replied.

The police officers arrived.

* * *

ED STOOD outside the room observing the evildwel. He didn't know what to do. Why wasn't Zelina responding to him? Suddenly, the evildwel and Eddie were gone. Ed checked the room, but didn't see them. *Now what?*

"Come on, Zelina! You must've known."

No answer.

"Great! Now what do I do? Eddie is cutting up his mother's and stepfather's clothes. Why?"

Ed knew the answer, though. It was because of what he'd done to Rachael in a jealous rage. Eddie was repeating his actions to get back at his mom. Eddie had been so young—Ed was surprised he remembered, but clearly he did. It was one of those wonderful parenting moments that Ed could reflect on. The snow globe, though—had he told Eddie about that? Ed had no memory of it, but that didn't mean it didn't happen. Ed had a feeling this would be added to his life's review. He knew he deserved every painful moment of it.

As for Rachael thinking he'd come back from the grave to do this to her, well, what did he expect? She was aware of what an angry jerk she'd married, but now she had to deal with her son acting the same way. Ed had two people to save. He didn't need Zelina to confirm that. The problem was how was he going to change his son and get rid of this misty evil thing?

Before Ed knew it, he was following Rachael and Tony to a higher floor. They walked into a large suite. *Not bad,* he thought. At least something good came from this.

"I WISH it was just us and I could carry you over the threshold again, Mrs. Battaglia," Tony whispered into Rachael's ear as he tightly held her hand.

Hank announced, "Here's your new room. A nice upgrade. Make use of the bar; there will be no charge. I'll be outside all night, if you need anything. I'm sorry for any worry this has caused you, and I'll make sure it doesn't happen again. I'll take my leave now. I know you must be exhausted after a wedding and long flight. Good night, and aloha." Hank shut the door.

Finally, they were alone. It was an amazing room, Rachael had to admit, and it had been a long day. She was exhausted, especially after the police. It was obvious they were suggesting that they had done this themselves to get better treatment. Hank stepped in and straightened that out, thankfully. They were lucky that Hank was at this hotel and helping them.

"What a day, Mrs. Battaglia. We'd be long asleep back at home, with this time change. I think we should get some sleep and see what tomorrow brings us." Tony kissed Rachael again. Even with all that had happened, she found herself responding quickly to the kiss. Tony checked the lock.

"Nice of them to give us champagne. Would you like to open it now or later?" Tony yawned.

"All I need is some sleep. We can drink it tomorrow and watch the sunset from our patio and private Jacuzzi, if that's okay? This room is like something a movie star would stay in. Someone may have tried to ruin our honeymoon, but all they did was get us this." Rachael smiled.

"More than okay. We have a plan, then. Yes, I do feel like someone important when I'm with you. I see another threshold I can carry you over." Tony picked Rachael up.

Even with her bad feelings about everything that happened, when she was with Tony, she felt completely safe. She giggled as he carried her into their master suite. There were rose petals on the bed, where he carefully laid her.

"I'll be right back," Tony promised.

"I will be waiting."

She quickly undressed and crawled into bed. Before Tony came out of the bathroom, Rachael had fallen asleep.

CHAPTER 4

$\mathscr{T}$he morning sun shot through a small opening in the tropical-print draperies, directly hitting Rachael. She was wide awake. Tony was unaffected and lightly snored next to her. Rachael stretched, feeling refreshed, and noted it was 9:00 a.m. (or noon back home). She carefully got out of bed and hurried into the bathroom. She'd missed the two peach-colored shell sinks last night when she fell asleep waiting for Tony. She'd love to have something like that at home.

She continued to study the bathroom. It was beautiful, the same size as her bedroom in her old apartment. Between the amazing sinks was a huge bamboo gift basket filled to the brim with everything she would need. Next to her was a phone and a small TV, but the most amazing thing was the shower. It was the focal point of the bathroom. It was peach, like the sinks, with a seat, lights, and speakers.

"Now, this is luxury." Rachael grinned.

She started the shower and found it was instantly warm, so she headed in. The large showerhead released a steady stream of water that mimicked rain. It soothed her as she lathered in shampoo that smelt of gardenias—her favorite scent and one that she always wore.

This was her honeymoon, and she had a wonderful man in her bed. Her life was perfect—except for a broken snow globe and someone breaking into their room and cutting their clothes.

Was this her punishment for finally being happy? No, she was past thinking like that. She did not deserve bad things happening to her. Not in her past, and not now. She had found her strength after she left Ed, and she wasn't going back to being that fearful young woman. No one was going to take her happiness from her. She and Tony would handle this together, and they'd be happy, she promised herself.

Now, back to this amazing honeymoon, Rachael thought. She pushed a couple of buttons in the shower to see what they did. The first one turned off the white light, and the second button was a blue light. She left the blue light on.

"That's cool."

She pushed the last two buttons with her still-intact fake pink fingernails. One was a heat lamp, which she didn't need, and the other one sent Hawaiian music through the speakers on either side of her. It was amazing.

"Got it all ready for me?" Tony stepped inside with her.

"We have to get one of these at home," Rachael teased.

"That's a very good idea. You know what another good idea is?" Tony asked as the water rushed down his firm body.

"What is that, Mr. Battaglia?"

"Kissing my beautiful wife good morning." Tony gently took her face in his hands and brought his lips to hers. The blue light reflected against the peach walls, making their shadow look like a moving work of art.

* * *

ED HAD BEEN WAITING in the bedroom, but when he saw Tony follow Rachael into the bathroom, he knew it was time to leave their hotel room again. He found Hank outside the room talking to a younger security guard named Charlie.

"I won't be back until tonight. I want someone here by their door all day. Even when they aren't here. In fact, *especially* when they aren't here. I'm going to interview all the employees and check their records. If you have any input to add, please let me know. Here's my number; you can reach me anytime. Have a good day, Charlie," Hank added.

"I will, Hank. You can count on me." Charlie's smile was so huge that it flared his already large nose.

Ed immediately did not trust Charlie, and with good reason, he quickly found out.

As soon as the elevator doors closed, Charlie was on his phone. Ed slid over to see who greasy-haired Charlie was texting.

"Can't help you. There are too many eyes now. I'll lose my job."

The response was from Snowman: "I paid you well. I expect you to help me when I need it. There will be an extra $100 in it for you if you keep me updated on everything. I mean, we aren't hurting anyone playing a silly prank. Besides, Mr. and Mrs. Battaglia got an upgrade from it. Nothing wrong with that. Keep your cool, and don't say anything. Understand? All you need to do is get me a key to the new room. I'll make sure it won't happen on your watch. Text me when they leave."

"Can't promise. Get back to you."

"There will be another $250 if you do, Charlie." Snowman replied.

Charlie started to sweat. Ed could tell he needed the money. He had a habit to support. Ed knew that look. Too bad—he seemed like a nice kid, if he'd just cut off his stringy blond hair. Probably a surfer who just moved here from the mainland. Well, he was when he wasn't at his new job or partying. *How did I know that?* Ed wondered. Maybe it was his build and deep tan.

Or maybe Ed didn't know all the things he was capable of yet. He didn't have to guess who Snowman was. That was his son. Ed worried that Hank might figure out it was Charlie, and then that would lead him to Eddie. Charlie started typing again.

"Will try."

Ed was sure he would. The evildwel was a few feet away from them. Ed moved closer, but it moved away from him as he approached it. He moved fast; it moved faster. *Okay, how do I get close to it?*

"I'm trying to introduce myself," Ed said.

It stopped moving.

"I used to have one of you with me, I'm told. Can I ask what you want with Rachael and my son Eddie?" Ed slowly moved closer.

He continued his dance with it, but it matched his steps. At one point the red eyes became a face. It was a man in his thirties with dark hair and a beard. He had no idea who it was, or if that was what the evildwel looked like. Maybe Zelina was wrong about this thing, although Ed doubted that. He certainly had a lot to learn and even more questions for Zelina.

Then the man in the evildwel frowned, right before he merged back into the mist. Red eyes were watching him now, and a dark mouth smirked at Ed. He knew he was looking at the face of pure evil. There'd be no reasoning with that. He wondered if he could get through to the man he saw inside of it. Ed continued inching closer, and it kept moving away.

The door opened. Out stepped Rachael and Tony, holding hands and smiling. At least they were blissfully unaware of what was going on, for now. When Ed returned his attention to the evildwel, it was gone.

* * *

"Good morning, Mr. and Mrs. Battaglia. I'm Charlie, Hank's day replacement. If you need anything, just ask. I'll be here all day. No one will get past me!" Charlie held out his right hand.

Tony shook the offered hand. "Good morning, Charlie. We'll be gone for the day, going on the Hana drive. My wife wrote down our cellphone numbers in case you need to contact us." Rachael handed the young man the carefully folded piece of paper.

"Hmm...I thought I had it here in my paperwork, but I'm not seeing it. Thank you. Have a wonderful day. Don't worry, your room is safe with me here," Charlie assured them with a large, toothy smile.

"Thank you, Charlie," Rachael said.

He seemed awfully young to be doing this. He had to be around the same age as Eddie, and boy, was he nervous. New?

"I feel better knowing you're on the job. Will Hank be back tonight?" Tony inquired.

"Yes, sir. He's the best around. He was a cop in San Francisco. We're lucky to have him, and I'm lucky to work with him." Charlie wiped the sweat from his brow.

"Lucky, indeed. San Francisco was my old stomping grounds as a kid. Beautiful place. You ever been there, Charlie?"

"No, I haven't, sir, but I'd like to see it someday. I want to get some of that famous chocolate and see Alcatraz." Charlie intently studied their door while picking at his fingernails.

"Yes, the chocolate swirling in those big containers at Ghirardelli always makes me hungry. Of course, it helps that I'm already waiting on the chocolate sundae I ordered." Tony paused and smiled for a moment, but got no response from Charlie, so he continued. "I agree—you can't miss seeing Fisherman's Wharf or the tour of the prison. Make sure you get your tickets for Alcatraz ahead of time. They sell out quickly. There's so much to see in San Francisco, so give yourself a couple of days, Charlie." Tony winked.

"I will, sir, thank you." Charlie smiled weakly while his eyes kept moving. He was unnerving to watch.

"No problem. Thanks for keeping an eye on our room. We'll see you later." Tony squeezed Rachael's hand.

Rachael and Tony stood quietly, waiting for the elevator. Rachael felt Charlie watching them. She wasn't so sure she trusted him, but if Hank did, she supposed he was okay. Maybe he was new on the job and trying to make a good first impression. Hopefully, he'd figure it out soon. She looked at her husband and raised her eyebrows. He smirked back at her. She loved how they didn't need to speak to communicate *that guy was strange.*

As soon as they got into the elevator, Rachael commented, "Nervous guy?"

"Yeah, he was. Bit of an oddball. Unless he's not used to seeing such a beautiful woman as my wife." Tony pulled her into a kiss.

Soon they were lost in each other again, and Charlie was forgotten. Rachael never knew she could want someone like this all the time. Their passion hadn't dwindled from that first moment their eyes had locked. It had been fireworks ever since; plus, it was a friendship. It was hard to explain to anyone, but it was definitely amazing.

Rachael and Tony had one stop to make before they headed out. They needed to replenish their clothes. They quickly found everything they needed. They ended up with three bags of new clothes, which they sent to their room, except for their new swimsuits, a new palm-tree button-up shirt for Tony, towels, and a yellow sundress for Rachael. They needed those for their drive.

"I'm going to put my suit and dress on," Rachael declared, heading into the hotel lobby bathroom.

"That's a good plan. I'll put on my new swim trunks and shirt. Meet you back here."

Rachael dressed in her new, black one-piece suit, which flattered her figure nicely, and threw the dress over it in record time. She glanced into the mirror and added some lipstick before hurrying back into the lobby. She couldn't believe she'd beaten Tony. She was still taken with how beautiful the hotel lobby was. There was a stunning fountain in the middle of the large, three-walled room. It cascaded down lava rocks into a pool filled with colorful koi. There was a fireplace with chairs surrounding it next to the open wall that faced the ocean. The pool below wrapped around two waterfalls.

Between that and the amazing ocean was a walkway. She wanted to make that walk at night after the sunset and then sit on the beach and watch the waves in the moonlight. Maybe check out the mall, too. She could spend the rest of the vacation here at the hotel, no problem. In fact, she was going to suggest that to Tony after today's excursion. Finally, Tony emerged from the bathroom wearing his new red palm-tree swim trunks and shirt with green palm trees silhouetted against the orange-and-red sunset.

"Perfect," Rachael grinned.

"Thank you, and that dress makes you look like an island goddess. Tony grabbed her bag of yesterday's clothes from her.

Rachael rolled her eyes at him and smiled. He grinned. Soon they were sitting in their rented blue Camaro with the top down. Rachael was navigating them to the Hana drive with a foldout map they had gotten from the hotel.

"This is it," Rachael said.

"It certainly is," Tony replied.

"Tony…" Rachael chided him and then giggled.

"I love when you giggle." he gently ran his fingers through her hair.

"Both hands on the steering wheel, mister," Rachael scolded.

"Yes, ma'am!"

They headed into the tourist-lined, green-canopied road after passing a town and houses. Rachael studied the map, finding the perfect place for their first stop. She quickly found a spot that had a bamboo forest and a waterfall. *Perfect,* she thought, and pointed it out as soon as they got to it. She grabbed her cellphone for pictures as Tony opened her door for her. He pulled her into another kiss just as a small white car pulled into the same parking area. They started their hike holding hands.

* * *

ED WAS TORN. He knew he was supposed to stay with Rachael, but he wanted to keep an eye on his son too. He'd noticed Eddie had been following them the whole drive. Ed was worried about what his son had planned as he watched Rachael and Tony walk into the tropical forest. They stopped and took a picture—even got someone to take a picture of them. Rachael seemed safe. The evildwel hovered around their rental, not following them.

"I think it's better I watch the evildwel now, Zelina. Rachael seems okay. If I don't hear back from you, I'll take that as a go-ahead," Ed tried.

Then he waited a moment. Nothing. So maybe it was up to him now, as long as he didn't break any rules. He sat, unseen, next to his son in his white car. The car wasn't clean, like a rental. That worried Ed. His son might have borrowed this ride without asking, but his biggest concern was how he could get through to Eddie and stop whatever plan he had. His son was texting away. Talking to Sasha, he saw. She *what?*

"It's going to be okay. I'm not upset; I'm happy. I've always wanted a kid. You take care of yourself. When I get back, we'll go see that first ultrasound together. With me in college and working, it'll be fine. I'm cleaning up right now. Things will be different. I'll control myself from now on. I promise. Love you," Eddie typed and hit send.

"Shit!" Eddie yelled. "A damn baby? How did she let that happen? Another mouth to feed! How can I change if shit keeps happening? Dumb bitch!"

He punched the dashboard, making his hand bleed. He didn't notice. Eddie sat there for a moment. The evildwel grew bolder and came closer, even with Ed there. Ed went toward it. It skirted around him to get to Eddie. That was when Ed saw it: a separate dark mist around his son, lighter and smaller, but still there. Eddie got out of the car with a knife and headed to Rachael's car. Ed thought quickly. Maybe if he focused on that rock, he could move it and distract Eddie. His experiment was a success. It was a direct hit. It stopped his son in his tracks.

"What? Who threw that?" Eddie looked around.

There was no one there to answer. Eddie started forward, rubbing the red mark on his arm.

"Maybe it was a bee or something."

Ed did it again, hitting him on the back of his neck just as a tour bus pulled in right next to the Camaro.

"Shit." Eddie grabbed the back of his neck and headed back to his Honda.

He opened a silver flask and took a long drink. Great, now Ed had to worry about his son drinking and driving. He knew he'd done that himself, many times. Well, until that time when it killed him. Ed had never felt so helpless, and Zelina still wasn't responding to him. He sat next to his son, helplessly watching him drink, until he saw

Rachael and Tony heading back to their car. Ed had stopped Eddie from what he was going to do this time, but would he be able to next time?

Ed made the decision to stay with Eddie. They followed Rachael and Tony. Angry music screamed from the vibrating speakers while Eddie kept drinking from his flask. Next, he lit up a joint with the windows rolled up, and soon the car was smoky. *Maybe this will calm him down,* Ed hoped. It didn't. Eddie pulled over and watched Rachael and Tony take pictures of a waterfall from a bridge. *They are so happy,* Ed thought.

"I'll get you, bitch!" Eddie took another swig from the almost empty flask. "You shouldn't have remarried. You belonged with my dad. You tore us all apart, and then he died. All because of you. You'll pay." Eddie smiled.

It was a smile Ed knew too well. He saw the dark mist increase around his son. Then he saw the evildwel behind them smile through its mist. He wondered if they could merge into one. Ed winced. He hoped not.

"Come on, Eddie. Fight it. I wish you could hear me. I love you, and I'm sorry for everything I did to you and your mom. Please don't hurt her. She loves you." Ed hoped that what he was saying would get through to his son.

For a moment Eddie paused. His mist lightened for a brief instant. Eddie turned to where Ed was sitting, confused.

"Come on, Eddie. Be strong, like I wasn't," Ed pleaded. He tried to reach out to his son but felt a shock from the mist or weaker evildwel. Eddie jumped.

"What the—" Eddie shook his head. "Some good Hawaiian smoke, I guess." Eddie laughed and took a drink from his flask.

Ed wished he could throw the flask out the window, but he would be breaking rules doing that and lose the chance to help by taking away Eddie's free will.

"She looks like a dog in heat. What would Dad think about that? I know he'd be proud of the snow globe and all their clothes. She isn't going to find her happy ending with me around, right, Dad?" Eddie held the flask up. "I'm taking care of business for you. I'm doing you proud."

Ed shook his head. "No, Eddie. You don't understand. I was wrong. You're wrong. Your mom deserves to be happy, and so do you." Ed started sobbing.

Eddie looked around, confused. "Some weird vibes around here. Must be near a damn burial ground. Ha! Okay, Battaglias, lead the way."

Eddie suddenly flashed back to when his mother had held him after he'd fallen and skinned his knee. He remembered the love he felt with her for a moment, before the darkness took over again.

"Good," Ed said to his son. "I can get through to you with memories. I'm not giving up. I'm declaring war on your evildwel. You're next, bigger evildwel—you hear me?"

They followed the blue Camaro through the narrow road filled with twists and tight turns. Ed nervously watched his son cross over the middle of the road more than once. Luckily, no one was coming.

Ed flashed back to his own mother driving down the street when he was eight years old. He was crying.

"Quit your bawling. I kicked the bum out. If you weren't so girly, Ed, it wouldn't have happened. I can't have their attention on you and not me, right, son? A girl has got to be taken care of, you know? Now I must put myself out there again and find another man to help us," his mother had said, taking a long drink from her cold red coffee cup. Ed knew that cup contained more than coffee because it always did—80 proof and cheap, like his mom.

The pain Ed had felt in that moment from his mother's words had been worse than what any of her boyfriends had done to him. Even at that age, Ed knew his mother should have protected him from being used like that. But she didn't. She never did. It was never brought up again.

If Ed had seen that man after he grew up, he would've killed him. Now, though, Ed wasn't sure if there would be anything left of that man if he was inside one of these things. Was his mom in one as well? Well, if either of them were, Ed hoped it was punishment enough for what they had done to him. What always nagged at Ed was how many other children that man might have done this to. He shook his head. Knowing about evildwels put a new perspective on how he looked at people, and if they weren't trapped in one of these monsters, well...

Ed glanced at his son. He wished he could tell Eddie what had happened to him. Maybe he would understand more. Rachael never brought men around who would hurt his son. She was the mother that his mother had never been. Ed had that much to be grateful for. Yet it was he who managed to hurt his son in new ways—not physically, but mentally. Ed gave his son a perfect example of how to be angry and bitter and hate the one person in the world who loved him most. Eddie was a fast learner. He'd learned to repress his emotions with drinking and stalk his mother on her honeymoon while his pregnant girlfriend sat at home alone. Neither woman deserved his son's anger.

Ed was determined to stop his son from making the same mistakes he had. Even though things had happened to Ed as a boy, he continued using that as an excuse for his actions to others. *Better late than never, figuring that out.* It only took his death and years of watching his life over and over to get there. Zelina was right—he did suck, but no more.

They pulled into a large parking lot at a beach. *Time for a swim?* He knew his son had other ideas from the knife in his hand.

"This'll be the perfect place to do it." Eddie watched them go to the beach.

"Not if I can help it, Eddie." Ed watched the evildwel follow them to the beach.

Ed sighed. He couldn't stay with Eddie and his weak evildwel if the main evildwel didn't stay. Ed realized the bigger mist was always where bad things were happening. A bus pulled in.

"Good. That should stop Eddie from doing anything stupid now." Ed exited the car to follow the main evildwel. He glanced back at his son, who was drinking from a new flask. Ed hoped Eddie would pass out, or else Ed would have to figure out a way to prevent Eddie from driving back—without breaking the rules.

"I'm going to follow Rachael, Tony, and the main evildwel and leave Eddie alone in the car with his misty buddy. Any input, Zelina?" Ed waited. "Nothing? Then I'll carry on."

* * *

"THIS LOOKS KIND OF STEEP, Rach. Be careful. I can help you down. Get behind me." Tony surveyed the path to the beach.

"The write-up said 'easy access,' too. Oh well, you lead the way, and I'll grab you if I need, or...or even if I don't need to." Rachael giggled. She had never giggled this much in her life.

"And I'll never complain when I am grabbed by you, trust me. Looks like there aren't too many people here, even with the number of cars in the parking lot."

"There are other people with us on this island, really?" Rachael stuck her tongue out at Tony.

Tony winked at Rachael. "Exactly." He kissed her. "I wonder if all the stories I hear about having sex on the beach are true?"

"Guess we should find out."

"Yes, we should. I'm sure we can find a nice, secluded spot some-where where we won't get arrested celebrating our honeymoon." Tony pulled away and headed to the beach.

"You lead, and I'll always follow."

"I feel the same way about you," Tony replied.

They quickly found a spot to set up their towels on the pristine black beach. Off to their right was a rock formation. This spot was more like a lagoon, and there were more people than they thought. Rachael wondered if there would be some privacy if they hiked into the rock formations. Or maybe they could swim out and find a private spot. Gee, she was thinking like a teenager! That thought made her giggle again.

"Ready for a swim, Mrs. Battaglia?" Tony was unbuttoning his shirt.

It took her breath away to watch. He was amazing, and he was hers. She hoped her body, after three kids, did the same for him. He had always acted like it did. She glanced at her belly. She was proud of how hard she'd worked to get it trim for her wedding, but she would gladly give it up to have a child with Tony. Even though he was going to adopt her children, he left it up to her to decide if she wanted any more.

She would never forget what he said to her: "I have you, and that will always be enough. A child would be a blessing, but then, so are your kids."

Then he'd added, "I'm not the one having to push a watermelon out of my body," and laughed. He also put adoption on the table.

Rachael worried she might not be able to have more kids after having such a hard time with Kelly. She had experienced some complications and an early labor. She was convinced they were being watched over that day, and the moment she heard Kelly's cry, she knew they were. The nurses rushed her new baby out of the room before she even got to see her. She remembered the look of relief on the doctor's face that day. It spoke for all of them. After a couple of weeks at the hospital, Kelly was ready to come home.

Rachael knew that the stress she had been under hadn't improved after leaving Ed, but with Tony, there would be no stress involved. Either way, they were sure going to try this week, she decided.

"I'm ready to swim, Mr. Battaglia."

She removed her yellow dress to reveal the daring black one-piece suit she'd bought that morning when they restocked their clothing. A two-piece would have worked better on a honeymoon, she realized. She'd get one later.

ED WATCHED Rachael and Tony run into the ocean, holding hands. They looked like the couple running off into the sunset together happily ever after at the end of a sappy movie. He wondered if they knew how lucky they were to have that. Well, he had a feeling Rachael understood. Ed noted the evildwel was off to their side, keeping its distance.

"What are you doing?" Ed asked the evildwel, who didn't respond.

As soon as they got into the water, the evildwel suddenly took off. It went back up the hill toward the car. Ed glanced at Rachael and decided she was safe with her husband. He hurried after the evildwel. By the time he got back to the parking lot, it was too late.

"It was a trick to lead me away," Ed sighed.

Eddie had done his handiwork on Rachael and Tony's blue Camaro. All four tires were flat. Eddie was in his car laughing, with his evildwel growing darker by the moment. The larger evildwel joined Eddie in the car. Ed was torn as to what to do. Something told him he needed to stay with Eddie, that Tony was going to take care of Rachael.

"Okay. I'm going to stay with Eddie and not Rachael. Any feedback, Zelina?" Ed waited for her to appear or answer. "I'll take your continued silence as a yes, then."

He got into the car with his son, who was slurring his words. He should've stayed and tried to disable his son's car, rules or no rules. Now all he could do was helplessly watch him. Any distractions on Ed's part now could be fatal.

"That'll show thh-hat itt-cchhh." Eddie started the car and headed to the exit just as a patrol car pulled into the lot.

Ed watched the patrol car approach the blue Camaro with its flat tires. The officer was already calling it in. Rachael would have help by the time she got back to the car. Good. Ed drove off with Eddie, who was at least driving better than he was talking. Maybe they would make it back safely. Ed knew he'd driven like this many times and gotten home in one piece.

* * *

"MAKING love to your wife on the beach, check." Tony pulled Rachael into a kiss.

"Making love on the beach wasn't as bad as I heard it was—in fact, it was pretty amazing. Just a little sand in unwelcome places. Nothing a swim in the ocean won't fix. Race you to the water," Rachael said as she pulled her bathing suit back on.

"Right behind you." Tony quickly had his swim trunks on. They both jumped in the water. As soon as they swam out, Tony asked, "Do we have any snacks?"

"We do. Chips *and* water!"

"Well, after that I need some real food. What do you say we find that little town we read about and try their burgers? We can always swim more after." Tony winked at Rachael.

"Yes, a burger sounds great! And you are certainly determined to conceive that child, Mr. Battaglia," Rachael joked, blushing.

"I'm only determined to spend every waking moment making my wife happy. If having a child together does that, then that is what we'll do. You do know you don't have to have any more kids if you don't want them, right? I'm happy no matter what we do." Tony pulled Rachael into a hug and kissed her.

"I know, and that's one of the many reasons I love you so much. So, that's a yes to more baby making? Great. Because I stopped taking those pills I've been on since I had Kelly. I wanted to surprise you. Since we're all married now and stuff, I'd love to bring a child into a loving house like ours. It would make everything so perfect, don't you think?"

"I can't argue with any of that. And if you want me to keep trying with you, well, I suppose I could." Tony laughed.

"We don't even know if I can still have kids. But yes, it's worth a try, I admit." Rachael swam away. She beat Tony to their towels and drank her bottle of water. They ate the bag of chips in mere seconds. Time to go get their burgers.

"Come on, slowpoke," Rachael called.

"I can't keep up with my young wife."

"You are doing well so far," Rachael replied. The smile fell off her face as she got to the top of the trail to the parking lot. "Our car..." was all she got out as Tony caught up to her.

There was a tow truck next to their car and a man working on their tires.

"What's going on?" Tony asked the repairman.

"Is this your rental? You are Anthony Battaglia?"

"Yes, but what happened?"

"Strangest thing. The police were patrolling this lot and saw your car with four flat tires. I've never seen them do this before, but they called it in. Someone from the department then called the rental company. It was your rental company that called me. I was already on this part of the island. The best part of this is I had four tires with me that matched your car. So I hope you don't mind, but I went ahead and fixed it so I could get to my next call. Like I said, the strangest thing I've ever heard of. You must have someone watching over you. The police calling the rental company and them calling me—why, something like this usually takes hours to resolve. Yes, very odd."

"Odd, indeed," Tony replied.

"So the car is okay?" Rachael asked. "They didn't see who did this, did they?"

"I didn't talk to the police directly, so I can't tell you that. But from what I can tell, someone slashed your tires. I fixed them all up. In the three years I've lived here in Hawaii, I've only seen this happen once before. If you'll sign here, I'll be on my way. Wait, maybe you should start the car, just to be safe." the man handed a clipboard to Tony.

Rachael grabbed the keys from Tony and started the car. It was running fine. Tony asked about burgers.

"Right down the road to the right—best burgers on the island."

"Thank you." Rachael waved.

"You're quite welcome," he said. A message blared from his dashboard. "Sounds like there's an accident. I'd better go. Aloha, and drive safe."

"Thanks! Aloha," Tony called.

They were alone.

"So someone cuts up all our clothes, and now they cut up our tires. Don't tell me you don't think that was directed at us." Rachael got out of the car. She had no intention of driving back after seeing how narrow the road was.

"Okay, even I admit that someone randomly cutting up our tires, after our clothes, seems personal, but, like the tow truck driver said, it happens. We can't assume it's related. I'll point out again—we are still safe. In fact, we were lucky that it was taken care of for us before we even knew. Someone seems to be watching over us."

"Well, I think it's more than a coincidence. We need to be more careful until we figure it out." Rachael put her seat belt on.

"I can agree with that, but we can't let it ruin our honeymoon, either."

"No, it isn't ruined," Rachael quickly added. She would let this go for now, but she wasn't going to let down her guard again. "Let's get that burger."

Soon they came to stopped traffic. There was the accident the tow truck driver had gotten the call for. He was backed up to it.

"I wonder if they're okay," Rachael commented.

"I hope so. Can you see anything?"

"There's a white car down the side of the hill. I can't see anyone walking around besides the police. Wait, someone is in the car. I can't see their face, but they look young."

A police officer came up to her window. "It'll be a moment until we can get the life flight in here."

"Thank you. Is the person okay?" Rachael asked.

"Well, the young man is alive, but not responsive. You have a good day, and drive safely. Aloha," the officer said and moved to the next car.

They watched the helicopter lower a board and the men extract the boy from the mangled car. They quickly covered him, so she couldn't see his injuries. Rachael was glad for that. She watched as the board, with the young man on it, was hoisted up to the helicopter. Right as it got to the top and they were ready to pull the board inside, Rachael swore she saw her ex-husband next to the poor boy. She shook her head to clear it. Must have been because she was thinking of him so much, with all the things happening—including the sliced tires.

She didn't say anything to Tony about it. Not that she didn't trust him, but it was just too crazy to believe or say out loud. Their mood was dampened on the way to get their burgers and for the rest of the drive. It had gone from one extreme to the other since they had been in Hawaii. The only consistent thing was her husband's love for her and her love for him. Rachael shook her head and then laid it on Tony's shoulder and fell asleep as they drove back to the hotel.

CHAPTER 5

*R*achael and Tony found their hotel room unguarded. Rachael waited in the hall while Tony carefully inspected the room. When he gave the all-clear sign, she entered. Now they could continue with their evening plans. She hoped this new development—no one at their door—meant that their room break-in had been resolved. She hurried to take a shower while Tony called room service to order their dinner.

She frowned as she started the shower. There were still unanswered questions about their slashed tires and clothes and the snow globe (which she knew she still needed to tell Tony about). Her hope was that they had nothing more to worry about, and the car tires really were a random thing, but part of her knew better because of the snow globe. *Someone is attempting to ruin our honeymoon,* she thought. Well, they weren't going to.

She rushed back into the bedroom to grab something to wear from the bags left on their bed from the early morning shopping spree. Nothing fancy, since they were eating in the room. She heard Tony ordering today's special. She smiled as she peeled off her new black bathing suit and hung it over the towel bar. Nothing could or would break them apart. They had each other. But there was someone who didn't see that—or perhaps they did, and that ended up being the problem.

Tony had earned her trust over the last four years. She knew she hadn't made it easy for him, either. She smiled. The man that had seemed too perfect at first—was perfect for her. They'd figure this out. She stepped into the warm water. Not bothering with the lights or music, she let the rainy flow soothe her worries away. She stayed in the shower longer than she had planned, and her hands pruned. She'd fully expected Tony to join her and waited a little bit more, enjoying the soothing peacefulness.

* * *

TONY SET THE PHONE DOWN. He heard the shower still running and smiled. He hurried to fill their ice bucket and add their champagne to it.

"Plenty of time to join my wife before the food arrives," he said out loud and grinned.

He pulled off his shirt and was heading to the bathroom when someone knocked at the door.

"Good timing," he mumbled to himself and threw open the door.

Hank looked around. "I just got here and wanted to check in with you. I'm sorry Charlie left his post. He's no longer under our employ. Unfortunately, I think he's the link to whoever broke into your room. He must have caught on that we figured it out, because he left before he could be questioned. Your room okay?"

Tony glanced behind him, glad he could still hear the shower going and that Rachael didn't have to be a part of this. He stepped outside the room and shut the door. "Our room is fine, but Charlie? Well, that kind of makes sense. He was a nervous young guy. I feel like if he was in on it, he was working with someone else. He didn't seem like the type to come up with this on his own, you know?" Tony glanced around the hall.

"I agree completely. I think he's the one who let whoever did this into your room. What I've found out so far is he came into some money two days ago. Money he didn't make here. He was flashing several $100 bills around. Not very smart, and I doubt he has any left. Still leaves us with who paid him. So is everything okay?" Hank asked again.

"Nothing happened here in our room, but we had an issue at the beach. Someone cut up all our tires. The driver who fixed our tires thought it was a random thing that happens in isolated parking lots from time to time. I wondered, though. Odd thing, too—it was called in by local law enforcement. Then the rental company was contacted. They got the guy out to fix it before we even got back to the car. Pretty amazing service." Tony smiled with a slight shrug.

"What? You're telling me your tires were cut now? I don't think that's a random thing, Tony. I'd be careful, if I were you. Someone is out to send you a message, and it doesn't seem to be a good one. I'll add that to my report and continue looking into this. I'll pass this on to the local police, though I doubt they'll consider the two things related, but I do."

"Well, honestly, this has bothered me. I don't want my wife worrying about this on our honeymoon. If you could keep this to yourself for now, I would appreciate that."

"I understand. I will do that, unless more happens. Then I think it would be important for her to be in the loop," Hank replied, flipping through his small notepad.

"Okay. I can agree to that. Here's our food—that was fast! Thank you, Hank. You are going way above your job for us." Tony opened the door and stood aside for the man to roll the tray in the room. Boy, it was lucky he hadn't joined Rachael in the shower...

"I may be retired from police work, but I can't change how I think or see things—even running this hotel. And I can plainly see something's not right here. Enjoy your evening."

"I will, thank you." Tony shook Hank's hand.

"Just call when you're done, and we'll pick up the trays," Pika said.

Tony reached into his pocket and pulled out a $10 bill. "Thank you," he said, but saw Hank shaking his head at Pika.

"No tip necessary, sir. My pleasure. Aloha." Pika hurried off.

* * *

RACHAEL PLACED a flower behind her ear as the final touch to her hair. She quickly applied mascara and lipstick. No need to go overboard with makeup tonight. She checked her nails. Still on, and her toes had the same color. Not even a chip yet! She was ready. She tugged at her yellow shorts. They were a bit shorter than she was used to, but she knew Tony wouldn't mind—in fact, he'd picked them out. Her white tank top was the first touristy purchase, which informed everyone she was "Just Mauied." They needed to get some more shopping done for the kids, her mom, and Ava. They had plenty of time, though.

She heard Tony talking to someone. The food was here. She rushed out and smiled at her husband. He looked amazing without his shirt.

"I'm starving!" Rachael exclaimed.

"Your dinner awaits, and, might I add, you look amazing in those shorts," Tony said with a sly grin.

"You did pick them out."

"Yes, I did. I have good taste. Oh, and Hank is back. I guess Charlie got fired. They think he's the one behind the room break-in. So, sounds like they have that completely under control." Tony sat at the small table Pika had set up for them overlooking the large balcony and the ocean.

"That young man—Charlie? Really? I mean, he had a weird vibe; but still—I guess you never know, huh?" Rachael joined her husband.

"Nope, you don't. Hank is staying, to be on the safe side, in case anyone else was involved. I trust Hank, and I'm glad he used to be a police officer. I'm beginning to wonder if he's more than the security guard or hotel manager. I think he might own the place."

"That makes sense, the way he took control and gave us all of this. You may be right, but how could an ex-cop afford a nice oceanfront hotel?"

"I bet he inherited it. We should look it up later and see," Tony shrugged and popped the cork on the champagne.

"Should I grab my phone?" Rachael smiled at her new husband.

"Let's do it together, after dinner."

"We will." Rachael sat at the small table overlooking the ocean.

"Yes, we will." Tony gave her hand a quick squeeze.

Rachael grinned at him. She knew he didn't mean looking up Hank on their phones. "The dinner smells amazing." Rachael took her first taste. "Wow! This tastes as good as it smells. What is it?"

"The guy called it moonfish, or opah. Freshly caught this morning. He even knew the guy who caught it." Tony took a bite. "Wow, you're right—it's great."

Dinner went by in comfortable quiet as the waves crashed against the shore. Even though they were surrounded by people milling about the walkway and beach and in the ocean, Rachael felt like they were on their own private island, sitting in their hotel room. The sun was starting to set as they finished.

"One of the best dinners I've ever had," Rachael said.

"This is a four-star hotel, where we are paying for a two-star stay. We should come back here for our anniversaries."

"I agree. Isn't the sunset beautiful?" Rachael watched the sky filled with pinks against the blue and a few scattered clouds reflecting off the ocean. *This is what heaven would look like,* she thought.

"Not as beautiful as my wife, but a close second." Tony sipped his champagne. "I forgot to order dessert, sorry. But I seem to remember a box of chocolate-covered macadamia nuts by the couch."

"I couldn't eat another bite. Maybe later."

Tony smiled and stood up. He quickly peeled off his clothes and slowly stepped into the hot tub on their private balcony. Rachael smiled back. She preferred the view of her husband over the sunset. She was in no hurry for him to submerge in the bubbling water. Without taking her eyes off him, she quickly dropped her new clothes on the balcony next to her husband's. She wasn't concerned about her hair or makeup as she slid into the warm, bubbling water. The flower behind her ear fell out, whirled around, and then was gone under the bubbles.

"Glad you could join me." Tony wrapped himself around her.

"Always."

Soon the water was sloshing onto the patio. They didn't notice. They didn't notice the pinks blend into orange and then fade away behind the ocean horizon. They didn't notice that the ghost in the room had left, either.

* * *

ED SIGHED. He hated leaving his son at the hospital, but he had to check on Rachael and Tony. They were fine, obviously. He studied Hank, who was sitting in the hall. He was looking at something on his cellphone. Ed was convinced he was one of the good guys.

"He is." Zelina startled Ed.

"Why haven't you replied to me?" Ed demanded. He regretted his tone when her eyes narrowed.

"You did not need my input, Ed. You had a few things you needed to see and work out for yourself. I kept an eye on Rachael when you were not around, trust me." Zelina crossed her arms.

Ed gulped and didn't know how to respond. He had so many questions. "I don't know what I should be doing," he finally said.

"I know," Zelina replied.

Okay, now what? That wasn't an answer, Ed thought.

"No, it was not. But I have already said you have a lot to make up for. You have not broken any rules yet, so I have not stepped in, although I worried for a moment with Eddie. You did the right thing, letting him make his own choice."

"Hardest thing I've ever done," Ed admitted.

"I imagine it was."

"He's doing this for me."

"I know he is. I want you to note that Hank was like you." Zelina changed the subject quickly. "He lost his family because of his anger. They also went on to be happy, but unlike you, he made amends and changed. He makes it his life goal to help everyone he can. He does what he can and leads a sober life. One of those people he helped owned a chain of failing hotels. This was one of them. When he died, he left Hank the hotel. He has built it up into a fine place to stay. Do you not think? I try to make sure things go well for him because he is one of my responsibilities, like Rachael."

"It's beautiful. I didn't know you took care of the living, too," Ed admitted.

"I do a lot of things you do not know about, Ed." Zelina grinned for a moment before continuing. "Although I am not sure if Hank will be here when Tony and Rachael make it back. His children might have to take over the hotel for him soon, if he does not sell it, that is. Not sure. Hank has repaired his past the best he could. You could stand to learn from him, but you do not have time. Go to Eddie, right now—and yes, I know he has his own evildwel. It is still very weak. When they are alive, you see the dark mist around them, not like the other one. It is not attached to any living human now. And Ed, your mother did not, nor does she now, have an evildwel around her, but your molester, Al, did, since you were wondering. It is time to forgive them both. What happens to them is out of your hands."

"Oh, yeah, well...I did wonder about that. I almost wish my mom had been under the influence of an evildwel. So that was all just her?"

"Yes, it was. Not all bad and misguided people have an evildwel. There is so much you do not know about her, and we do not have time to go into that now—what she had to do to survive. It explains how she is, but, as you know, does not excuse it. Forgiving them will help you, not them." Zelina shrugged.

Ed sighed. He knew he had more work to do to get to that point.

"Just know I am keeping an eye on things here with Rachael and this evildwel. This is when it will get tricky, but ultimately you must help them both. First, start with Eddie. Only you can get him to change. If he does, he lives. If not, he will end up like you." Zelina looked grimly at the evildwel.

"Are you saying I can make a difference in whether my son lives or dies?"

"Yes, that is exactly what I am saying. He is in a coma. Reach out to him. Push his evildwel away by finding him. You stay with your son until this is done. He needs you now."

"Wait, what about Rachael? Now that Eddie is out of the picture, she will be okay, right? I mean, no one will hurt them now?"

"No, I do not think you understand. Eddie was not the problem. He only made it worse—or really, it made him worse. Depends on how you look at it, but Eddie will have a daughter who needs him. That is important, but that powerful evildwel still wants what it wants. Eddie is a part of it, but not all of it. When Rachael and Tony get back home, the real battle begins. The evildwel has been having fun up until this point. After that there will be some prices to pay. Now go. I have this for the next few days. If we are not here when you are done, come back to the Battaglia house. I have a feeling you will understand more soon. Good luck, Ed." She added, "Do not fail your family."

"I still don't know what I'm supposed to be doing." Ed threw his hands up in frustration.

"I know, but that does not matter."

"Well, okay. I'll try to save Eddie."

"I would do more than simply try, Ed."

Ed frowned, unsure how to reply to that. Zelina didn't comment further, so he quickly left to be with his oldest son.

* * *

ZELINA SIGHED and shook her head after he disappeared. *Maybe I have finally saved this family, if he is strong enough. Just maybe.*

Zelina stayed with Hank. She was proud of him. Most humans could not make the changes he had while they were alive. He was one of a kind. She would be glad to have him on her team. Unfortunately, that time might come sooner than she hoped, if things played out the way it appeared they might. It was unfortunate that she could not help Charlie, but he had had more chances than most. He did not even have an evildwel inside him; this was all him. She was not sure how the evildwels chose their victims. Maybe they would still come after the boy. She did know that Charlie had one more chance, but if he made the wrong choice or was not stopped—well, she saw no other options for this boy. He would have a lot to answer for.

Zelina was always hopeful. Sometimes her hope was misplaced, but that never deterred her. If this ended badly, perhaps with Charlie in jail, maybe she could get through to him, finally. She would have his lifetime to try, if only an evildwel did not interfere. So much depended on two bad-decision-making men. One scenario was Hank getting married, but the more likely one was him dying within the next few days. She sighed and radiated some of her light to Hank and put her trust in Ed. More depended on him than he realized.

ED RUSHED to his son's bedside. He was glad to give his son his full attention, although he wasn't sure what he could do for him. Eddie had monitors and tubes all over him. He wasn't breathing on his own. It looked grim. A doctor came in and checked him, listening to his heartbeat, checking his eyes, and shaking his head at the nurse.

"The longer he stays in this coma, the less chance he has to come out of it. Sad, such a young man like this—drinking and driving. We see it all too often." Dr. Max sighed. "I don't like this part of my job. What makes this sad is no one knows who he is."

"We've made calls. No one is reported missing. The car was stolen, and there was no ID on him. I'm sure someone will come looking for him." the older nurse smiled.

"I hope so. There's nothing more we can do for him with this head injury. It's amazing the rest of him is in good shape. It's up to him and God now. Keep him comfortable, and we can take comfort that his actions didn't hurt anyone else. Call me if there's any change. And keep someone monitoring his brain patterns, too. I refuse to lose another young person to drinking on my watch. Keep the police out. Unless they plan on filing charges, they have no reason for being here. Stealing from an ex-cop. Not the brightest of kids, but I'd rather see him serve a couple of years in jail than dead. Keep me posted." The doctor looked at his watch, shook his head, and pushed back his black-rimmed glasses.

"I will, doctor; but did you hear who the ex-cop was? It was the guy who owns that Wily Hotel. I overheard the two officers talking. They said he doesn't want to press charges. From what I hear, he's big on helping whoever he can." the nurse adjusted Eddie's sheets.

"I've heard of him. Helped some hard cases the last few years. There are some good ones on this planet, right, Blanche?"

"Right, doctor."

"Well, keep me posted, Blanche. I have a date with my wife. Our thirtieth wedding anniversary and one year living the island life. Big night." Dr. Max winked.

"Will do, doctor. Happy anniversary on both accounts."

"Thank you." Dr. Max hurried out the door.

An ex-cop who owns a hotel? It couldn't be, Ed thought, but he knew it was. Eddie stole Hank's car? If Eddie gets out of this, he must make amends to Hank, too. *If,* Ed thought. *So many coincidences.* Or maybe there always were, and he'd never noticed.

"Come on, Eddie, fight this. Wake up."

Ed noted again that the dark mist around his son lightened when he spoke affectionately. Like the other evildwel Ed was dealing with, this new one wasn't a fan of affection. He was sure this was important to know, but was not sure what to do with that bit of information yet.

"Eddie, it's Dad. I'm sorry for the things I did to you. Please let me make it up. Let me show you how sorry I am and how good your mom is. You have it all wrong, Eddie. I was the bad guy."

He saw a young face looking at him.

"Eddie?" Ed stood up.

Only Eddie was still in a coma, with all the machines beeping in rhythm. Nothing had changed, but he could see his son's face. He wasn't dead, but he was locked in that dark mist. Ed knew what he had to do—he had to get him away from that thing. Before Ed put any more thought into it, he jumped into the mist. That move surprised the evildwel, and it reacted too late in trying to move away from him. It was a direct hit. Ed was inside. He was immediately hit with icy pain. Ed screamed until his voice was hoarse. He pushed down the pain and fear and moved toward the center. In the middle was a face —his son's.

"Eddie!" he reached out for him.

"Dad?" Eddie asked, obviously confused in the dark mist. There were no red eyes watching him, like the other one. "What are you doing here? I'm not dead, am I?"

"No, Eddie. You're in a coma. I'm trying to get you to wake up."

"Wake up? Wake...wait. I remember driving. Yes, I was following that bitch. You would have been proud of me." Eddie puffed up and smiled.

"Don't ever call your mother that again. You have it all wrong. I was the bad one, not her. You must stop trying to punish her. Please. I'm trying to fix it. I was wrong in what I did to you and your mom," Ed pleaded.

Eddie's eyes widened, and his jaw dropped. Ed knew Eddie had never heard his father say anything good about his mother. The mist was lightening. Was the evildwel leaving Eddie? This was going to be easy. Ed kept talking.

"Eddie, listen to me. Since I died, I've been watching all the horrible things I've said and done over and over. I have changed, and I've learned a lot. I regret so much, and I'm being given a chance to help your mom and you. An angel named Zelina is helping."

The mist darkened again, and Eddie smirked at his father. "Okay, you expect me to believe you are my dad and there is an angel named Zelina helping you? That everything I've thought my whole life is wrong? I don't think so, old man. You need to leave me alone. Get out of here!" Eddie finished, screaming.

Ed felt the air grow heavier by the second. This wasn't going to be as easy as he'd thought. He wondered if he could win against this thing.

"I will not leave you this time. I'm going to stay here with you, even if that means I'm stuck in this misery with you. I'm going to show you what love looks like coming from me. Your mother certainly has shown you. Too bad you didn't pay attention, but you will now." Ed tried to move close enough to touch his son. "Trying" was the key word, because it seemed like he wasn't getting any closer to him.

Eddie looked puzzled for a moment, before his eyes narrowed. "You have no idea what it was like to have to hear how horrible you were my whole life. That I was exactly like you. Therapist after therapist. They all gave up on me. Mom was there, pretending to care, but I knew she hated me because I was like you. She only loved Stevie and Kelly. That left me alone. All I could do was be what you taught me to be. You made me this way, old man. So, yes, go deal with that. Listen to those words over and over. Watch your life again and again. I don't care."

Eddie finished in a voice so low that Ed could barely hear him. It was like it was fading away or maybe fading back into the evildwel—into the numbness. Eddie's eyes shut. It had to be a shock to have to confront himself again, even for a few moments. Ed waited patiently. He wasn't leaving without his son.

Ed inched closer to his tuned-out son. The pain made it almost impossible to even move. That didn't stop him. Ed felt like he was being ripped apart. Maybe he was, but at least he was trying to help. He got within inches of touching Eddie. There was air in this dark place where you could hear, but there was no light, no goodness, at all. It was a dark, empty place full of hate, and he was going to pull Eddie out of it. He reached out and grabbed hold of Eddie's arm. Pain shot through his hands like they had been sliced off with a knife, but he didn't let go. Ed knew that if he did, Eddie would be lost forever.

Ed couldn't talk anymore. The weight of the evil kept his voice inside. He had been in this place before, but Zelina had been there for him when it had abandoned him in the moments before his death. Ed had wanted to be saved, though—did Eddie? Ed wasn't sure. Hate was powerful.

Ed tugged at his son. It was like trying to pull a house off its foundation with his bare hands. But in the place he was now, maybe that was possible? He wished he knew. Ed continued pulling, but dark memories started flooding his mind. He felt that his son was not engulfed in a numbing peace. That had to be a good sign, but it also meant Eddie's memories were pounding him too, trying to get both of them to give up. *No thanks,* Ed thought. He had no intention of letting the darkness consume him again, although having his feelings go away was attractive, but he wasn't going to let anything control his actions. This parasite was not going to feed off him or his son anymore! He knew there were empty promises, along with empty peace, for the privilege of being its pawn. Ed wanted no part of it. He had learned too much to go back. He fought and pulled. There was more to life than that empty existence, and he wasn't giving in.

Ed wasn't sure how long this went on. Hours, days, weeks? He kept fighting and pulling, inch by inch. At the same time, memories of hitting his ex-wife kept coming. The fear and pain in her eyes were because of him. He meant to love her, but he hadn't known how. More than once, his grip on Eddie almost slipped away. He shook his head. *No,* he reconfirmed, he wasn't going back. He stood tall and strong and pulled. He forced different thoughts into his head. He thought about how happy Rachael was now, how good his kids and his grand-daughter were, and what he was fighting for.

That worked for a while, until Eddie's images started coming at Ed. Eddie watching his dad hit his mom. How afraid he was. Eddie wanted to help his mom, but he loved his dad, too. In the end he chose the stronger one—his dad. It got worse from there. Eddie slipped and finally hit Sasha. Ed watched Eddie promise to never do it again. He also heard him warn Sasha not to make him mad like that, just like Ed used to do with Rachael. Ed refocused those dark thoughts on good things like Sasha and Eddie's new baby. All Ed could hope for was that the good would cross over into Eddie's thoughts.

He shivered and kept pulling on his son. He started to notice people coming and going from the room: doctors, nurses, and he thought he saw Hank, too. Time was a blur. Sometimes the room was dark, and sometimes there was light coming in from the window. None of that mattered in the evildwel. Only the pain and darkness did. Yet Ed hung onto his son with all the love he had, and he found there was a lot of love to tap into. He saw

Kelly's sweet face and Stevie's smile. He thought of a new baby coming into that family. It would be loved. He loved his children so much.

Finally, the mist was fading. Ed felt stronger. The evildwel that had his son was losing. *I love you, son,* Ed thought over and over. He focused all his energy on pulling his son free. He set his feet and pulled and pulled. At the final tug, both fell out onto the bed. The empty evildwel floated in the corner of the room, a mere mist of what it had been, and then it was gone.

Ed had done it, but Eddie wasn't out of his coma. His eyes were still shut, and all the machines chirped away. His son was like him, but not. He had a hold of his son's soul while his body fought to live. *Now what?* Ed thought as he pulled his son into a hug.

"Dad? How? What happened?" Eddie hugged his dad tightly.

"You were in a place much like I was. Controlled, fearful, and angry. It's called an evildwel. It feeds off your negative emotions, but it's gone now. You have a chance. I thought you would wake up from your coma if I saved you from that. But you're still with me. An angel named Zelina has asked me to save your mother."

"An angel is helping my mother?" Eddie asked. "I'm in a coma?"

"Yes, to both questions. Do you remember anything I said to you or what happened before you ended up in a hospital bed?"

"Yeah, Dad, I do. I remember slashing the tires, missing a corner—oh, the accident. I remember some men cutting me out of the car, and I thought I saw you. Did I?" Eddie asked.

"I was there." Ed watched the hospital monitors. They were unchanging in their rhythm, and Ed began to wonder.

"Well, then, after I saw you, there was darkness until you started pulling at me. The pain was incredible until I was out, but the love I felt when I was free was amazing. I wonder if that's how a baby feels when being born?" Eddie frowned. "I don't have to go back into that thing, do I?"

"Not to that dark place, but I think you're meant to go back to your life. You have a lot you must do and make up for, Eddie. You have a wonderful girl who has tried to help you and stood by you.

Then there's that matter of your baby girl." Ed paused and smiled at his son, who took those words in.

"A girl?" Eddie repeated.

"Yes."

"Cool. Eddie smiled.

"It is. I think some therapy and love will certainly help you have a happy life with your family. I'm confident you can do this, if you remember that Sasha has some healing to do with you. She is stronger than you ever were. Drugs, drinking, and stealing must remain in your past, but at the same time, you can't run from them. You must own up to what you did and pay for it. I want you to be the man I never was. Raise your baby with love. First, though, I'm starting to think you're supposed to go with me. To help...yes, maybe that's how you're supposed to change," Ed said and smiled.

"Help you? Change? I'm confused."

"Since you didn't wake up like I thought you would—well, it all makes sense what Zelina said, about helping you change. I think that means you're supposed to help me fight the other evildwel."

"Other evildwel? Whose?" Eddie asked.

"I don't know. It's following your mother and stepfather around right now. No idea why, but it's much stronger than yours was. I think we should go check on your mom. You will go with me, won't you?"

"Leave my body there? Seems kind of strange, Dad. But, well, what else have I got to do besides watch myself breathe?" Eddie smirked.

"Are we doing the right thing, Zelina? Is he supposed to go with me?"

"Who are you talking to, Dad? I don't see anyone."

"No response, of course. I was asking the angel for advice. I've concluded that if I don't hear from her, I'm going in the right direction."

"Okay, I guess," Eddie said.

"I know this is odd to you. It is to me, too. But I think together we can do anything."

"Odd it is. What are we going to do, Dad?"

"Good question. No idea. But the first thing I want to do is check on your mom. I don't know how much time passed while I was in that thing with you. They might still be on the island. Let's check their hotel room, first."

"Sure, and is that angel gonna fly us there?" Eddie smirked again.

Ed responded to his son's smart-ass remark with a glare. *Wait until you meet her...* He glanced at the young man in the narrow bed with its side railings up. A white blanket covered his body. His chest went up and down as his body got the oxygen it needed to heal. *He will heal,* Ed thought, because now he believed in miracles.

"Oh well, it's weird looking at myself in a hospital bed," Eddie said sheepishly.

"Yeah, 'weird' doesn't even cover it. Let's go."

"Nothing bad will happen if I leave?" Eddie frowned and reached toward his still body.

"I know the soul and body can be apart. Besides, if Zelina didn't want you to leave, she'd let us know." Ed grabbed his son.

"I hope you're right..."

"Why wouldn't I be?" Ed grinned.

That only got an eye roll from Eddie.

"Come on, Eddie."

The pale body in the hospital bed didn't even notice when they left.

* * *

RACHAEL FASTENED her seat belt on the plane. She couldn't believe how fast their honeymoon had gone. Nothing else had happened, though, but marital bliss. Each day was spent in each other's arms, either in their room or in the ocean. They only took the car out for drives after sunset. The rest of the time they never left the hotel area. The part she enjoyed the most was snorkeling. It was a new experience for her. First time out, she got saltwater down the air tube more than once. She didn't care, though, even after a long coughing fit, because of the new world it opened up to her.

It was a liquid world filled with coral and several different types of fish ranging from yellow and black to blue and green, but the large sea turtle quickly became her favorite. Next time, she would have an underwater camera to record the undersea life. It was like they had traveled to another planet, but it had always been right there under the water's surface.

While Rachel and Tony were enjoying each other and nature, Hank had made sure they were safe. Rachael was surprised that Charlie had escaped and avoided arrest. She knew Hank had talked about dropping the charges, and if he did, she would too. Too bad they never found who he was working with, even though she had a pretty good idea.

Tony and Hank had become fast friends and promised to keep in touch. In fact, Tony had invited Hank to join him and Patrick on their upcoming fishing trip.

"Maybe," Hank had replied with a sad smile.

Rachael wondered about Hank's family. All he had told Tony was that he and his wife were divorced and he didn't see his kids enough. He hinted that he had a lot to regret. Rachael thought he was doing a good job on his end. *Too bad he doesn't see that,* she thought.

Today's newspaper, in the seat pouch in front of her, caught her eye. She quickly scanned it like she had been doing since she had seen that horrible accident. Nothing new. The poor boy was still in a coma, and they weren't sure if he would recover from his severe head injuries. The worst part was no one knew who he was. The only description the paper had was that the young male, who appeared to be in his late teens or early twenties, had short brown hair, brown eyes, and an average build. Did he have any moles, tattoos, piercings, or anything to identify him so his family would know where he was? And why didn't they just post a picture of him? She had been tempted to go see him at the hospital but didn't know if they would let her in the room. She hated thinking about how that boy was all alone after making a stupid mistake.

Drinking and driving had cost her ex-husband his life. She never drank and drove—in fact, she hardly ever drank. She was going to talk to her kids about that one more time. Make sure they knew they could call for a ride, no questions asked, if they drank, so they wouldn't get behind the wheel of a car while drunk or be the passenger of a drunk driver, either.

She sighed as she looked out the plane window, watching them rush to load the last-minute suitcases. She was going to miss Hank, Maui, and the aloha spirit she'd run into every day on their honeymoon. Even with her clothes and tires being cut up, there was so much more to balance that out. Tipping the scales was the beauty of not only this island, but its people. She couldn't wait to see Hank and the island again.

Rachael smiled at Tony, who shook his head at her with a grin. He was still trying to find an open spot to place their slightly too large overnight bag. She wouldn't let Tony check it because it contained all the treasures and gifts for their family.

Rachael yawned. She had taken the pill from her doctor, which made her groggy and would allow her to sleep on the flight. She studied her fake fingernails—they were still on. If she wanted to keep them, she'd have to go in for her next appointment. She would see. They were such an extravagance for her.

Before they took off, Rachael laid her head against Tony's shoulder. She was out before the plane leveled off. Next thing she knew, they had landed at San Francisco International Airport.

* * *

"WHERE ARE THEY?" Ed exclaimed when he saw the empty room. Eddie shrugged.

All signs of the couple were gone. No shoes or bags—nothing. *Maybe the room has just been cleaned really good,* Ed thought. Hank entered the room without knocking.

"Have they left, Zelina?" Ed called out.

They waited for an answer that didn't come. Hank headed to the TV and jiggled the cable. He was here to make repairs.

"Maybe we should check the bedroom. If nothing is in there, we should go," Ed said to Eddie without moving. He felt they weren't alone and was on alert.

"Yeah, we should. Who's that?" Eddie asked.

Ed saw Charlie silently exiting the bedroom and said to Eddie, "Uh-oh, it's Charlie."

"What? Who?"

Charlie was right behind Hank as he bent down working. Ed recognized that look on Charlie's face—hopelessness. His intention was clear. In a moment Charlie would put that shiny knife in Hank's back.

"Look out, Hank!" Ed yelled.

Only Eddie heard him.

"What can we do?" Eddie asked.

"I'm not sure."

Ed didn't know if this broke the rules or not, but he went into action and focused on a water glass by the coffee maker. He wanted it to crash to the ground, getting Hank to look in Charlie's direction. It wobbled and then hit the ground, breaking into several pieces. That was all it took for Hank to turn around and see Charlie directly behind him. Ed watched Hank quickly disarm the boy and pin him to the ground. Charlie couldn't move. He burst into tears.

Charlie pleaded with Hank. "I was only looking for something to sell. No one was supposed to be here, Hank. You surprised me, is all. I needed some money because I lost my job. Let me go. I won't bother you again, I promise. I'll clean up. I was only looking for something to sell. Just this one time…please…"

Hank didn't respond as he grimly called the police from his cell-phone. Charlie had stopped struggling and talking. Now he looked like a small boy. Hank looked around the room and shook his head.

"I tried to help you, Charlie. Nothing I can do for you now. Sorry."

"I'm sorry, Hank. I shouldn't have tried to kill you. I promise it won't happen again."

"No, it won't." Hank searched the boy for more weapons. All he found was a small pocketknife, which he threw over by the discarded knife.

"Gee, I'm sorry I tried to kill you." Give me a break, Ed thought. The kid obviously had a drug problem, but Ed thought it better to keep all of this to himself. His son had the same issues, he knew. Glad he could see this. Might wake him up. Ed glanced at his son, who looked confused. *A good start,* Ed thought.

Ed called out again to the angel. "Well, Zelina? No comment again? Fine. At least Hank is okay. I think he knows he can't help the boy now." Then Ed turned to Eddie. "Come on, Eddie, let's find your mom."

"Okay, Dad, but what just happened? That wasn't the guy who helped me, was it?"

"Yes, it was. I'll explain on the way."

They left Hank to deal with Charlie. Ed knew Charlie would spend several years paying for this attempt on Hank's life. Too bad. Hank would feel bad about that. It wasn't Hank's fault; it was the choice Charlie made and had to live with. Ed understood that better than most now and wanted his son to learn that lesson, too.

* * *

ZELINA HAD BEEN WATCHING. She smiled. Ed had succeeded with both Eddie and Hank. Ed was surprising her in a good way. But the worst was coming. She hoped he was up to it. All his children depended on him. She watched the police enter the room and handcuff Charlie. Zelina was glad that Hank was not coming to her just yet. Now he could stay, do his good work, and then meet that lucky lady.

This was the part that scared her. She got to the Battaglia house right as Tony carried his bride over the threshold. The evildwel was right behind them. It was growing stronger and bolder by the moment.

* * *

ED AND EDDIE WATCHED QUIETLY, unaware that Zelina was watching them, as Rachael and Tony entered their home. The evildwel followed them in. Would Ed and his son be enough to fight it? A face peered through the red-eyed mist. Ed could make out brown eyes and a groomed beard before it faded back into the darkness.

"What—and who—is that, Dad?" Eddie asked.

"That's what I was talking about. It's an evildwel. What you were in. I have no idea who's inside of it, though. It's something we need to figure out, Eddie."

Eddie nodded. They watched their family reunite. Ed felt shame when he saw Rachael's mom, Mae. He owed her an apology for what he had done to her daughter. He couldn't imagine how he would feel if someone treated his little girl like he had hers.

CHAPTER 6

*R*achael and Tony were smothered in warm hugs from Mae, Kelly, Stevie, and Ava. Rachael felt safe and loved, as though nothing could ever harm her new family, but at the same time, she felt a cold presence that she couldn't explain. Perhaps it was because they were coming from the tropics and it was a temperate June day, she tried to rationalize. It was more than being cold, though. Rachael felt chilled on a deeper level. She sensed evil around her, amid all the love. It didn't make any sense, she knew. It had to be her fear of being happy, something she thought she had worked through. Guess not, thanks to Ed. *Yes, that's it,* she thought, and she shivered. She still hadn't told Tony about the snow globe; plus, their clothes and their car tires being cut up had revived old feelings that she hadn't left behind on the island.

She met Tony's inquiring eyes. She smiled to reassure him as he rubbed her icy arms. He smiled back. She knew he was worried about her, even though the rest of their honeymoon had gone smoothly. She could tell that more was happening than he let on. It was obvious every time Tony and Hank spoke. She saw his grimace when he got a message from Hank. It was not a "checking to see if you got home safe expression," or that he fixed the bad cable on the TV in their hotel room, either, like he'd tried to convince her. A sudden crash got everyone's attention.

"Oh no!" Mae cried. "I even used a picture hanger on that. I've never been good at hanging things on the wall. Your father always used to do that. I'm sorry."

"Don't be. You've done so much for us. I can't thank you enough, Mae." Tony bent to pick up the picture. "This is beautiful, thank you. The frame is fine; it just needs some new glass."

"Yes, thank you, Mom," Rachael chimed in, picking up the broken pieces to throw them away. The overwhelming urge to run away was stronger than ever. She felt like someone, or something, did not want her in this house. "Ouch!"

"Careful!" Mae warned. "Let me clean it up with the shop-vac."

"No, I've got it, Mae." Ava smiled and handed Rachael a tissue. "Then I'll head out, after I give Tootie one more treat. Rach, let that big man of yours take care of that cut. Just ignore me. I'll be gone before you know it." Ava winked.

"There has never been a way to ignore you, Ava." Rachael grinned.

"True. I'm pretty unforgettable." Ava laughed.

"You are," Rachael agreed and then added, more seriously, "Thank you for all you did and do for us."

"Anytime. I had fun with Tootie and doing some cleaning. You know I love to clean. Now hurry and fix your wound before you bleed all over my clean floors. I'll get this glass cleaned up and be on my way." Ava gave Rachael and Tony another hug.

"Thank you for all your help, Ava," Tony said.

"No prob. Glad I could help the happy couple." Ava headed to the kitchen.

"Wait for me, Ava. I'll show you where I moved the shop-vac." Mae was testing the other pictures. She seemed satisfied and then followed Ava into the kitchen.

Tony smiled and turned to his wife, "I have a feeling things will be hard to find for a while."

"I think you may be right, but it could be fun. Like a treasure hunt," Rachael said with a forced cheerfulness.

"I know where things are," Kelly said. She'd been unusually quiet up to that point.

"I even know where a few things are," Stevie added with a grin.

Tony smiled. "Perfect. No worries, then. If the Band-Aids are still in the same spot, I can fix your mom up, like Ava said."

"They are, but I got this, Dad." Kelly held her hand up. "You and Stevie unload the car, please."

"Yes, ma'am." Tony bowed to Kelly.

Kelly rolled her eyes and added, "I just want a moment with Mom. She's going to love what we did with our rooms." She paused. "So will you, but Stevie's going to show you." Kelly glared at her brother before grabbing Rachael's arm. "Wow, you're cold, Mom!"

"I know. It was so warm where we were. I have to get used to our cooler coastal weather again," Rachael said with a smile that she didn't feel.

"Uncle Patrick put a coat hanger for you in the entry. Here's a sweater, Mom." Kelly handed her a gray sweater that Tony had gotten her last Christmas.

"Thanks, Kelly. What would I do without you?"

"I have no idea, Mom." Kelly smiled and tugged her mom up the dark wooden stairs as they heard Ava pull their old shop-vac across the wood floor to clean up the broken glass.

Rachael overheard Ava saying in a hushed tone, "They are going to love him, Mae."

Rachael didn't hear the response because Ava started the vacuum.

Love him?

Kelly said, "Come on, Mom. First, a Band-Aid."

"I'm coming."

Kelly smiled, but then glanced back at Ava and her grandma with what Rachael would call a *look*. Rachael studied Ava and her mother. They both waved, with huge grins on their faces. They were up to something. Rachael waved back as Kelly tugged her up the stairs. Rachael could smell the fresh paint. They'd been busy. Kelly ran into the main bathroom, which still had its sterile white counters and toilet. The old pink-flowered shower curtain had been replaced with a tropical sunset. The towels were peach, and the old wooden toilet seat was replaced with a new light-peach one.

"Looks nice in here," Rachael commented as Kelly dabbed her finger with some alcohol and quickly slapped on a clear Band-Aid.

"We didn't do much in here, but Stevie wanted no part of the old pink-flowered shower curtain." Kelly smiled.

"I can imagine. I'm surprised the shower curtain isn't silver and black for his team." Rachael grinned.

"He tried, Mom, trust me." Kelly rolled her eyes. "Come on, I want to show you my room!" She tugged Rachael out of the small bathroom and threw her bedroom door open in a grand gesture.

What used to be in the room wasn't there anymore. You couldn't even tell it had been the mauve guest room.

"Wow. You guys made this beautiful."

"We did. Aunt Kathy got all the supplies, but Grandma showed us what to do. I painted my room and picked out some new things. Stevie painted his own room, too. We both did this after school and during finals, mind you. Aunt Kathy did the cleanup and coffee runs, too. Uncle Patrick worked late into the night. No one really slept last week. Ava and Tim helped, too. It was a group effort, I guess. I really love it here, Mom."

"I'm glad you like your new home." Rachael smiled at her daughter and then added, "You know, Kelly, you might have a career as an interior designer."

"Yeah, that'd be fun, but I still want to be a biologist. As soon as Stevie brings Dad up, we have another surprise for you." Kelly grinned without making eye contact.

"I'm not sure I can wait."

"Gonna have to, Mom, because Dad has to be here."

Rachael knew she wouldn't pry from her daughter what the surprise was, either. An A student, editor at the school newspaper, motivated, friendly, and caring, Kelly had never given Rachael a day of worry, even with her stubborn streak or strange obsession with ghosts and the supernatural.

"Then I'll wait. Kelly, this room looks so much better white."

Rachael studied the room. "That mauve made it feel heavy to me. Your bed fits perfectly, like I imagined it would, under the window. I love the shelving here. I assume you designed it and Uncle Patrick made it for you?"

"Yes, he was a huge help. I like how he made it into a large K. He started on these projects a while ago, you know. We've been making plans." Kelly raised her eyebrows before she continued. "My computer desk was a tight fit. Uncle Patrick had to cut off an inch on both sides, but now it works. Oh, Aunt Kathy got the Wi-Fi set up. I'm not sure how Dad lived without it before, but we are here now to bring him into this century, right, Mom?"

"We'll take good care of your dad now. And I'm sure he'll be taking great care of us, too. Great rugs."

They were thick and plush and reminded her of a picture she had seen of the universe: yellow, blue, purple, and green, with a bright white coming through. It was a serene effect.

"It's the universe. Cool, huh? Lightens up these dark wood floors. I know I'm too old, but I kept my kitten pictures. I couldn't get rid of them, so I added them to my paranormal posters. Oh, speaking of kittens, Tootie is around here somewhere. She's been hiding all week," Kelly said breathlessly, looking under her double bed, which had a comforter that matched her throw rugs.

"It's perfect. I love how it turned out—kittens with ghosts, UFOs, vampires, and werewolves—it fits you," Rachael said. This room was bigger than her room at the old apartment, where her stuff had been boxed up. Tony's house was a perfect fit for them. No, not again —*their* house was a perfect fit for all of them. Then she added, "I owe her, your uncle, Ava, Tim, and Grandma a huge thanks for helping you guys settle in. I think we should throw a party to thank them."

"This house is perfect for it!"

"It is. We're so lucky to have found Tony. He's giving us so much," Rachael added, getting teary-eyed.

"Oh, Mom. I know he is, but he gets all of us too, right?"

"Yes, right."

"Wait until you see what everyone did for you!" Kelly rubbed her hands together.

"What? Should I be nervous?"

"Nope. You'll see." Kelly looked away.

"I guess I will. What about Stevie's room?"

Kelly shrugged mysteriously and smiled.

"Follow me, Dad," Rachael heard Stevie say.

"I'm right behind you," Tony said.

Kelly and Rachael followed them into a room that used to be Nora's pink flowered hobby and sewing area. Now it was a sleek, silver-and-black room for Stevie's favorite football team, the Oakland Raiders. He had shelves shaped like an S filled with Raiders memorabilia, including cups, pictures, books, and mementos from games he had gone to with his grandpa and Tony. The thing he was proudest of was a signed football from the team that Tony had gotten for him last Christmas. It helped that Tony had gone to college with someone who worked in the team's front office. The throw rugs were black, and his bed was silver. His Raiders flag was behind his bed. Football gear was in an old locker that was painted black. His computer desk had a fresh coat of black paint on it. Rachael was surprised his walls weren't silver, but they were white like Kelly's room.

"It looks completely different. I love it," Rachael said.

"Yeah, you guys did an awesome job. This is exactly how I'd picture your room, Stevie." Tony grabbed Rachael's hand.

"Thanks. Yeah, it fits me now, not that I'm into decorating or anything," Stevie mumbled. m

He was exactly like Rachael's dad. Her dad was always so proud of all his grandkids and especially the fact that one was a clone of him. Stevie got by in school, enough to stay on the football team, but he was better with his hands. He loved to build stuff, and he loved to have fun. Lately he had been having a lot of fun, which lowered his grades at school and got him into trouble more than once, but nothing too bad. Yes, she would have to have the drinking-and-driving talk with him again. She knew Tony would be a good influence on him. Besides, Rachael had a hard time getting mad at her younger son.

"I made this locker. What do you think?" Stevie asked with his lopsided grin.

"I had a feeling." Tony placed his free on his Stevie's shoulder. "It looks like something you'd pay hundreds of dollars for at a store."

Stevie puffed up. "Yeah, well, it was nothing."

"Just like something your grandpa would make—I love it. He'd be so proud of you, Stevie." Rachael choked up.

Stevie was studying his desk intently when Kelly spoke. "Hey, don't forget my room."

As soon as they had fully admired the kids' new rooms, they passed by the extra room, which had stacks of wedding gifts in it. "After we open all these presents, we could make this into an exercise room—or maybe something else." Tony winked at Rachael.

"I'm hoping for the something else," Rachael said.

"Something else?" Kelly repeated.

"Yes."

"Sewing room? Office? Guest room?" Kelly asked.

"We hope we can turn it into a baby's room someday," Rachael said.

"A baby? Really? At your age?" Stevie turned red and added, "Well, I mean, you aren't too old, but we are—well, it would be cool, I guess."

"Oh, that would be so cool. I'd love a little brother or sister. So would you, Stevie!"

"We'll see what happens, but that's my hope."

"Right, awesome." Stevie seemed unconvinced.

Rachael was sure he'd change his mind the moment he saw a baby —or at least, she hoped so.

"We'll love you guys the same, no matter what. I promise," Tony added.

"I know you will, Dad. Don't forget, I want to watch you open all your wedding presents," Kelly said.

"We'll open the gifts as a family later," Tony promised.

"Okay. Grandma! Are you coming up now?"

"Be right there. Just finished, and I'm saying goodbye to Ava. You wouldn't believe the places we found broken glass," Mae yelled back.

"Are you guys ready for the final surprise?" Kelly asked. She was visibly excited.

"We are." Tony released Rachael's hand and put his arm around her shoulder.

"Yes." Rachael nodded. Stevie wouldn't look at her, and Kelly had that silly grin on her face. They stood outside the master bedroom door. It was shut. So they must have worked on Rachael and Tony's room, too?

"I'm glad we didn't do anything to the spare room. We didn't know what you planned to do with it. Grandma thought an office for you guys—a baby's room never came up. Oh, we put some of the extra furniture out in the garage to throw away and the rest in the attic for you to go through later. I picked out the best pieces to use in this house. Aunt Kathy spruced it up with new throw rugs and lamps. Of course, you can change anything you don't like, but honestly, I think you'll like everything. I know your taste well, Mom. The kitchen got a new coat of paint, too. There's still more to be done, but we all hope you like what we did," Kelly chattered on, watching for her grandma.

"Okay! I'm here," Mae smiled broadly. "What do you think of the kids' rooms? They did a great job, didn't they?"

"We're impressed," Tony said, while Rachael watched the sly looks between her mother and kids.

"Ready?" Kelly asked.

"Ready," Rachael confirmed.

Stevie opened the bedroom door. Their bedroom had been painted a cheerful yellow. Gone was all the dark wood, which had included a lot of mauve with ivory doilies. In the room now was a new king-sized bed that replaced the old double Tony had been using. On the bed was a new bedspread with sunflowers on it that matched the throw rugs. *Thanks, Kathy,* Rachael thought. There were yellow-and-white lamps on the new pine end tables and a new white leather padded headboard—the very same headboard she had pointed out to

Tony once while shopping. But what was above the headboard caught her eye.

"This is amazing! How did you guys have time to do this too?" Rachael asked.

"This was Ava and Tim's project. Tony had ordered the new bedroom furniture before you left—and that amazing picture above your bed," Mae said.

"It is *amazing*. Thank you. And that picture—it looks like the beach where we swam on our honeymoon. Wait, is that our names in the sand?" Rachael looks at Tony, who nodded at her with a huge grin.

"'Tony Loves Rachael.'" Tony winked.

"Oh, Tony. Thank you!" Rachael hugged him. If her family hadn't been standing there, their honeymoon would have continued.

"Yeah, well. You know..." Tony sounded like Stevie, and then he blushed.

"I do know."

"There is one more thing," Kelly spoke up.

"What?" Rachael asked, looking around the room. Everyone had a goofy look on their face, including her husband. They were all in on something together.

"Go look," Mae encouraged.

"Check out the bathroom," Stevie urged with a sly smile.

Stevie's look reminded her of the time when he broke his bedroom window throwing his football to a friend. That look made her nervous. What was behind that door? She carefully opened the door, not knowing what to expect. *What was that?* A golden blur raced out of the freshly painted yellow bathroom and jumped up on her.

"A puppy?"

She couldn't believe it. She'd always wanted a dog but never lived anywhere they could have one. Tony never had pets because his mom was allergic to fur. Rachael and Tony hadn't talked about adding to their family right away, but she'd never had a better surprise.

"A puppy," Tony confirmed.

Rachael's mother was beaming. She loved puppies. Well, she loved all animals, but now only had a cat named Lester. Rosy, the sweetest black-and-white Jack Russell, had died last year. Maybe this would encourage her to get another one.

"I assume you were in on this surprise?" Rachael asked her new husband.

"You assume right, even down to the fact that he was from the local shelter, and a mutt, just like you always talked about. A retriever mix, we're told. Three months old. The litter and the mom were found abandoned. He was the last little guy to be adopted, by us!" Tony started to pet the puppy, who couldn't decide who to visit first.

"What's his name?" Rachael asked.

"We left that up to you." Kelly bent down to pet the pup who immediately raced off. "Although I kind of think he looks like a Sammie."

"I was leaning toward Raider." The puppy ran between Stevie's legs.

Rachael bent down, and the puppy licked her face. She picked him up, and he nestled into her neck. She fell in love with him in that moment.

"You're so perfect," Rachael said. "Any names, Dad?"

"Well, I always thought Cogburn would be a good name for a pet." Tony grinned.

"Like Rooster Cogburn?" Mae asked.

"Who?" Kelly frowned.

"It was a John Wayne movie. Grandpa and I used to watch it." Stevie rolled his eyes at her.

"Oh." Kelly smirked back at him. "I still think Sammie works the best."

"Well, we have some good names so far. Maybe we should try the names out on him and let him pick," Rachael suggested.

"You haven't picked a name yet, Mrs. Battaglia." Tony smiled at Rachael.

"Um, well he kind of looks like a Pluto to me."

"Pluto? Like Mickey Mouse's dog?" Tony patted the little dog's head.

"Yes, little Pluto." Rachael laughed when the puppy licked her nose.

"Well, Pluto, Sammie, Raider, or Cogburn probably has to use the restroom. I'll take him out back while you finish your tour," Mae said, taking the wiggling puppy out of Rachael's arms.

Soon the family was back downstairs, and Mae met them outside the kitchen. "I've got a couple of things to do in the kitchen before I go. Look at the family room first." Mae rushed into the kitchen.

Rachael shrugged and followed her family into the huge family room. She was amazed at how different it looked with some of her furniture added and new rugs and curtains. The mantel already had the family pictures on it from the wedding. The old mauve couch still sat in there—that would have to go. Rachael wanted a sectional sofa that would accommodate her family.

She turned around, observing the biggest TV she'd ever seen. "You're kidding! Do we really need a TV this big?"

"We do, Mrs. Battaglia," Tony confirmed with a sly grin. "Got it on sale right before our wedding, in fact. Your brother did the rest. The couch won't be delivered until next week, sorry. It was that huge forest-green one we looked at a couple of months ago—the one you loved. I ordered it right after, but because it was on sale—well, we had to wait. So, we're all ready for family movie night, right, kids?" Tony asked.

"Well, if I'm not busy..." Stevie added. Kelly elbowed him in the side. "Hey, I was just telling the truth, you know. I *am* pretty busy most of the time."

"It's okay. It's not required, but we should make some time to do it before you're grown and go away to college," Tony said with a wink.

"Yeah." Stevie looked away.

"We will," Kelly added.

"Yes, we will, but you spoil us with all of this. And what a sneak with that couch. I know the exact one you're talking about," Rachael said. "But right now, let's enjoy our first day and night as a family. How about dinner and then presents after—we have some gifts we got for you guys, too. I'd better get Grandma's before she goes. It's a sparkly pink Hawaiian dress, of course. I forgot to give Ava her gifts. Oh well—next time. So does everyone agree on pizza?"

"Yes!" Kelly and Tony replied.

"You don't need to ask me," Stevie said. "I'll even go pick it up for you."

"You will? What? How did I forget—you passed?" Rachael asked.

"Yup." he grinned. "No more getting up early and driving me to football practice."

"Oh, Stevie! I'm so proud of you! I'm so sorry that I forgot to ask," Rachael said. She had completely forgotten about his driving test on her honeymoon!

"I knew." Tony winked.

"Come on, Mom." Kelly pulled on her sleeve. "The kitchen."

Rachael walked into a room that had been painted yellow over the drab olive-gray it used to be. There was a brand-new stainless-steel fridge with a bottom-drawer freezer like Rachael had once pointed out to Tony, a new dishwasher, and a new glass-top stove. The cabinets had been stripped of their old, dark paint and were a bright, shining white. The only thing left was the kitchen sink that had, luckily, been stainless steel.

Off to their left was a new bench table that fit into the corner perfectly. Rachael was thankful they'd gotten rid of the old table and four rolling chairs that matched the walls.

"How did you do this in a week?" Rachael asked.

Mae spoke up as she shut the new fridge. "Well, this took more work and time than we had, so your brother hired someone to redo the cabinets and paint the walls. Since the floor looks like stone, Tony thought it might work. I think the floor looks great, but it's up to you. Kathy picked up the table at a garage sale, if you can believe it, hardly used, from an older couple who preferred TV trays to a table."

"This looks like a different kitchen. It's amazing. I wouldn't change a thing." Rachael looked around. She noticed that around the top of the walls was all the artwork from her kids growing up, just like she'd had at the apartment. "Thank you, everyone."

Everyone chimed, "Welcome!"

Mae removed the faded red apron. "Your little Raider, Cogburn, Sammie, or Pluto did both number two and one. He is all set for a bit.

I just finished filling your new fridge with supplies. You're all set, I think. The puppy food is in the pantry, and I got you lots of paper towels and wipes, just in case."

"We're having pizza, Mom. Why don't you stay for dinner?" Rachael asked.

"Oh, no. Not tonight. I have a date with a bubble bath. This has been rewarding, but it's been a long week for me. I want you guys to enjoy your first night together as a family. I love you."

"We love you too, Mae. Thank you for all you did for us. We'll never be able to repay you," Tony hugged her goodbye.

"Of course, you will. Repay me by being happy." Mae smiled and hugged everyone else goodbye and headed for the front door. "Night!"

"Thanks, Mom. Night, and drive carefully."

"I always do." Mae waved and shut the door.

"Well, who's hungry?" Tony asked.

"I am." Rachael held up her hand.

"Like you need to ask me." Stevie grinned.

"I could eat. Make sure you get me the vegetarian," Kelly said.

"All meat, for me." Stevie smirked at Kelly, who rolled her eyes at him.

Rachael smiled and said, "I'm going to unpack and get a load of laundry started."

Tony shook his head. "No, *we* will unpack and start the laundry together. You guys don't mind ordering, too?"

"We got it, Dad," Kelly said. "And we'll watch Sammie."

"Yup. I might need some money, though," Stevie said.

"I have a hundred-dollar bill from vacation that—" Tony started.

There was a crash in the other room.

They rushed back into the family room. There was another picture of the family from their wedding on the floor. The frame had shattered this time, along with the glass.

"Oh no!" Rachael rushed in to pick up the puppy, who'd followed them, before he got hurt.

"How did that happen?" Kelly asked.

"Maybe Tootie?" Tony looked around.

"Tootie isn't a fan of the puppy yet. She's been hiding under the beds all week, but maybe she came out..." Kelly replied. "I'll clean this up. You guys go unpack. We'll call you when the pizzas are here."

"Maybe we should leave the puppy in the kitchen for now," Rachael said.

"I'll put him in there when we get the pizza." Kelly kissed the top of the puppy's head.

"Or we could take him along," Stevie suggested.

"Or not. I can't hold him and the pizza." The puppy licked Kelly's chin.

"The pizza doesn't need to be held. It's not going anywhere." Stevie smiled.

Tony interrupted. "Just leave the little guy here. Thanks, kids."

"Yeah, thanks. Now, let's go unpack, Mr. Battaglia."

"Yes, let's," Tony replied with a slight grin.

Their unpacking was interrupted by a long kiss. They were soon entangled again. After Stevie and Kelly left to pick up the pizzas, the puppy slept quietly in the kitchen, and Tootie watched from under the bed. Her ears were back as she observed the corner. The dark mist left the corner and exited the room while the newlyweds christened their king-sized bed.

CHAPTER 7

*E*d watched the group respond to another picture being knocked down. They had no idea it was intentional or that something evil was around them. He shivered. He felt helpless watching the evildwel move freely around the house. He had to figure out something, quick. He sighed and watched Eddie head for the kitchen. At least Ed felt like he was getting through to his son. Eddie clearly loved his brother and sister. Ed knew that Eddie would do anything to protect them. He had to remind Eddie how much he loved his mom and how good his stepfather was. But even with making that part of this right, they still didn't know how to fight this evildwel.

Right now, though, the puppy was attracting his son's attention. Ed felt remorse, remembering the promise he'd made to Eddie about getting a puppy when he was around four years old. It never happened and was one of many broken promises Ed had made to his son. So now he gave Eddie some time with the puppy while he watched the evildwel. It was the least he could do. Then he had to figure out a way to get rid of this misty monster and make sure his son woke up from the coma.

"Come on Stevie, the pizzas will be ready in ten minutes."

"Hang on!" He sighed and continued texting. Ed could see it was to someone named Cassie. They were planning to meet up tomorrow night.

"I'll meet you in the truck." Kelly headed to the front door.

Ed felt pride rush through him when he watched Stevie drive off with his sister. He knew it was a feeling he had no right to. All the credit went to Rachael. And that evildwel had no right to be around those incredible kids. Ed went to check on Rachael and Tony. They were busy unpacking.

"I wish you'd point me in the right direction, Zelina." Ed waited. No response. "Guess I'll figure it out," he said sarcastically, hoping for a biting response from Zelina. He didn't get it.

"What?" Eddie called from the kitchen.

"Nothing, Eddie. Just thinking out loud. Puppy okay?" Ed shouted, heading back downstairs.

"Yup. He's sleeping. When he woke up for a moment, I swore he knew I was there," Eddie yelled.

How did Rachael and Tony not hear something when they shouted? "Maybe he can see you."

"Cool."

The evildwel was back. Guess the newlyweds needed their privacy again and weren't going to be doing any laundry today. Ed watched the evildwel hover at the kitchen door. What was it waiting for? He didn't like the fact that Eddie was on the other side of the door, but so far it wasn't interested in them. *The puppy?* Ed wondered. He hoped not. He was going to find some way to protect his children and their pets.

Ed heard a thump coming from upstairs. He tried not to think about what was going on behind closed doors. It wasn't getting any easier for him to see how much they loved each other, even though he was happy for her. *The new and improved Ed,* he thought with a grin. He wondered how long it'd be before she was pregnant by her new husband. Or was she already?

Ed had a feeling that her fears about being unable to have more kids weren't warranted. One born of pure love between Rachael and Tony would be amazing. He wished he'd experienced that. Not that he hadn't been proud of his own kids, but back then, they put a damper on his lifestyle. Ed sighed. So many mistakes—but his children weren't, nor was his granddaughter. He hoped they all realized what a miracle she was.

Ed was going to make sure Eddie knew how lucky he was going to be—if he came out of his coma. The only thing they had to do was beat this evildwel. *Gee, is that all?* Ed shook his head. Even though Zelina had told him it was all up to him, he wondered. He knew she didn't share everything with him.

Well, the only thing he could think of to fight this thing was this newfound love he'd acquired. How cheesy did that sound? But it might be the only way to take down this red-eyed dark cloud. He hoped he was as strong as his thoughts were. Bravery, strength, and love were things he knew little of in life. They might be the center-piece to saving his family, though. *Just great.*

* * *

ZELINA SMILED. He was starting to get it, although he had a lot of work to do. And this evildwel was one of the oldest and strongest she had ever encountered. So much hate in the man it had joined. Zelina shook her head. Even with her quietly helping, it was going to be a fight, but ultimately, everything really did fall on Ed. His ex-wife, his children, and his grandchild all depended on him. One of the most important things that could come out of this, besides saving lives, was Ed's change.

Ed had been a success in many ways, and if anyone could pull this off, it would be him. She reflected on the day when his evildwel left him as he slowly died in the twisted car wreckage. She had watched him take his last jagged breath. Then she took him to where he would watch his life, hopefully to learn from, but at least take responsibility for, what he had done. She never knew if it was going to make a difference or not, but now she saw a changed man, not the selfish, greedy, and angry one who had died in front of her that night. He was not the same man who had treated his wife and family so poorly.

Even with Ed's success, Zelina's biggest concern was the two unborn children—Rachael and Tony's little boy, especially. He was going to be important to their world. He would save a lot of people if what she saw went as it was supposed to. But, of course, he needed to be born, and they all needed to survive this evildwel. Zelina hated that she could only do so much with all her information, but that was how it was for an angel

She was trying to revive a practice that went beyond seeing what they did in life and the outcome and allowed them to try to fix things as much as possible, to undo some of the harm done by misguided people. The practice had been abandoned when one being had not recovered enough and tried to do more harm.

Zelina was taking a huge chance on Ed. She hoped he would not let her (or his family) down in the end. So much was depending on it, with the sudden increase in evildwels in the world. They had only seen this a few times in the past, but nothing like the scale they were seeing now. When they did see a huge increase in evildwels in the past, well, nothing good ever came from it. If they could battle some of that darkness, maybe they could prevent the coming events, or at least make them less deadly.

All she knew was this had to work, and if it did not—well, she had angels to answer to. They would take nothing less than a positive outcome to consider this a success. So basically, Ed had the world riding on his shoulders, but he had no idea. She hoped she had made the right choice when she picked him for this. She sighed and threw her hair back over her folded wings. No, it had to work, and he was the right person to do it. She would believe in nothing less.

Zelina went back to work. She checked on Eddie and saw he was sitting next to the puppy. A good sign. She sent some love to him. She knew Eddie had a lot of healing to do before (or if) he could go back to his body, but she was hopeful. She smiled fondly at Eddie and went back to Ed. *Come on, Ed,* she thought. *If you do this, you can change the outcome of this battle. You can do this, Ed,* she thought and sent him love, too. One thing would never change: She would never stop believing in love.

* * *

ED STUDIED THE EVILDWEL. He slowly approached it. It didn't move away from him this time, like it had in Hawaii. It seemed stronger here. Ed stood in front of it. The fear and anger flowed off it and into Ed. He slowly backed up until he felt normal again. Two feet away, he was okay. He hoped he wasn't required to go inside this one. He didn't think he would make it out this time.

Eddie was suddenly next to him. "What are we going to do about this thing?"

"I'm not sure. I think love might have something to do with it, as stupid as that sounds," Ed said as the evildwel entered the kitchen. "It would help to know who the person inside this thing is. Any ideas?"

"No idea. Actually, the whole love thing doesn't make me feel like I wanna puke." Eddie grinned.

"Well, that's good, I guess." Ed smiled back. "I think the only way to beat this evildwel is to know who—and what—we're fighting."

The quiet in the house was unnerving to him. Something was coming.

"How do we do that? If—" Eddie was cut off by a sudden crash in the kitchen, followed by a yelp.

Eddie pushed past his dad. They discovered the microwave had fallen off the counter and narrowly missed the cowering puppy. The evildwel was right there, and they could see the bearded face again, along with its glowing red eyes. It was smiling.

* * *

RACHAEL HAD FALLEN asleep when a loud crash from downstairs woke her up. "What was that?"

"What?" Tony sat up. "I didn't hear anything."

"I heard a bang from downstairs. I hope the puppy didn't get into anything." Rachael hopped up and got dressed.

"Probably dreamt it. It's quiet now. Come back to bed." Tony grinned. "I'm sure we have a bit more time before the kids get back."

Rachael's heart was racing, and she felt cold. Something was wrong. She could feel it, but couldn't explain it without sounding crazy. "They could be back any moment, silly. I want to go check in case the puppy got into who knows what. You know puppies."

She quickly ran a brush through her hair and kissed her husband, who wasn't moving from his spot in their messy new bed. He sunk back down, pulled the covers up, and burrowed into the yellow pillows. She hurried out of the room and took the stairs two at a time. She shivered. She still felt like she was being watched, the feeling that had started on the day of their wedding.

She hurried into the kitchen and saw the puppy hiding under the table in the furthest corner. It was terrified. The microwave was on the floor next to a puddle of pee. How did it fall off the counter and onto the floor? Could the puppy have pulled it down? *Doesn't seem likely,* she thought. She heard Tony come into the kitchen behind her. He had thrown on his jeans and shirt. His hair was more tousled than usual, and he had never looked so handsome to her.

"What happened? How did the microwave get on the floor?" Tony scooped up the shaking puppy. "Did you do this, little guy?"

"I don't see how. Unless it wasn't on the counter all the way?"

"I don't remember seeing that, but then, there was so much going on. Here, you take little Cogburn, and I will see if this still works."

Rachael grabbed the puppy, but he began to wiggle, so she set him down. He went right back under the table. Rachael shrugged and mopped up the pee as Tony plugged in the microwave. Nothing.

Tony shrugged. "Well, looks like we need to replace this. It was old, anyway. Maybe Tootie knocked it down."

"I haven't even seen Tootie since we've been back. She's hiding. And, besides, she has never knocked things down before. Of course, we've never had a puppy before, either," Rachael admitted and then added, "Still, how would she have gotten in here? The door was shut. This is strange, Tony. I don't like the fact that 'strange' has followed us home from our honeymoon."

"Well, it wasn't where it was supposed to be, that's for sure. If it was, it never would've fallen. Don't worry. Everything is fine. They probably rushed, and this didn't get put back right, is all. Then maybe the cat or puppy did something, and off it fell. Been known to happen. I'm thankful the puppy didn't get hurt. We'll go microwave shopping tomorrow." Tony ran his hand through his bedroom hair.

"Yeah, that's a possibility as to why it fell." Rachael quickly changed the subject. "We could look at refurbished microwaves instead of a new one. They're cheaper. With all the money we're spending already on the house—well, I don't need anything else new."

Tony shook his head. "We could, but we aren't. This is your house as well as mine. You'll have everything you need to be comfortable here. I might have overstepped getting some of this without you, but I tried to get everything I thought you'd like. I've been saving money my whole life. It's about time I put some of it to good use. And you know my mom left me a little, too. Don't worry about that, Rachael. Spending a little money on my new family gives me great pleasure. Let me enjoy being able to do a few nice things for you and our kids for a bit."

"I know, but I've had to be careful with money, and spending it kind of makes me nervous, is all," Rachael admitted.

"Don't be nervous. There's plenty of money left for our old age." Tony laughed.

"Well, if we don't get all sour like that couple at the airport."

"Impossible, Mrs. Battaglia, because you enchant me." Tony drew her into a kiss.

Right then, Tony's truck pulled into the driveway.

"Pizzas are here." Tony added in a hug. "I love you. Don't ever forget that."

"I won't, if you remember how much I love you," Rachael responded, blushing.

"I hope to still make you blush in thirty years." Tony winked. "I'll get the plates if you grab the napkins—and Rach? Everything is going to be okay. You're safe with me, I promise. They're a few random events that aren't connected."

"I hope so, and I do trust you," Rachael said with a fake smile on her face. She knew this wasn't right. She was going to figure it out, even if Tony didn't believe her. She had to tell him about the snow globe. He'd see that someone was after them. As she set out the napkins and added some soda from the well-stocked fridge (thanks to her mother), she missed Tony's face when he turned away from her, or she would have seen the fear on it.

* * *

"THE PIZZA'S HERE," Stevie called out as they entered the house in a flurry.

"In here," Tony responded, petting the small golden ball of fluff in his arms again.

The puppy was still shaking as he nuzzled his head under Tony's hand. Tony knew the puppy was too small to pull the microwave down like that, but he didn't want to worry Rachael. First thing in the morning, he was going to change the locks. Someone was playing tricks on them, and he was over it. Bad things had followed him his whole life. No more. It was time to install those security cameras. No one was going to mess with his family, he promised himself.

* * *

STEVIE ATE what everyone else didn't, except for Kelly's veggie pizza. It felt normal to sit around the table, the four of them. Even the puppy ate some pizza toppings. Rachael warned that it might bother his little stomach, but she knew they wouldn't believe her until it was time to clean up after him. The puppy licked her arm from Tony's lap.

"He needs a name," Kelly insisted, pushing her plate away.

"He does. We have four. Let's put him on the floor and see if he responds to any of them," Tony suggested.

"Well, that might work," Kelly conceded as she carefully wiped her mouth with a napkin.

"Good. If he responds to one, that's his name—agreed?" Tony gave a thumbs up. Rachael held back a smile. Sometimes he was so silly around the kids; it was endearing.

"Agreed, if you let *me* do the asking." Kelly's grin was endearingly lopsided. "And I promise I'll say the names the same. No playing favorites."

"I completely trust you." Stevie rolled his eyes. Kelly ignored him.

"Yes, we all trust you, Kelly," Tony said with a quick glance to Stevie, who had his innocent face in place and nodded in response. "Okay, let's try it." Tony put the puppy on the floor. He looked so tiny and scared sitting there. It broke Rachael's heart.

"Here, doggie." The puppy ignored her. "Okay, well, then...here, Raider." He still ignored her.

"Fine." Stevie shook his head.

"Here, Cogburn," Kelly tried. Still nothing. "Here, Pluto?"

No interest. In fact, he lay down.

"Here, Sammie," Kelly tried.

The puppy put his head down on top of his golden paws.

"None of those worked," Tony said. "Any other suggestions?"

"Leo?" Kelly bent down to the puppy.

The puppy suddenly looked up at her.

"Leo?" Stevie repeated.

The puppy looked at him and wagged his tail.

"Leo it is." Tony threw his hands up. "Where did you get the name Leo, Kel?"

"No idea. I thought of Leo the Lion when I looked at him."

"I know where you got it. Do you remember that book I used to read you guys when you were little?"

"Oh, yeah!" Kelly agreed. "Leo the Lion!"

Leo got up and wagged his tail and then pooped right on the kitchen floor.

"Gross, Leo!" Kelly hurried out of the room with her brother following.

"Well, I will clean it up, Mrs. Battaglia. After all, I'm the one who fed him all the table scraps," Tony smiled.

"Thanks. I'll get the dishes."

"Deal." Tony scooped her into a kiss, making sure they didn't step in the puppy's accident.

The rest of the night went quietly. They spent it as a family watching Tony's all-time favorite movie, *Star Wars*. The kids had bought it for him as a welcome-home present. "A classic," Tony always insisted, and he said so again after it ended. It always made Rachael smile. She loved her sweet, nerdy husband, although she never got tired of watching the movie either, not that she would admit it.

Rachael yawned. "Do you guys mind if we open the presents tomorrow? It's been a long day for us."

Tony looked at Rachael and nodded.

"I can wait. We'll all be here tomorrow night, right, Stevie?" Kelly asked with a smirk.

"Well, tomorrow night? I...um...well, I kind of had plans." Stevie's face reddened. "Could we do them before dinner? The movie I'm going to starts at seven thirty."

"Going alone?" Kelly pressed.

"She told you?"

"She did."

"What's going on?" Tony looked confused.

Rachael had a pretty good idea.

"He and Cassie are going to the movies tomorrow," Kelly announced.

"Oh." Tony glanced at Rachael.

"She's a nice girl." Rachael smiled.

"Still—weird, going out with my best friend." Kelly scowled at her brother.

"Well, we are just friends, really."

"Sure you are..."

Stevie, for once, was speechless. He suddenly found some lint to pick off his shirt.

"Well, I'm sure you'll have fun." Rachael yawned again.

"Yeah, well, she's picking the movie, so..." Stevie mumbled.

"A chick flick, Stevie. That's what you call it," Kelly teased.

"It looks interesting, and I like the actors in it, so..." Stevie was still intent on making sure his green T-shirt was lint-free.

"Bet you won't even watch it." Kelly continued her badgering.

"Why would I go to a movie if I wasn't going to watch it?" Stevie protested.

Kelly smiled.

"Glad she's nothing like you," Stevie muttered.

"Whatever."

Rachael cut in. "Well, I'm going to take the puppy out one more time. I think we can leave him in the kitchen tonight."

"I'm staying up late. I'll do puppy duty later. We could take turns, right?" Kelly looked at her brother.

"Yeah, I could help, sure," Stevie agreed.

"Thanks," Rachael replied.

She had a feeling that with Stevie dating one of Kelly's friends, things would get interesting.

"Night, kids." Tony grabbed Rachael's hand.

"Night," Rachael added.

"Yeah, night." Stevie had already changed their new big screen TV over to his video game.

"Night, Mom and Dad." Kelly picked up a remote.

Tony almost pulled Rachael up the stairs, after they got the puppy settled. When they got to their bedroom, he scooped her up. "I haven't carried you over this threshold yet, Mrs. Battaglia."

"Oh, Tony." Rachael giggled as he carried her into their room.

She had never felt so loved in her entire life. Like Ava said, she had the entire opal mine. They didn't go to sleep right away, though, as he pulled her into his embrace.

The rest of the night was uneventful. Rachael popped awake once during the night and sat up. Her heart was racing, but Tony was sleeping soundly next to her. Her first thought was that this night of peace would be their last. Trouble was coming. She fell back into a restless sleep, unaware of how right she was.

* * *

ZELINA WAS TRYING to prepare Rachael the best she could by warning her in a dream. The evildwel was in the corner, and on the opposite side were Ed and Eddie. Both sides were watching and ready for battle. Ed had to figure this out soon. Zelina knew who this evildwel used to be. She was not allowed to tell him. It made it hard to help, but the rules were in place, and she could not bypass them. She could certainly lead them in the right direction, though. She smiled and got to work.

* * *

ED WAS WORRIED. They were watching the evildwel grow stronger. It was darker and took up more space than before. Ed felt there was a clue somewhere in this house as to who was inside this thing. A flash of light illuminated the trapdoor to the attic. *Gee, does someone want me to go into that attic? Zelina?* Well, it couldn't hurt to look around while they slept.

"You stay here and watch them. I'm going to investigate. See if I can find a clue as to who we're dealing with. Maybe our bearded man used to own the house or something, because it sure seems stronger here. I'll be right back." Ed headed to the door.

"Okay. Be careful, Dad," Eddie warned, never taking his eyes off the evildwel.

"I will. You stay away from that thing. I don't want to have to pull you out of one of those again."

"I want nothing to do with it, trust me."

"I do trust you, Eddie. I want *you* to trust you now, okay?"

Eddie didn't reply. Ed wasn't sure he was completely getting through to him. But Eddie at least was on board for helping his family. A good first step—if he learned to control his anger and his drug addiction along with that, then he would be set. Ed had observed in the kitchen earlier, when they were naming the dog, that Eddie kept calling out the name Leo to his family. He watched Eddie whisper something into Kelly's ear. Ed thought they couldn't hear them, but surprisingly, Kelly suggested that name. On some level the family was hearing them. Ed had that on his side, and it might come in handy soon.

Ed glanced back at his son one more time before he entered the attic. He looked so young and fragile sitting in the corner, watching the evildwel. He felt a tug in his chest as he remembered the young boy who had wanted to name a puppy Leo. Ed had missed so much of their childhood. This was the only way he could make up for all that. He sighed and hoped this was all going in the right direction, because everything that had ever been important to him while he was alive was affected by what he could do for them now, when he was dead. It was a scary thought for him that people depended on what he did. He shook his head and hoped Zelina was nearby, helping.

As he entered the dark and dusty half-finished room, a feather floated by.

"Zelina?" Ed asked.

Nothing. Over to his left was a stuffed white chicken. Strange. Ed felt like it was staring at him with those glassy eyes. *Who'd want that?* Ed wondered. Well, it explained the feather. He got to work. Everything was covered with dust on one side of the room. The other half was covered in pink sheets and not dusty. The feather floated and twirled around the room and landed in the middle of the dusty and undisturbed part of the room.

"Okay. The chicken wants me to start over here. Thanks, Zelina," he added, if she was the responsible one.

He'd learned, since his death, that there was more meaning to not only lives here on this plane but those around him, too. If he thought about it too much, his head hurt. And he wasn't even sure why it hurt, because there was nothing to hurt like when he was alive. Another mystery for him to figure out after this.

He could see that the stuff under the pink sheets had to belong to Rachael and the kids. Old toys and some secondhand furniture. He headed over to the other side of the room with the old sheets that used to be white but were gray now, covered in dust from years of sitting. Nothing unusual was here. Old toys, lamps that looked like they had seen better days, boxes of clothes, a typewriter, a beta video player, and an old TV with the antenna still on it. *Just old junk,* Ed thought. What did he think he would find up here? This side had to be Tony's mother's stuff, or maybe even from the previous owners. Then Ed spotted a pile of photo albums behind the boxes of clothes.

"Well, that looks like a good place to start."

He examined the top album. He found pictures of Tony and his mom going back to when Tony was a small boy. Nothing of him as a baby. Ed kept looking. Tony on Christmas morning, playing with a small red train, with his mother in the background, smiling. She had been a beauty in her day, he thought, but her eyes looked sad. He recognized that look. He had seen it in Rachael's eyes. Maybe because she was a widow, or was it something else? He continued through Easter and the Fourth of July, where Tony was holding a sparkler, with a huge grin. Then he was Batman, but what did this have to do with what was going on?

Ed saw another box under all the others. Maybe it did have something to do with the original owner of this house. This box was old and beat up, like mice had found it. Its label said "Tax Papers." Ed could see it wasn't tax papers, since the box had opened a bit. It was more pictures.

Intrigued, Ed dove into this box. There was Tony as a baby, with his smiling mother holding him. Okay. Again, there was that look on her face. It wasn't a happy wife and mother looking back at him; there was fear in her eyes. Chills went through him as he finally saw a picture of Tony and a man. The man was holding the baby and smiling. That face had the same smirk and groomed brown beard as the face they had seen in the evildwel.

"There you are!"

He quickly looked for any information on the picture. Nothing. He kept looking until he found a picture of Tony's mother and this man under an arch. "Mr. and Mrs. Wayne Battaglia," it was captioned. It had to be their wedding day, and this man who was trying to harm them—their enemy—was Tony's dad. What was going on?

"Zelina, it's Tony's dad, Wayne Battaglia, who's doing this. Do you know why?" Ed asked. Silence.

Ed continued to look. He saw a picture of the three of them right after Tony was born. They were smiling. On the back, it said "New Beginnings."

"New beginnings?" Ed asked. "A new beginning from what? Or because they had a baby?"

Ed knew Tony's father had died when he was young. There had to be more to this. Ed kept searching. The feather floated by again and landed on another box.

"Okay. Thanks, feather."

Inside this box, which was labeled "Old Junk," he found an answer. It was a thirty-eight-year-old article from the *San Francisco Chronicle*. He quickly started reading and saw it was about an unidentified man who was killed in a car accident that involved another family. Driving under the influence was suspected in the fatal crash. The family of the suspected drunk driver was found safe after a concerned neighbor called the police upon hearing a woman cry out for help. Both suffered minor injuries, including a non-life-threatening knife wound to the woman's leg and some cuts and bruises on the sleeping child. The story continued on the back page. He quickly flipped through and continued reading.

The child was released to his mother from protective custody. No further information was available on the identity of the family or the driver.

"How does this apply to what's going on, Zelina?"

He shook his head. He quickly found another newspaper with a follow-up story about Wayne Battaglia, the drunk driver, and the Jones family.

"So Tony's father was abusive to them and a drinker? Just like me, huh?" Ed wishes Zelina would answer. She didn't.

Ed kept reading. He couldn't believe what the words were telling him.

More details were released in the accident that killed the Jones family and Wayne Battaglia. David and Sissy Jones, along with their two-year-old son, Bobby, had just moved to this area to be closer to family. They left the local pizza restaurant and only were one mile away from their home. Their car was struck head-on by Mr.

Battaglia's truck when he ran a red light. Everyone was killed instantly. Battaglia, who worked at the local school as a teacher was found to have a very high level of alcohol in his blood. He was also implicated in a domestic dispute, although wife and child were found safely later. Mrs. Battaglia had been restrained in their home while their child slept in the next room. A neighbor, who wished to remain anonymous, confirmed they had heard fights coming from the Battaglia house more than once, and more regularly, lately.

"We would make the call to the police, but the wife would never press any charges. I saw bruises on Mrs. Battaglia on several occasions. The child seemed healthy and happy, though, so I figured it was none of my business. Maybe he just overdrank sometimes." The neighbor further explained that Wayne Battaglia was a quiet man, but was always friendly.

A second neighbor, Mrs. Calli, stated: "While Nora was loading suitcases into the car, her husband came home. They started talking loudly. I overheard her say to him she was tired of his drinking, cheating, and anger. She wanted a divorce. He should go be with the other woman now. Then he stood there smiling. You know, it sent chills down my spine, and he replied to her, 'There is no other woman now. You are the only one, and you are not leaving me or taking my son anywhere.'

"I guess he meant it, because they went back into the house. So I turned on my TV. I figured they were working it out. You know? It wasn't until later, when I heard her crying out for help, that I knew something wasn't right. I never liked that man. Why that sweet woman stayed with him, I will never know. Glad she's okay."

The wife had been cleared and declined to be interviewed. There was a continuing investigation into another murder that Mr. Battaglia might be implicated in. The officer at the scene, Hank Borders, declined to comment. The identity of the other possible victim was unavailable.

Ed couldn't believe the name he saw for the officer: Hank Borders, the man in Hawaii.

There were no other articles in the box. Ed wondered what had happened with the other charges. Next he found Wayne's obituary, along with a woman's, Stacy Smith. She died on the same day as the Jones family and Wayne. Was she his mistress? Did he kill her too? Her obituary didn't say much. She was twenty-nine years old and worked as a waitress at a local bar. No cause of death. Just a request to donate in her name to the local charity she was involved with, the Cancer Thrift Store. She had no living family. *Odd,* Ed thought.

"So you knew Wayne Battaglia is in that evildwel, didn't you, Zelina?" Ed called out. "And now I know. Not sure what I'm supposed to do with this. He was a bad man. He drank and killed that family in a car accident and hit his wife. He did what so many dumb men like me have done. I got lucky, and no one died because of me. What am I missing? Why is his evildwel so bad? What more did he do? Did he kill his mistress?"

No answer, but the feather landed near another box. He opened it. He found the answer he was looking for in a diary kept by Tony's mother. Wayne Battaglia was so much worse than Ed imagined. He couldn't believe what he was reading. Tony's father had planned to kill him that night. He was going to hang Tony by his feet and slit his own son's throat in front of his wife to punish her before killing her too.

Ed shuddered, reading Nora's account. *What kind of man does that?* Tony and his mother were lucky Wayne died that night. Too bad that other family had to die. There was nothing good about any of what he was reading.

"He was a monster, Zelina." Ed shook his head, trying to release the graphic images in his mind. "I can't—I have to fight that?"

Ed's question was met by silence. He sighed and went back to reading, hoping to find a clue that would help his family.

Although the physical abuse had ended with his death, the mental abuse continued after he died. Nora believed Wayne was punishing them both, and she was right. She never said anything because she knew how crazy it sounded, but she believed in ghosts. Nora was aware of what her dead husband was capable of, but unfortunately, Tony didn't know. Now Wayne, with this creature, was trying to take down Tony and his new family.

Ed paused from his reading for a moment. "That's *my* family you're messing with, Wayne." Then he went back to the journal, the most helpless he'd felt since he was a small boy who couldn't fight back against that man, Al. He understood Nora's fears and pain.

"My biggest fear is for my son, Tony. I know it doesn't make any sense. None of this does, but I believe Wayne is setting Tony up. Watching him. Waiting for him to be happy so he can take it all away. All the damage my husband did while he was alive can't compare to what he can do now. He plays with us for his amusement. It would have been easier to have been killed by him years ago, but then my son would have never had a chance at life. Tony is my everything and my joy. It's the one good thing Wayne did in life.

"I just wish that detective Hank Borders had connected Wayne to all those women he'd had affairs with, who all passed away from 'accidents.' It would have given those families some closure and maybe some peace to know the truth. I know he did his best, but he came up short. Wayne outsmarted them. At least the detective listened to me when no one else would. I'll always know, in my heart, the truth, and so does Mr. Borders. We both live with that, but Tony didn't have to. I hope I have the strength to continue protecting him."

This was all too brutal for Ed to even think about. He understood that Tony's mother was trying to protect him by not telling him, but he didn't have a clue that his father was a serial killer.

Ed kept reading through the night. What he was reading might have been considered crazy rantings from Tony's mother. That was what any sane person would think. Too bad Ed knew the truth. Mrs. Battaglia wasn't crazy, and that evildwel was very real. Ed had answers, but he had to figure out what to do with them. There were more victims than anyone knew, including two men she had tried to date. Both met with unfortunate accidents and died. She stopped dating.

Tony tried to date, but the girls always ended up leaving him. The last one was killed in a boating accident while she was skiing. A boat ran over her, killing her instantly. The driver of the boat claimed there was a dark mist over her. He didn't see her.

Ed came to the last passage of Nora's journal.

"April 5: I can't live with this anymore. Too many people died because I kept silent. Because I was afraid. I know Wayne got the best of me, but he won't get the best of my son. He's not going to ruin his life. Tony is already afraid to date now. Who could blame him, either? If he did find someone, the right one, well, then, she would either be taken care of, or my worst fears would come into play. Wayne would take his revenge and play with her for a while, just like he used to do to me when we first got married. It was worse than the beatings. I must tell Tony tonight. He needs to know what his father really was and did. Then maybe we can fight off this dark ghost who was his father—together. This is my last hope and the only thing I can think of to do. Tonight, after dinner, I'll tell my son his father was (and is) a monster. No one should ever have to do that. It will break Tony's heart, and I know mine is breaking, knowing what I have to do. I will make Tony his favorite meal, and I'll sit him down after the dishes and tell him. I hope he doesn't hate me."

It ended there. Ed looked for more, but there were just blank pages. He guessed that conversation never happened

The feather was floating around again and ended up on top of another box. Ed quickly opened it and found her obituary notice. He noted it was the same date as her journal entry, and she'd died of a heart attack.

"Aw hell," Ed said. "Did Wayne have something to do with that? To prevent her from telling his son the truth?"

Ed knew the answer to that. Tony met Rachael right afterward. Tony's mother's greatest fear was being played out. Wayne was playing with his son before the kill, and he had involved Eddie in it, and now the rest of his kids. This thing was enjoying its last hunt with Wayne's remaining family. Soon it would grow tired of all of this and end it. This was what Ed had to stop. There would be no more deaths because of Wayne Battaglia. He grimly closed the diary.

CHAPTER 8

*E*ddie watched his mother and stepfather sleeping while the evildwel sat across the room from him. He felt its pull, even though he wanted nothing to do with it. The numbness he felt while he was inside of his evildwel was calling him back. All his memories were raging in his head. He hated remembering the look on Sasha's face when he hit her. He had never intended on doing that, but she pushed and pushed. Really, it wasn't his fault—or was it, when she wouldn't shut up? *It isn't right,* he thought. If it was his fault, like his dad was preaching to him, then how could he change now, while his body was in a coma? Besides, wasn't he exactly like his dad? So it wasn't his fault. Not really.

His excuses fell flat as he watched that dark mist swirl around, hypnotizing him. It was making him question everything he had learned, including what his dad had said. If he could just get all those images out of his head. Why wouldn't they stop? He sighed and grabbed his knees, bringing them up to his chest. He was trying to make himself smaller—less of a target—but it wasn't working.

Sasha's beautiful face. A face he loved, but a face that had been so sad and disappointed in him. He felt a strong surge of love for her that was quickly overridden with anger. Well, if she'd controlled herself, she wouldn't have made him lose it like he did. No, that wasn't right. He closed his eyes. He had seen what love could do. What his dad did for him. What Sasha did for him. This thing was messing with his head. He wasn't strong enough to fight it. He glanced at the door. Where was his dad? He needed to talk.

Eddie could feel the evildwel's attention on him. It was getting stronger by the second. It called to him to go over and merge with it. He would be free and wouldn't see Sasha's sad face anymore; he would be numb, like before, swallowed by his pain until he felt nothing. No one else mattered when he was in that darkness.

Eddie shook his head to clear it.

"No!" he said to the evildwel. "I won't go back!"

Its red eyes pierced him. It smiled in response. It thought it had won, but it hadn't—yet. Eddie didn't want to go back to that numb place, because of his dad. His father had pulled him out of that cold emptiness. He couldn't do that to his dad or himself, no matter how familiar it was, or how safe.

"I can fight you," Eddie assured the evildwel.

It only continued smiling, but stayed where it was. Eddie tore his focus away from the evildwel and watched his mom's steady breathing. It was soothing to watch, and he started matching her breath. She was peaceful, lying next to her husband. Happy. She had no fear when she looked at Tony. As much as he wanted to hate the man, Tony wasn't the problem—he was.

Suddenly Eddie remembered the hopeful thoughts of his youth and smiled. One of his ideal dreams he'd had for his family was simple. He'd wanted them all around the kitchen table, laughing and eating, while a new puppy sat under the table eating scraps he would sneak to it. The puppy would be tan, with huge brown eyes. He knew this smiling group would decide what to name this new puppy. He'd watched this desire from childhood happen right in front of him earlier today.

Instead of it being his mom, dad, him, and baby Stevie, though, it was a new family that included a stepdad and his little sister. Eddie saw that it could include him, if he wanted. Unfortunately, up until now, he hadn't wanted that. That was in the past. He was going to fix that—if they would accept him. That idea made him sad and excited at the same time. He'd had a dream come true, even though no one knew he was there.

Eddie had carefully watched the puppy reject all the names they had for him. He got carried away and forgot they couldn't hear or see him as he shouted out the name he wanted for the puppy. When he whispered "Leo" into Kelly's ear and she repeated it, making it all real for him in that moment, he had almost clapped with childlike joy. He caught himself when he saw his father standing next to him, smiling.

That showed Eddie everything he could have. Even if his family didn't know he was there, he was. Kelly heard him on some level. It wasn't a coincidence that he could explain away this time. He felt he was a part of that family sitting around the kitchen table. It felt good, and he loved them. He hung on to that feeling as the evildwel still pulled at him. His family was getting harder to hang on to, so he switched to thinking about Sasha and the most important thing— their baby. He hoped she would look exactly like her mother, with her white-blond hair and oval blue eyes. Sasha was the most beautiful woman he had ever seen. He couldn't believe his luck when she fell in love with him. He knew he'd never told her that. He sighed.

"Stop messing with my mind!" he told the evildwel. That eerie smile continued.

He thought about his body in Hawaii, fighting to stay alive while he sat across from something that wanted to end that struggle. If he gave in to this evildwel, these new feelings and that body and life would be gone—including Sasha, their baby, and his family.

Eddie wanted and needed this chance. He was making a promise to himself that maybe, for once, he didn't want to break. He was going to be good to Sasha and their baby, provide for them and love them. He intended to make up with his mom and be a part of this family and sit around the table with them. He was going to quit drinking and stealing, and he'd do things like Tony did. He knew he had used the idea of college as an excuse to party. It had been the perfect plan to continue having fun and getting money to do it. Inside him, his dreams lurked, one of them from when he was a boy. He'd wanted to be a fireman. He'd never told anyone, but he still wanted to be one. His friends would have laughed at him. Only Sasha knew. She believed in him, and he'd made her pay for that.

That night when he lost control with her—he could still see the look of fear on her face after he hit her. He never again wanted to see her look at him like that. His empty promises to change had never meant anything. This time, they meant everything. If he gave in to that empty side that the evildwel offered to him, he'd be lost in that dark thing forever.

Eddie was lucky that he had his father and an angel named Zelina on his side. He didn't know or understand much, and he was okay with that, for the first time. His dad being by his side and changed— well, Eddie felt like he had a chance. He smiled, but it faded away as he saw the bearded man in the evildwel. That familiar pull. Just let go. Forget all of them. It would be so easy to do. Eddie felt like he was being torn apart. There were two sides to him, and he was rooting for the good side to win, even if it meant he'd have to pay for the things he did. It was a crazy situation, one where he might have more control than he realized.

"Come on, Dad." Eddie closed his eyes again. He didn't want to look at the evildwel anymore. It was like sitting in a bar with a drink in his hand but not drinking.

Dawn peeked through the uncovered bathroom window. Eddie watched his mother and stepfather slowly wake up. He left the room to give them privacy, followed by the evildwel.

"Come on, Dad," Eddie said as he hurried into the kitchen to check on Leo. He'd had two accidents, but both were on the newspaper. Leo was sleeping soundly on his towel. *He will need a bed,* Eddie thought.

"Sorry I took so long, but I now know," Ed said grimly as he suddenly appeared next to Eddie, startling him.

"Dad! Finally! That thing…well, it was a tough night," Eddie admitted. As the evildwel moved back, Eddie added, "You know what?"

"I'm sorry, Eddie, but I trusted you to work through it. I'm proud of you." Ed smiled and then became serious. "I know who is in this evildwel." he looked at the thing.

"Thanks, Dad—who?"

"Come with me, and I'll fill you in." Ed met the evildwel's red eyes. Eddie could have sworn the thing shrugged at them.

* * *

THE EVILDWEL WATCHED them leave the bedroom. It smiled again. It didn't care. It knew there was nothing they could do about it. It had been planning this for a long time. This was the final course to its meal—the dessert—and it would enjoy every moment of it.

It's going to be a long day, it thought. Tony was finally going to pay, and pay hard. No one would be left after it was done: the final revenge before moving on to its next waiting resident. Too bad it couldn't get Eddie. That would have been fun. But it would really miss Wayne Battaglia when he finally was absorbed with the rest of its guests. Yes, it had had so much fun with him. So much fun that Wayne had no idea he wasn't really in control. *They never do*, the evildwel smugly thought.

* * *

AFTER A LONG AND STEAMY SHOWER, submerged in each other, Tony and Rachael rushed downstairs to make breakfast before the kids got up. Tony got the puppy's accidents cleaned up while Rachael started the bacon. It was their first cooked meal as a family. Rachael wanted it to be perfect, and it was.

Stevie practically inhaled breakfast, wiped his mouth, and declared, "I'm going to fill out a couple of job applications today. There are a couple of places that will work around my football practice schedule. Can I borrow the truck, Dad?"

Tony glanced at Rachael, who smiled at him. She loved how natural that word sounded to her.

"If it's okay with your mom."

"It's fine. If you're sure you can handle working and keeping your grades up, along with your practice?" Rachael asked.

"I can. Several players work. Nice to have some extra cash, now that I drive. You know, for gas and stuff."

"Extra cash for Cassie," Kelly teased.

"You know, whatever. You'll see when you get your license." Stevie smirked at her.

Kelly smirked back at him. "Yes, I suppose I will, big brother. Just so you know, Cassie really likes you. I mean, she wants you as her boyfriend. So don't hurt her."

"Oh, well, I kind of thought so, but...well...I won't." Stevie replied. Rachael wasn't used to her younger son being at a loss for words. "So, can I borrow the truck?" Stevie changed the subject.

"I don't see why not. All you have to do is be here for dinner and presents, and then you can go to that movie." Tony smiled.

"Yeah, I'll be here, thanks. I shouldn't be any later than three." Stevie grabbed the keys off the wall peg.

"Please be careful, Stevie. Call us if you're going to be late," Rachael warned. She suddenly wished she'd had that talk again with the kids about drinking and driving. *Well, he won't be drinking during the day.*

"Kay, bye!" Stevie slammed the front door.

Kelly was texting away furiously. She looked up and smiled. "Do you guys mind if I leave too? Brenda and Cassie want me to go swimming with them. Brenda's mom will drive us to the lake. I'll be back for dinner and presents, too."

"Sure. Your mom and I have some shopping to do today. Then tonight we can have our first home-cooked dinner together as a family. I think you'll like what we got you." Tony winked at Rachael.

Tony had insisted on picking out gifts for the kids while Rachael covered her mother, Ava, and her brother's family. She kept it simple with mugs, magnets and candy, but Tony put a lot of thought into his selections. Kelly got a book on Hawaiian myths and a tiki statue made out of hapa wood. It was guaranteed by the sales clerk to bring good luck. The grimace on the tiki's face was supposed to scare away all bad spirits. Perfect for Kelly and her paranormal hobby. Stevie's gift was a kit to build a Hawaiian canoe. Tony said that someday they could build the real thing together. That had made Rachael smile.

"Okay. I can't wait to see it. Oh, I don't need any food; Brenda's mom has that covered. They'll be here in ten minutes. I'd better grab my suit and towel." Kelly rushed out of the kitchen, not giving Rachael a chance to say anything more.

"Teenagers are good at that." Tony read her mind.

"At what?" Rachael asked with a grin.

"Avoiding full conversations." Tony laughed.

They dove into doing the morning dishes. Just as soon as Tony dried the egg pan, Kelly's ride pulled up.

"Bye!" Kelly called, rushing out the door.

"Bye! Be careful!" Rachael warned.

"That leaves just the two of us to continue our full conversations." Tony kissed her. His kisses always left her breathless. Leo barked.

"Someone has to go outside." Rachael giggled.

"If you do that, I'll lock up the house. I believe we have some microwave shopping to do, Mrs. Battaglia." Tony kissed her again.

"You're right, Mr. Battaglia. Plus, I have a few things I'd like to pick up. You know, stock the pantry. I hope you're in the mood for shopping. It might be a long day."

"I have no place I'd rather be than with you," Tony smiled.

"Likewise."

Leo barked again.

"Out you go, little guy."

Rachael watched the puppy run around on the lawn. She had never felt more content. Leo did his job while Tony made his rounds, shutting off lights and locking the doors. Her kids were bad about that, but if that was all she had to complain about, she'd take it. Soon Leo was back inside. Rachael locked the back door and gave the puppy some more water and food. Tony came back into the kitchen.

"I hate to leave the little guy alone," Rachael said.

"He'll be fine. His dishes are full. We'll put some newspaper down over there again. He did good last night. Used the paper and didn't tear anything up. Of course, it helped that the kids checked on him, too. We can always come back and check during the day, and on Tootie, too. Don't want to leave her out, even though I'm beginning to think that's exactly what that cat wants."

"I would have to agree with that. Might take a while for her to warm up to all this change and a puppy. Did you leave her more food and water?"

"I did. Back door locked?" Tony asked.

"It is. I'll meet you at the car."

"'Kay." Tony was at the front door when the phone rang. He looked at Rachael, curious. She shrugged and almost didn't answer, until she saw who it was from: Stevie. *Wonder if he forgot something?*

"Hi, Stevie. What? Oh no! I only care that you're okay. We'll be right there." Rachael hung up the phone, and Tony immediately had his arm around her.

Soon they were on their way to the hospital. Rachael couldn't believe the words she had heard her son say: "Mom, I'm okay, but I've been in a car accident. My brakes failed, and I'm sure the truck is totaled. I'm sorry. Can you come to the hospital and get me?"

Their day of shopping was forgotten as they brought Stevie home. The ER had checked him out. Nothing was broken, just some bumps and bruises. The doctor said he should rest the next day or two, but he would be fine after that. Tony had his key in the front door when the phone rang. A surge of fear ran through Rachael. She pushed past him the moment the door opened and answered the phone breathlessly.

"Mom? Don't freak out. I'm fine now, but Brenda's mom is taking me to the ER to get my foot checked. I slipped on a rock when we were hiking down to the swimming hole. Brenda's mom is convinced it's broken. She wanted to know if you could meet us there."

Shocked, Rachael managed to remain calm. "I'm not freaking out, Kelly. I'm glad her mom is taking you to get checked out. We'll meet you there." Rachael would wait to tell her in person about her brother's accident. Both kids hurt at almost the same time? What were the odds of that happening?

"Is Kelly okay?" Tony said, knitting his brows together.

"Yes, she slipped and hurt her foot. We need to head back to the ER, or should you stay here with Stevie?" Rachael asked.

"No. I'm going with you," Stevie said.

"They said you should rest," Rachael said.

"I'll be sitting in the car, and I'll rest at the hospital. Plus, I'd be in a place where they could take care of me if anything happened, right?" Stevie tried to joke, but his face said it all. He looked very young and pale.

"I think you should stay here with me," Tony said.

"No, Dad. I'm okay to go. I want to go," Stevie insisted. He added, "Besides, that doctor was being cautious. He's a fan of our football team.

"Well, it's up to you, Stevie. I did notice you got really good treatment there. That explains it. I'm glad everyone is okay. That's what's important."

"Yes, it is." Rachael sounded more confident than she was.

"What are the odds you'd both have accidents at the same time? This will be a day we won't soon forget," Tony declared, a bit too cheerfully.

"Right." Stevie frowned when he thought no one was looking, but Rachael was.

Something or someone was out to get them. Rachael firmly believed that. She wished Tony did. Perhaps he was in shock. No one could deny that what was happening was more than mere coincidence.

"We should go," Rachael said.

She knew they wouldn't be able to talk Stevie out of coming. He was stubborn, like his grandfather. That was why he was so good at playing football. Tony smiled at Rachael. She didn't notice; the smile didn't make it to his eyes. The weight of the moment was making it hard to leave the house. Luckily, Tony grabbed her hand, giving her strength. She felt an evil presence that she couldn't explain without sounding irrational. There had to be a reasonable explanation, but she had no idea what it was yet.

Stevie said, "Let me grab a clean shirt. You know, it was the police that insisted I get checked. I knew I was fine. I'll meet you at the car."

Soon they were on their way, just in time to see Brenda's mom wheel Kelly to the ER entrance. Kelly smiled and waved at them as the security guard pushed the button for the automatic door. Seeing her in good spirits helped. Rachael could see that Kelly's foot was swollen already as she hurried to her daughter.

They relieved her. "Thank you for taking care of her, Sally," Rachael said.

"No problem. I hope she didn't damage it too badly, but she is young and will heal fast. We were just walking along. Next thing I knew, she was on the ground. When she couldn't walk on it, I knew we had to get her to the doctor. Let me know what they say. Take care, Kelly," Sally added.

"I will. Thanks, Mrs. Wright." Kelly waved.

"Yes, thank you again. I'll call you when we know her prognosis."

Cassie and Brenda both hugged Kelly goodbye.

"Call me," Cassie insisted.

"I will. Now go swimming for me, okay?"

"Well, I don't know if we should..." Brenda said.

"I insist." Kelly crossed her arms.

"I'll still take them if they want to go," Sally Wright called from their blue pickup.

"I want to go." Cassie smiled at Stevie, who blushed.

He has it bad for that girl, Rachael thought. She grinned at Tony.

"Maybe you can come over later, or tomorrow?" Kelly replied.

"Sure. As long as there are no more ghosts." Cassie strolled by Stevie, who could barely look at her.

"I can't guarantee that." Kelly grinned.

Rachael shrugged at Tony. Kelly and her ghosts. What could she say?

The group quickly left, and the staff registered Kelly with what Rachael thought were some awfully strange looks. They quickly got Kelly into x-ray and away from her family. Rachael felt like they had some questions to ask her about how she got hurt. Did they really think she and Tony had anything to do with Stevie's or Kelly's accident? *Maybe her ghost stories will help them with that,* Rachael thought with a slight smile.

After x-rays the family waited in the nearly empty white-and-blue waiting room. They were unusually quiet as the TV blasted a nature show about sharks. Rachael was feeling like sharks had attacked her family today. Fortunately, they'd gotten away from the feeding frenzy. She didn't want her kids out of her sight. It would be like entering the ocean waters again, not knowing if the sharks were nearby and waiting.

Finally, the nurse wheeled Kelly back into a room, and her family was allowed to join her. A new doctor entered their room, not the football fan that Stevie had gotten. The thin young man with glasses (who had to be newly out of medical school) quickly informed them that Kelly had a broken bone at the top of her foot. "Follow up with the orthopedic doctor," he advised and left. Another person came in to wrap it up. Then Kelly got crutch lessons and some instructions for care before they left. She managed well with her new crutches.

"I'll go get the car," Tony said.

"I'll help," Stevie added.

"I didn't want to say anything in front of Dad, but they asked if you guys hurt me in any way. I almost told them it was a ghost, but I thought it would look bad for you and Dad, so I told them it was an accident. I'm pretty sure they believed me," Kelly said.

"I guess I can't blame them, but it *was* strange to have two accidents at once."

"I bet they talked to Stevie, too," Kelly hopped across the room on her crutches.

"Maybe they did earlier, when he was in here. We weren't with him the whole time when they checked him out, although his doctor turned out to be a high school football fan and knew Stevie from that," Rachael said. She gave Kelly a distracted smile.

"Yeah, Stevie is a big deal on the team, but to me he's just my brother. Mom, you understand that I'm not kidding about a ghost pushing me? Something pushed me, but there was nothing there."

Kelly turned, twisting around on her crutches to better look at her mom.

"Something? Sally said you slipped on a rock, which would be an accident." Rachael studied her daughter.

"Right, because what really happened sounded crazy. Cassie and Brenda know there was no rock. That's why they brought up a ghost, because I was pushed," Kelly insisted.

"Oh, honey, you probably slipped. Ghosts don't go around pushing people off hiking trails."

"They can, and they do. You know there are things we can't see. There is so much information out there about it. And don't you think it's odd that something happened to both Stevie and me at almost the same time?" Kelly asked as their car pulled up. Stevie quickly jumped out to help his sister.

"It's strange, but I doubt a ghost is after us."

"Whatever. I know what happened to me. You can choose not to believe me, like Mrs. Wright," Kelly slid into the car and then pulled her foot in. Stevie glanced back at his mom and shook his head before following her into the car.

They didn't say anything else about it on the way home. Kelly closed her eyes the minute she got in the car, and Stevie soon followed. They were both quickly asleep. Rachael knew Kelly was mad that she didn't believe her. Her daughter had some unusual ideas when it came to ghosts. Kelly even tried to talk her into going to a haunted house so she could study it, but Rachael had finals at school that week.

Kelly read her books, watched her shows, and Rachael knew she was active on the internet in her quest for information. *It's just a phase,* Rachael thought. It never interfered with her schoolwork or friends. A ghost pushed her? If she really believed that, then Rachael thought that perhaps it had gone from a hobby to something more. That "more" wasn't what Rachael wanted her family's lives. Perhaps she had let this phase go on for too long. She would talk to Tony about it later.

Rachael sighed. She hoped Kelly wouldn't blame a ghost for the brakes failing on the truck, their clothes being cut up, and the tires on their honeymoon, too. That hadn't been a ghost. Yet something was going on, and she had a feeling she knew who was responsible—she just didn't want to admit it.

* * *

ED HAD DONE his best for his children, trying to keep them safe. Although he couldn't stop Stevie's accident, he did get him to slow down. Scaring that squirrel in front of Stevie got him to slam on his brakes the moment before they completely gave out. It could've been so much worse than it was. Fortunately, the tree and the solid older truck took most of the beating, not his son. He wasn't sure how Wayne or the evildwel got the brakes to fail, but he was going to figure it out so he could do some things himself. The police and ambulance arrived quickly, so Ed and Eddie followed them to the hospital. It was there that the evildwel took off. Ed knew he had to follow it.

"Stay with your brother. I'll meet you back at the house," Ed called back to his son as he left.

Ed had arrived just in time to see his daughter being pushed off the side of a dirt trail, and he sped into action. He heard the snap as she landed. She had a broken bone, but she seemed fine otherwise, which was a good thing given the steep cliff she'd narrowly avoided falling over. Ed had used all his energy to stop her from rolling. He had no idea whether it worked or if she stopped rolling on her own, but one more roll and she would have plunged down the rocky hill. There would have been more damage than one broken bone, then. The evildwel had watched as Kelly's friends Brenda and Cassie and Sally Wright rushed to help Kelly.

"The closest cell signal is up the road about a half hour out. Take it slow, Kelly. We'll get you to the hospital," Sally said.

"It only hurts when I try to walk on it."

"That's hopeful, but it looks broken to me," Sally said through tight lips.

"Yeah, I heard a snap."

Sally didn't reply. Brenda and Cassie were both pale and quiet. The group focused on carefully helping Kelly walk, bit by bit. It was going to take a while, Ed realized, to get to the car without any help. He saw they were alone, besides the evildwel. They had this under control, but why was the evildwel sticking around? Did it have more planned?

Then, as if it knew what he was thinking, it suddenly took off. *We are just chasing this thing around, but not stopping it,* Ed thought in frustration as he followed it back to the house. This was where they had been sitting on the front porch, observing each other. Ed hated not knowing how his kids were, but he didn't want to let this thing out of his sight. Finally, Eddie showed up. Ed turned his back on the black mist.

"Are Kelly and Stevie okay?" Ed asked.

"Yes. Stevie is fine, just some bruises, and Kelly has a broken bone. They're on their way home now," Eddie responded. "Did you see what happened to her? She's insisting it was a ghost who pushed her. No one believes her, though."

"They should. That's exactly what happened. Our friend the evildwel pushed her," Ed replied grimly.

"I should've gone with you."

"No, I'm glad you stayed with the family. Thanks, Eddie."

"I'm afraid of what this thing will do next." Eddie's eyes narrowed as he studied the evildwel.

"Me too. If we hadn't been there for Stevie, who knows how bad that accident would have been? As for Kelly, she was very close to falling off a cliff. I tried to stop her from rolling off. I'm not sure if I did or not. I think we got lucky this time."

Eddie shook his head. "Crap. This is getting scary. I couldn't believe it—the moment they got back home with Stevie, they got the call about Kelly. I stayed with them, but I wanted to be where the evildwel was, too. But the good thing about this is if anyone can figure out why some ghost-like thing is after her, it's Kelly. She's been obsessed with ghosts since she was little."

"I saw the pictures in her room earlier. That might work in our favor, although *I* wouldn't believe her if she told me that." Ed's brows furrowed together.

"Yeah, well, I'm sure I wouldn't have, either, but now… Hey, what's that?" Eddie asked as the gate opened and the puppy ran out.

"No idea. Great! Our creepy creature is gone."

"You go check on the house, Dad. Leo got out front. I'm going to stay with him." Eddie hurried to the puppy.

Ed saw the puppy looking at Eddie. It lay down next to him, five feet from the street, and fell asleep safely behind some bushes. Ed smiled at his son and then hurried toward the house. He shivered when he got to the back door.

"Call me if you need some help," Eddie yelled.

Ed waved and quickly found the evildwel in the kitchen. The lights were flickering on and off. What was it doing? Then Ed saw.

"Stop that!"

It didn't stop. It had shoved something into the exposed outlet and was now gnawing on it. It began to smoke. Ed rushed it and was pushed back. The smoke thickened, and the smoke alarm went off. The evildwel's red eyes were focused on Ed now. It smiled and then headed outside. Flames were shooting out of the wall. There was nothing he could do, so he followed the thing outside and looked over at the white house across the street. Someone was home.

"Stay there!" Ed yelled to Eddie. "I got this."

"You sure?" Eddie called. Ed waved back.

Ed hurried across the street. The man was sitting at his kitchen table, eating a sandwich and watching his very loud TV. You couldn't hear the smoke alarm over it. Ed had to think fast. He was going to break a cup by the window that faced the house. It was the only way to get this older man's attention.

Crash!

The man wiped his mouth carefully and got up to see what happened.

"Damn it!" he said. "That was my favorite cup! I'd better sweep it up."

The man in the old gray sweats glanced out his window and saw smoke pouring out the open back door of the kitchen. He opened his window. The smoke alarm was blaring.

"Oh no! A fire! No one is home. I'd better call 911!" the man picked up his phone.

Good, Ed thought. Help was on the way. Eddie was still sitting with the puppy. Ed went back to the house. The smoke had slowed down, but the wall was scorched from the flames. The evildwel was gone again. Ed looked everywhere for it. Nothing. With the evildwel gone now, his kids were in danger, and no one was guarding them, but he had to find the cat first.

Ed found her under the bed upstairs. She wasn't budging. He heard a siren in the distance. He thought the cat would be okay for now and left her. He would come back and make sure she moved if the fire got worse. He looked at the wall. The fire was smoldering, almost like it was going out. The evildwel suddenly appeared at the back door. Ed followed it outside.

"I know who you are! I know what you did to your wife, mistress, that poor family, and all those women. But your son? Why do you want to hurt your son and his new family so badly?" Ed demanded.

The face looked at him through the dark mist. It was smiling, but it didn't answer as the smoke poured through the door at a stronger rate again. The fire engine pulled up. Ed knocked over a lawn chair and got a firefighter's attention. They rushed in through the back door and got right to work. They had it out before it got any further than the wall. The cat was still safe upstairs and the puppy out front.

Holy smokes, Batman! That was too close. Ed shuddered. *Quoting the old* Batman *show?* Ed thought. It had been his favorite as a boy, holding at least one good memory of his childhood and his mother, who'd watched it with him. Right then, Rachael, Tony, and the kids came home. The look on Tony's face was of disbelief. No matter what Tony said to Rachael, Ed knew that he was worried too.

ZELINA STOOD BY EDDIE, watching him interact with the puppy while the fire crew rushed into the house. He was petting it, and even though the puppy could not feel it, she knew he sensed Eddie's presence. Dogs were smart like that. *There is hope for you, young man,* she thought. She had taken a chance sending Eddie all those memories when the evildwel was tempting him. It could have gone either way, she realized, but sometimes she had to do things she should not.

Zelina had gotten to the evildwel just in time. She could not believe it was so bold as to try to burn the house down. It was doing things she had never seen an evildwel do before. Zelina had a trick that sucked oxygen away. That was enough to bring the flames down. Otherwise, they might not have had a house to come back to. She watched Ed try to stop the evildwel, with no luck, but at least he had been successful in saving Stevie from further damage with that squirrel and had gotten the neighbor to call 911. That was quick thinking. He had shown some strength with his daughter. If he had not, she might have gone off the cliff. It could have been so much worse. He was slowly learning what he could do.

Zelina studied the evildwel. It had no fear of Ed, but she thought perhaps it might, soon. Yes, things were going better than she could have hoped, but this last part was up to them. You never knew with all these emotional beings what would come of something, but she had high hopes since they finally knew who was in the evildwel.

Tonight, Zelina knew, everything would come to a head, and all their fates would be decided. She extended her wings and hovered above the house. She watched. It was all she could do, or was supposed to do, she knew. She never broke the rules—she bent them a bit, but never broke them.

This evildwel had led her to do things she normally would not. It had caught her eye years ago. The thing had stayed relatively quiet while Tony grew up, unless the mother tried to date. Two of her boyfriends had met quick endings. One was a car accident where the brakes failed, a special trick of this evildwel. Another drowned swimming, and he had been on the swim team in high school. These were not things Zelina could prevent.

All those years, the evildwel with Wayne Battaglia inside watched his wife and son until it scared his wife to death on the night she was going to tell Tony the truth. It kept Tony single too, until he met Rachael. Tony fell in love with her immediately, and then this evildwel began to work on her family instead of getting rid of her. That was when Zelina knew things would get serious. First, it started with Eddie, who was easy and ready to accept his evil side, and found a fellow evildwel to take residence in him. It was patient, but now it was ready to finish the game.

Zelina shivered. The day she had brought Ed into this, Rachael's wedding, was when things went to another level. The evildwel used Eddie and his own evildwel to do things with and for it. She had never seen evildwels work together before. It frightened her and her superiors; if this happened more, how could they fight it? This family was the experiment. Reluctantly, it was given the green light. Now it was in its final stage. Wayne wanted them to pay. He was patient and waiting for revenge. *Not this time*, Zelina thought.

* * *

RACHAEL EMOTIONALLY SHUT down as they pulled into the driveway, finding the firetruck there. She couldn't believe what she was seeing. She was quickly assured by a firefighter that it was limited to a wall. Stevie and Kelly sat dumbfounded in the car. They were lucky, she was told. Old houses can have bad wiring. They should have an electrician look over their house.

"Thank you," Tony said.

"Glad we got here when we did. Your neighbor called it in. Saved your house," said the man with the tag that said "Harrison."

"At least no one was hurt, and we're all okay." Tony wrapped an arm around Rachael.

Rachael wanted to scream. Why did he keep saying that? Didn't he see something was going on? She knew it was time to talk about Eddie.

"Did you see a puppy?" Rachael patted Tony's hand and pulled away from his comfort.

"No, we didn't, but we weren't looking for one," Harrison said. "I wouldn't use the kitchen until you get someone up here."

"We won't." She hurried off to find the puppy while Stevie helped Kelly out of the car.

"Here, Leo!" Rachael called and ran into the kitchen. She found the expected huge mess in her newly redone kitchen, but she couldn't worry about that now. She needed to find Leo. Where was he? The back door was ajar. She ran outside, calling him.

"I can't find him, Tony!"

"Try out front. I'll check with the neighbor, and I'll thank him for the call, too. Stevie, you help your sister into the house. Open some windows and air it out, okay?" Tony said.

"Kay. And Dad?" Stevie asked.

"Yes?"

"Don't you think it's strange, all the things happening today?" Stevie handed his sister her crutches.

"Yes, it's strange, but I feel lucky too, Stevie. We're going to be okay. I promise." Tony's smile didn't make his eyes.

"Something that I couldn't see pushed me, you know," Kelly added. "We aren't dealing with a living being. This is a ghost. A very mad ghost."

"I think there is a logical answer, Kel." Tony nodded to Stevie who shook his head in response. "We will figure this out. But first, get your sister into the house."

"Ghosts are logical, even if you can't see them." Kelly hobbled off on her crutches. "I don't need any help."

* * *

STEVIE QUIETLY FOLLOWED behind his sister. She did need help up the steps, Tony noted. Stevie was right there, helping her, and she looked completely displeased. She was stubborn, like her mother, but ghosts were something his mother had believed in too, he thought with a shiver. He wanted to remain logical, but it was becoming harder by the moment. Maybe it was time to tell Rachael about his past bad luck. She needed to know the truth.

Tony watched Rachael make her way back out front after finding the gate open. "Here, Leo!" she called.

"Here, pup!" Tony joined in.

Tony saw the bush move at the same time Rachael did. She rushed over and pulled him out of the hedge. He was wagging his tail and snuggled into her arms. He began licking her face. *At least he's okay,* Tony thought.

"I'm going to check on the kids and the cat. We need to talk about what's going on, Tony." Rachael sped off cradling the puppy.

We're all okay, Tony thought again. He couldn't get those words out of his head. He knew Rachael hated it when he said that—even he got tired of hearing himself say it. How did he tell Rachael that this wasn't the first time people around his family had met with accidents? What if Kelly was right? What if there was some unseen thing after them? Well, he hadn't said anything because it sounded ridiculous. He didn't want to sound like his mom when she talked about ghosts and haunt- ings. She believed their other house was haunted. That was why they moved when she got some money.

Bad things had started happening when he was a baby, beginning with the car accident that took his father away. Then there were the two men his mother had dated—both died in accidents. But it was the girl he had been serious about, who had broken up with him in their last year of college, who had broken his heart. She'd said she needed to explore what was out there. He remained hopeful that they would work it out. He was willing to go anywhere with her. The very next day, she died in a freak boating accident. His mother died in a car accident too, after a heart attack. So many accidents, but that really proved nothing.

Yet Tony had finally found his soulmate late in life. When he met Rachael, he'd thought that part of his life was in the past. Here was history, repeating itself. How could he protect them like he'd promised? They were his mother's words he was repeating to himself and his family: *At least we're okay.* She would just brush off all his concerns, growing up. Now he was doing the exact same thing to Rachael and his new family.

What happened on their honeymoon had alarmed him, but when things settled down, he thought that perhaps everything really would be okay. Since they had come home, though, it had only gotten worse. Tony knew he had to get them out of there if someone like Eddie was after them. That was the only logical answer for what was going on. He couldn't (and wouldn't) accept that it was something unseen, but he had certainly had his share of bad luck. That was all it was, he assured himself. No need to worry Rachael.

Besides, if he was to believe his mother's theories (and he didn't) that their first house was haunted, what were the chances this second house would be? He was letting his imagination take over, like his mother had. Doors and stuff didn't get moved without someone moving them. There was always a possible explanation, even if they didn't have one now. His past was just bad luck.

This house had always been a peaceful place for him and his mom. They'd left the sad memories of his father's death behind in the old house. His mother had always been so brave. He felt like she held much of her grief inside so she could focus on raising him. But Tony always understood she'd lost the love of her life, and maybe that was why she believed in ghosts.

Even though he understood her reasoning, he had a family to protect. He wouldn't and couldn't believe it was a ghost, like Kelly had suggested. He wished it was, because it was worse to think that it was Eddie. Yes, much worse.

Tony began to plan. First, he had to get them out of there. They wouldn't tell anyone where they would be. *Try to find us then, Eddie,* Tony thought. There were a couple hotels that took dogs, too. *Yes, we will be safe there,* he thought, but a small part of him worried that running wouldn't matter.

* * *

Ed and Eddie stood together on the front lawn. They felt as helpless as Tony did. Ed wished there was a way to tell Tony the truth, but maybe it was better he didn't know yet. Someday he might see what was in the attic. He'd learn what a monster his father was, how he'd tied up his wife and was about to kill his son in front of her. That part wasn't in the newspaper, but in the journal. How he'd run out of his booze, or the sleeping baby would have been brutally killed. That man made Ed look like a saint.

"We have to do something. It's getting stronger by the moment. I tried going at it when it was starting the fire. It pushed me back," Ed said.

"What if we went at it together, Dad?"

"And do what? I went in after you. I fought hard and almost didn't get you out. I'm not sure we can separate Wayne from this evil thing now. I mean, we could try, but then what? We'd have Wayne Battaglia the evil ghost *and* a mad evildwel?"

"Yeah, but if we do that, then we wouldn't be fighting something powerful like we have here. We might be on the same level, huh? My evildwel left when you pulled me out. I assume this one would leave, too? We must do what you did. You can trust me. I know its power. I have a lot to come back to, but if we don't make it, at least we tried to save our family." Eddie half smiled.

"I've been trying to avoid this, but I think you're right, Eddie. We should do it sooner rather than later. I think this thing is merely playing with them before it goes in for the kill. I won't let that happen," Ed said grimly as a strange car pulled up.

* * *

Tony explained his theory to Rachael, and Rachael added in the snow globe incident.

"I was going to say the same thing to you, Tony, but I couldn't," Rachael admitted.

"I'm sorry about the snow globe. No wonder you got so upset when he cut up our clothes, too. I didn't want to start our life together blaming Eddie for all our troubles, but it's the only logical explanation. I'm glad we're on the same page, even if neither of us likes it." Tony put his arm around her.

"I don't believe this house is haunted or that Ed is back from the dead, which leaves Eddie as the only possible suspect." Rachael snuggled into her husband's embrace.

"We agree on that, too. Kelly is the only one who believes in ghosts, like my mother used to," Tony added.

"I thought Kelly would outgrow her ghost ideas—that it was more of a hobby to her than real." Rachael looked at her husband as a small smile briefly passed over her lips.

"It's a hobby that she believes in right now. She has a good head on her shoulders. I'm not worried about her, nor do I think she was pushed. That was probably the only true accident that happened to us. The rest—the truck brakes, the fire, the clothes being cut, and our car tires—are all the work of Eddie. Maybe someone is helping him?"

"That would explain a lot. One of his friends? I couldn't see Sasha trying to hurt us, could you?" Rachael asked.

"No, I couldn't, but we don't know what goes on when they're alone. We have to keep that in mind and pray Eddie hasn't taken after his father." Tony looked away from Rachael.

"I've tried to help her, but, well, she didn't want my help."

"We'll get this sorted out, but we'll do it from a hotel room. We should call the insurance company first." Tony gave her a gentle squeeze and pulled away.

"Okay, you oversee the hotel, and I'll contact the insurance folks and see how this is handled. I'm hoping we can choose who we want. Remember I went to school with that guy who was becoming an electrician—Dan? I'll try to hunt him down. I'm pretty sure I still have his number in my cellphone, unless you have someone you use." Rachael rubbed her arms.

"I don't have an electrician. Never needed one until now. Sounds like a good plan. The insurance information is in the top drawer of my old desk. I want to go check on the kids, and then I'll look up which local hotels take pets. And Rach, let's not keep any more secrets from each other," Tony said.

"Agreed. We can handle anything if we do it together," Rachael said, more confidently than she felt.

"We can. I'll be right back."

She quickly found the insurance company's phone number and made the call. She got transferred to another agent, who warned her that their deductible was $1,000. If the damage was under that, she wouldn't have to file a claim. She was welcome to call repair companies of her choice and get estimates or repairs, she was told. She answered a few questions and was given a claim number and instructed to have the bills sent to the insurance company. The claim would be reviewed. That was easier than she thought it would be. Soon she was on the phone with Dan. He was available and would be there within the hour. She quickly updated Tony when he rushed back into the kitchen.

"I'm not a fan of waiting to leave. I thought it would be an appointment for later," Tony protested.

"The sooner I get it checked out, the better I'll feel about it, and besides, this will give me some time to clean up the mess."

"I understand, but I won't relax until I get you guys to the hotel—which, by the way, I got us a suite that takes pets. It's the new one by the highway." Tony folded his arms.

"I hear it's fancy. Thanks. And Tony, I know—I want us to all be safe, too. This is a bad situation all around. To think my own son would try to hurt us like this! It's hard for me to process. I guess I need to feel in control of something right now." Rachael's eyes filled with tears.

"I know. I'm sorry, Rach. If you feel better doing it this way, then we will make it work. I'll go pack up some things to take to the hotel. The kids are playing games, or resting, as they call it. They've been through enough today, without adding to their stress by telling them about their brother." Tony kissed Rachael and left the kitchen.

* * *

THE SOUND of Stevie and Kelly playing their game made everything seem normal for a moment. Their laughter gave him hope. Tony rushed upstairs and quickly packed for each person a change of clothes and all the toiletries he could think of. Boys in one bag, girls in the other. If they needed anything else, he could come back and get it. They'd leave extra food and water for the cat. She'd be fine for a day or two, and things would be sorted out by then, he hoped.

* * *

WHILE TONY WAS PACKING, Rachael did a quick cleanup. The smell was the worst part. The kitchen would need a new coat of paint, and the wall needed a lot of patching, but the closed door to the kitchen had probably saved the rest of the house from smoke damage. She tucked her hair behind her ears, pushed up her sleeves, and got to work cleaning up the mess.

It didn't take her as long to clean as she'd thought. Soon she was finishing up with a mop after wiping off the counters, refrigerator, stove, table, and cabinets. *That will work for now,* she thought. After making herself a cup of Earl Grey tea, she sat at the table. She studied the kids' artwork at the top of the wall. Some of it was ruined, but she couldn't bring herself to take it down yet. Right as she put the mug in the dishwasher, she saw a familiar car sitting in front of the house. It was Sasha's.

CHAPTER 9

*R*achael froze. What did Sasha want, and how long had she been out there? The girl sat frozen in her car. She looked like she wanted to leave, but she didn't. Instead, she finally got out of the car. She was still as pale as her platinum hair. She had on bright pink sweats and Eddie's old Oakland Raiders sweatshirt. She looked like a lost little girl with her straight, long hair pulled into a ponytail. Although Rachael's heart went out to her, she had to wonder why Sasha was here, and if Eddie had sent her. She hoped he wasn't using her to get to them.

Rachael wanted to believe the girl was as clueless about Eddie as Rachael had been when it came to Ed in the beginning. That idea could excuse how Sasha had acted toward Rachael the last time she tried to mend the rift between her and Eddie. Sasha had made it clear that Eddie didn't want Rachael around. She hadn't allowed Rachael to leave a present or message for her son because it would upset him. That exchange had hurt Rachael deeply.

Rachael sighed and hurried to the front door. She could hear the TV and Kelly's laughter. She couldn't remember the game they always played together, but at least two of her kids got along. Rachael opened the door before Sasha knocked.

"Oh!" Sasha exclaimed.

"What can I do for you?" Rachael asked quietly, stepping out onto the porch with Sasha. Rachael shut the door behind her and stood facing Sasha. She wanted to figure out what her son's girlfriend was doing here before the rest of the family saw her.

"I was hoping—well, I'm sorry to come by without calling. I was wondering if you've heard from Eddie?" Sasha could barely contain her tears.

"Eddie? No, but I was going to try to talk to him. Strange things have been happening, and I hope he's not involved," Rachael blurted out.

"So you haven't heard from him," Sasha repeated, her shoulders slumping in defeat.

"No. Why would I? He wanted nothing to do with me, remember?" Rachael immediately felt guilty about her tone. The girl was obviously upset.

"I remember. I'm sorry, Rachael. Maybe I shouldn't have come." Sasha backed away.

Rachael couldn't let her leave without finding out more. "No, I'm sorry. Please tell me what's going on."

Sasha was silent for a moment, and she began to pick at her short red fingernails. She took a deep breath, and in a quiet voice she answered, "Last time I saw you, I told you his plans to go to school and go to a rehab to get a handle on everything. He told me he wouldn't be able to contact me for the first week, except through text. It's been over a week, and it's been days since he texted me. He never told me the name of the place he was going—always said he couldn't remember it but knew where it was. So I started looking. I can't find any information on where he is. I've called all the rehabs, saying I was his wife so they'd talk to me. No one's heard of him. This isn't like him, Rachael. He always kept in contact with me. I'm worried something has happened to him." Sasha burst into tears.

Rachael pulled the frail girl into her arms. She didn't know what to think. Maybe her son had just decided to leave Sasha and didn't bother to tell her? *How to put this delicately?* Rachael thought. "What if he...well, decided he needed a break? Maybe he wasn't ready to do this and is staying with a friend?"

"No. I tried all his friends and people who weren't his friends. None of them have heard from him. In fact, some of them were looking for him too. It's not like that, Rachael. This was his idea to clean up. He really did want to do good for us. You don't understand," Sasha finished, standing a bit straighter and meeting Rachael's gaze now. She realized how much this girl loved her son in that moment.

Rachael sat on the new porch swing and indicated that Sasha should sit next to her. "No, I don't understand. Bad things have been happening around here. Unfortunately, well, the things happening could have only been done by him. So Eddie missing might mean he has been, um, trying to hurt us," Rachael said. Watching anger light up Sasha's eyes, she quickly added, "You know how much it hurts me to be saying this. I didn't want to believe it, but it all adds up. I'm sorry, Sasha, but I think you might be better off without him."

Sasha's anger dissipated quickly, and her face fell. The girl in front of Rachael now bore the face of someone who was devastated. Sasha's body seemed to crumple into itself as she wrapped her arms around her legs. It was like she was trying to hold herself up, which only made her look more wretched. Rachael quickly regretted her choice of words and hated the pain she was causing the young woman. Sasha could have been Rachael once, but the globe, the clothes on their honeymoon, and then the house fire and the truck brakes failing all pointed to Eddie. Even if Rachael didn't want it to be true, it was.

Sasha quietly replied through tight lips, with an unsteady gaze, "I don't know what's going on here, Rachael, but Eddie wouldn't hurt his own family. He may have had issues, but he was working on them and getting better. Just because he didn't want to see you—well, that was his choice. Whatever these things are that you think are being done to you, they aren't being done by Eddie. You need to understand that things between Eddie and me were improving. He was stepping up and doing what was right for our family. He's missing, not hiding. I'd bet my life on it. I only came to you because I was desperate. The police won't help me, and his friends—well, I need you to believe me,"

Sasha finished as the tears flowed freely down her face. She wiped them away with the back of her hand.

"I—What? Your family? You're pregnant?" Rachael asked in disbelief.

"Oh, I...well, yes. I didn't mean to tell you, but yes, I am. He was happy about it when I texted him. I wanted to wait until he got back home, but I thought it would give him something to fight for. After that I never heard back from him. His cellphone goes to voicemail. I checked his messages, but the only ones I found were from his friends, who were also looking for him. Rachael, Eddie even mentioned making things right with you before he left. You understand what a huge step that is for him?" Sasha folded her hands over her chest.

She was getting defensive again, so Rachael tried a new approach. "I'm very happy to hear about the baby and that Eddie wanted to make things right. You were right in coming here. I'm sorry for my first reaction, but you understand I'm on edge with all the things happening to us. I think we should sit down and talk with Tony about this, get everyone on board. You can't do this alone, and you need to hear what's been happening here." Rachael smiled at Sasha, who reminded her of a wild animal ready to bolt.

"You're okay about the baby? I thought you'd be furious. Well, then, that's such a relief. And you'll help me search for him?" Sasha paused and looked hopefully at Rachael, who nodded, so she continued. "I know something's wrong. He left in his car with a suitcase the day of your wedding. He said he would be back in a week. He isn't. I've tried all his friends and people that shouldn't be his friends. Nothing. Their messages indicated they didn't know where he was, either. I've driven past all Eddie's friends' houses to see if I could find his car. Nothing. I drove past all the other people he associated with. Nothing. I checked all the rehabs and hospitals in a hundred-mile radius. Nothing. No accidents of someone fitting his description, either. Plus, I've been having the most vivid dream. He comes to me, telling me he is so sorry. He hopes I can forgive him, and Rachael, he's wearing a hospital gown," Sasha finished, studying Rachael.

Rachael wasn't sure what to make of all of this. Eddie being missing, to her, meant that he was up to no good. Rachael wanted Sasha to remain calm in her condition, so she was going to calmly stick to the facts. Sasha could believe what she wanted after that. It wouldn't change the reality that these things were happening.

Rachael spoke in her "everything is going to be all right" tone. "Okay. You've checked a lot of places. Maybe we should extend out a bit further. Who knows what rehab took him in on such short notice? I wouldn't read anything into that dream, Sasha. Don't worry. We'll pull together and figure this out. I think you need to know what's been happening here, too. It's been unnerving for me. The day of my wedding, a snow globe came with the word 'remember' on it. It was the exact same gift Eddie's father gave to me on our wedding day. In Hawaii someone broke into our room and cut up all our clothes—the same thing Eddie's father did to me the day I left him. Then, on a drive, while we were swimming, we came back to a man changing all four flat tires on our car—they had been slashed. The police had let the rental company know." Rachael looked at Sasha, who listened to this wide-eyed.

"Wow, I had no idea. I'm sorry, Rachael. Who would do this to you? Wait, you really think it's Eddie?" Sasha shook her head.

"I don't want to, but, as you say, he's been gone. The only thing that made me question that it was him was the cost of getting to Hawaii. I mean, how would Eddie get money for that trip? Do you have any ideas?" Rachael finally asked. Tony's theory was that he'd gotten the money from robbing a house or selling drugs. Those things could have very well happened but she hoped Sasha would have an answer for it. More than likely, she wouldn't have a clue.

Sasha was frowning. "Extra money? No. We've been barely making ends meet since he stopped his illegal activities. You know, well, it's been rough. We're behind on a couple of bills and late with rent," Sasha admitted with a shrug.

"I know 'tough,' Sasha. As a single mom in school, I had to shop at thrift stores and sometimes go to the food bank to make it through the month. I know my parents would have helped, but I wanted to do it alone, you know? Are you positive, Sasha, that Eddie had nothing to sell to fund a trip?"

"Nothing," Sasha confirmed and added shyly, "I've always admired you for how hard you worked as a single mom. I know you don't think Eddie appreciated it, but I think deep down he knows how lucky he was. It was just how he felt about his father and all that seems to mess him up sometimes. He admired his father, and your marriage breaking up—well, it bothered him."

Rachael quickly cut her off. "Yes, his father did a number on him. That's for sure. I'm sorry for that." She paused, expecting an argument, but Sasha only frowned. So she continued. "There's more, Sasha. Since we've been home, things have been happening to us. Stevie's brakes gave out, and he got into an accident."

"What? Is he okay?" Sasha gasped.

"Yes, luckily, he is, but the truck isn't. We wondered if someone tampered with the brakes. We'll be hearing more about that when the mechanic calls, and the police want a report as well. Then, at the same time as the accident, Kelly fell as she was hiking with a friend and her mother to a swimming hole. She almost fell off a cliff, and she broke her foot."

"Kelly too? Oh no! I'm so sorry, Rachael. Eddie would want to know about all of this. I know he would want to help. He's different now. You'll see when we find him." Sasha gently rubbed her slightly bulging belly.

"I'm glad to hear he was having a change of heart, honestly. There's more, though. After all of that we came home to a house fire. Fortunately, a neighbor saw the smoke and called it in. We could have lost the house, our puppy, and our cat. I found our puppy—Leo had escaped outside through a door that was left open. I'm positive we locked it before we left to buy a new microwave. Our other one ended up on the floor, broken. We can only conclude that someone wants to hurt us. The only person who makes any sense, given the snow globe and clothes, is Eddie." Rachael was unable to look at Sasha. She quickly added, "Right now, we're considering staying somewhere else until we figure out what's going on. Nothing strange has been happening to you, has it?"

"No, and I know it isn't Eddie. There has to be someone else doing this," Sasha insisted. She was a pale shade of green. She looked like she was going to pass out. Had Rachael gone too far? She put her hand over Sasha's cold hand and lightly patted it.

Rachael was trying her best to remain calm and not upset Sasha, but the truth was it was even scarier to think that it wasn't Eddie. She was convinced it was him, though. She felt cold, suddenly, and the hair on the back of her neck and arms stood up. She realized that, as careful as she was being with the girl in her condition, Rachael wasn't 100 percent sure about Sasha. She was seeing a girl in distress, unless she was a fantastic actress. Rachael didn't know what to think, but if the story about the baby was true, then her grandchild would need her help, along with its mother.

Rachael took a deep breath, and put her arm around Sasha. "That's what we are trying to figure out, Sasha. Tony and I had a talk about this earlier today. Believe me when I say I don't want it to be my son doing these things, but these are things only he would know about. The one thing we can both agree on is that we need to find Eddie. Come in the house, and we'll talk about this some more. And Sasha, when is the last time you ate?" Rachael noted her frail appearance.

"Ate? I...well...last night?" She shrugged.

"I can't cook you anything in the kitchen because of the fire, but I can offer you some cold pizza, if that sounds good to you, or a sandwich?"

"The pizza sounds good to me," Sasha said.

"Good. I'd heat it up, but, like I said, our microwave fell on the floor, narrowly missing Leo. Along with pictures falling off the walls. This is getting stranger to me as I say it out loud." Rachael shivered. She felt something evil and cold flow through her. Then it was gone.

"Did you feel that?" Sasha asked.

"That cold?"

"Yes, and evil. Leaving the house might be a good idea, Rachael.

Something doesn't feel right here. I, um, think I'll wait out here, if you don't mind." Sasha looked as completely freaked out as Rachael felt.

"Okay, well, I'll grab you some pizza. Be right back." Rachael hurried to get Sasha some food.

The electrician, Dan, was talking to Sasha on the front porch when she returned with the rest of Kelly's pizza. Kelly would understand once she heard Sasha's news. Rachael was going to be a grandma—she hoped! That was an interesting piece of information. She should be happy, but part of her was worried, too. This was getting more and more confusing.

Rachael left Sasha to her pizza, which she was nibbling at, to show Dan to the kitchen.

Dan looked surprised at their scorched wall. "Wow. Let me take a quick look."

"Wow is right." Rachael watched Dan examine it.

"Found your problem," Dan informed her rather swiftly.

"What?" Rachael hoped it was something normal. It wasn't.

"There was a long piece of metal jammed into the outlet. It's melted and scorched. Easy to miss if you weren't looking for it. Do you have a baby or toddler who would do this?" Dan asked.

"No. We have a puppy, though."

"Well, you never know. He could have been playing, and it got wedged in there somehow. Luckily, he didn't get shocked or hurt. I can fix this right up. Where's your fuse box? I might have to turn your power off for a bit. Hope you don't mind." Dan paused, and she shook her head and pointed to the pantry. Dan continued, "And Rachael, I think this was your lucky day. It could have been so much worse."

"Yes, I have heard that more than once today." Rachael forced a smile, adding, "Thank you, Dan, for coming over so quickly."

"No problem. I was glad you called me. It shouldn't take me too long, unless there's more damage in the wall from the fire. I'll rewire, and you are good to go. So, depending on what I find, we are looking at a job in the $300 range. That okay? I could write out an estimate, if you like."

Rachael quickly let him know an estimate wasn't necessary

because she trusted him. She listened as Dan kept talking. She heard herself respond in a cheerful voice she didn't recognize. Standing in their scorched kitchen discussing family and Hawaii was surreal to her—like she was watching a movie.

Finally, she was able to get back to Sasha when Dan got to work. She wouldn't have been surprised if the girl had bolted, but she was still there.

* * *

EDDIE STOOD SILENTLY, listening to the exchange between his girlfriend and his mother. Sasha was so loyal to him. He was ashamed to think about all the lies he'd told her, including the one about him going into rehab when instead he had gone to Hawaii. It hurt to hear his mother say she didn't want to believe it was him, but who else could it be? She had a point, he had to admit. But it wasn't all him, and he wished he could tell them that. He would even take responsibility for what he did so they would know the truth. It was strange seeing himself through his mother's and Sasha's eyes, unclouded by whatever that evildwel did to his already messed-up mind and his own stupidity.

He felt remorse, but he also felt love for Sasha, their baby, and his mother, too. He was glad Sasha didn't know his real reaction to her news. If he got out of this, she never would.

What really ate away at him was how he'd gotten the money to follow his mother and stepfather on their honeymoon. He was too embarrassed to say it out loud to his father, but Eddie had helped a couple of his friends break into two local businesses by driving the car. They were small places that didn't have good security. He hoped they had insurance and that the burglary didn't put them under. Why hadn't he thought of that before? His cut hadn't been all that much, and his two friends had ended up in jail. He walked free because he talked. They had no idea. They were convinced he had gotten away. They stayed loyal to him, but he hadn't given them back the same loyalty. He got lucky there. What he got out of it had been disappointing at the time, so he continued finding ways to get more money, including making and selling methamphetamines, pain pills and weed, until he had enough for the flight and some extra expenses.

That wasn't even the worst part of it. He pretended to be broke all the time, having bills, but he'd never clarified to Sasha what they were, claiming repairs on his car that had never happened, all the while pretending to be on the right path. Poor Sasha worked as many shifts as she could get at the fast food place to make ends meet. He barely contributed anything—he never had. She always took him at his word. Either they didn't give him the hours they were supposed to (they did), or he had to pay some old credit card bills (he didn't), or whatever else he thought of at the moment. He was creative, and Sasha was completely trusting. He used to be proud of how clever he was.

Now he was filled with shame. It was a new feeling for him. He'd basically abandoned Sasha and his baby to get revenge on his mother. Looking at it now, it didn't make sense to him. He wasted so much time trying to make his mother miserable. All she did was raise him the best she could. Yeah, their family hadn't been together, and he had blamed her, but his father had admitted his own guilt, and that got Eddie to thinking. If his mother hadn't been at fault, then he had no reason to do what he did. It was crazy to think about. This pretty much made Eddie a huge and stupid asshole just like his dad had been, but on a bigger scale. He felt like he was seeing things clearly for the first time in his life.

Eddie would earn Sasha's praise and make amends to his mom and his siblings. He was going to take care of his child, too, if only he got the chance. He knew he would have to pay for his stupidity—probably jail time, or at least probation, for stealing the car. He'd pay the people back in full that he borrowed money from to make the trip to Hawaii. He wondered if his mom would press charges against him. He realized he didn't know. He would gladly do what it took to make it right and take care of his family. But it wasn't going to be easy, he realized.

The first thing would be working on his anger. It was never about Sasha; it was directed more at himself. It bled over onto her for being dumb enough to be with him. But she wasn't dumb, he knew, just full of love. He was going to cherish that, even if he only had now.

Eddie observed the evildwel hover around Sasha. She felt it. His mother felt it. It was getting stronger. His dad was watching the guy fixing the outlet. His dad didn't trust anyone right now. Although Eddie still felt that pull to the evildwel with Tony's father in it, he was also learning to protect himself from that familiar calling. Eddie wanted no more of what that dark cloud offered or his old lifestyle. He was changing for the better, finally. He was proud of that. He just hoped it wasn't too late, especially once everyone found out what he did. None of that mattered right now. Only stopping this evildwel did.

ED KNEW ENOUGH about electrical work to know that this man was telling the truth. He also knew about his history with his ex-wife. He had been kind to Rachael when she needed a friend, before she met Tony, even walking her to her car late at night. He was one of the good ones. Ed immediately knew that when he met him. How did he know so much about the man? No idea. Zelina wasn't exactly handing out information. Ed sighed. How did the evildwel get the metal into the outlet? It was very handy. It messed with the truck brakes, pushed his daughter down a rocky, steep hill, and, of course, killed people, too. Who knows what else it was responsible for, or what it was capable of? All Ed knew was that this red-eyed Wayne-thing had almost killed both of his kids in a matter of moments, while Eddie's body clung to life in a coma in Hawaii.

Ed had to find a way to get Rachael to check on Eddie, but how? All he could do was hint or leave clues. He watched her check into it on the island, but she'd never made the connection. Maybe it didn't matter now, or Sasha would figure it out. Ed knew Eddie used cash on the whole trip, but perhaps he'd slipped up and used his ATM for something? Worth a try. Although, Ed thought, maybe Sasha would have seen that. He frowned and puzzled over how to fix that problem.

* * *

ZELINA WATCHED it all play out. She knew Eddie had slipped up once and Sasha had missed it. It was time for Rachael and Sasha to bond, and hopefully, Rachael would feel she could trust the girl. Either way, they would both soon find out where Eddie was.

Zelina was afraid for Ed, and for Eddie too, for what they had to do. No one had survived taking on an evildwel this powerful. Together, she hoped, they might be able to. *Love is stronger than hate,* she thought and smiled. Basic Angel 101. She knew Tony had some painful news about his father to endure, but together, Tony and Rachael would be stronger.

That was what people tended to forget: how strong love is. Most of the time Zelina enjoyed helping people find their way through life, but this was one time she wished she had more of an idea of how this was going to turn out. *Yes, even angels get frustrated, but they do not give up,* she reminded herself. *Only humans do.* She waited and watched.

CHAPTER 10

$\mathcal{T}$he sound of Stevie and Kelly's laughter echoed on the porch and then fell into the silence. Rachael's two youngest children played their game, completely unaware of what was going on around them. It was pure innocence, and she wished she could join them. She knew she would soon have to pull them into reality—just not yet. She quietly sighed. Sasha was staring at her half-eaten pizza.

"I'll be right back," Rachael informed Sasha, who responded with a slight nod.

Rachael hurried to check on Dan and found Tony helping. She heard Dan repeating to Tony how lucky they were. Rachael whispered into Tony's ear to come out onto the porch after Dan left. He agreed, but looked confused. She hurried back to Sasha. Rachael filled the uneasy quiet by recapping her happy honeymoon to Sasha, who acted interested, but both knew it was filling the time until Tony could join them.

Soon Dan followed Tony out. Tony's face clearly showed the shock of seeing Sasha sitting on the front porch swing. Rachael should have warned him, but she didn't want to say anything in front of Dan.

He had a forced smile and said, "Oh, Sasha. I, um, am glad you could stop by. I'll be right back. I'm going to walk Dan to his truck."

"Let me grab my checkbook, and I'll meet you there," Rachael said.

When she got to his truck, Dan had completed his bill but seemed reluctant to let go of it, saying, "Well, I gave you a discount, and it came in a little under what I quoted—$275. I'll bill your insurance."

"Thank you, Dan."

"Yes, thank you. You can be sure we'll be using you again and will be recommending you," Tony added.

"I'd feel better if we paid you today, though," Rachael insisted.

"No, no. Let's wait and see what the insurance does first. I trust you. Well, I have to get going. I'm supposed to pick up some milk and bread. The wife is waiting, you know. Please keep in touch, and thank you for thinking of me." Dan hopped into his white work truck.

"I'm glad I got to meet you," Tony replied.

"Yes, glad to meet you too. Have a good rest of the day."

"Tell your wife hello, and give your son a hug from us," Rachael called as he started backing up.

"Will do!" Dan replied and drove away.

Rachael's stomach was heavy. She felt like that was their last grasp at normalcy. She smiled at Tony, who returned her smile with raised eyebrows. Tony grabbed Rachael's hand and squeezed it as they headed back to their guest.

Rachael started. "Um, well, you know Sasha, Tony—well, she came here looking for Eddie. He's been missing since our wedding day."

"Missing?"

"Yes," Sasha finally spoke up. "He was supposed to go into rehab, but he isn't at any of them. He's changed. He didn't do the things you think he did. He wanted to make everything right."

"Rachael told you about the things going on?"

"She did, but it wasn't him," Sasha insisted.

"One more thing you need to know, Tony." Rachael looked at Sasha. "She's pregnant."

Tony opened his mouth and then shut it. The hardness in his eyes disappeared and was replaced by confusion. Rachael understood that and quickly filled him in on the rest of their conversation.

146

Rachael could see that Tony was struggling to absorb it all. "Okay. You don't want to tell Stevie and Kelly yet, do you, Rach?"

"I want to wait...well, until we can't."

"I can agree with that. Sasha, I'm glad you came to us," Tony began. Rachael knew her husband well enough to understand he was carefully picking his words.

"Yes, I am too. She knows what has been happening here and our concerns, like I said. Sasha brought up a valid point: What if he was a victim in this too? So how should we proceed?" Rachael asked, not believing for a moment that Eddie was a victim.

"Well, yes, there is that chance Eddie is a victim." The word "victim" seemed forced to Rachael, but she didn't think Sasha noticed. Tony continued, "I believe, Sasha, that you've covered everything I'd have done to find Eddie. The next step should be to file a missing person report as a family member. Frankly, I'm surprised they didn't suggest you do that." He paused and looked at Sasha, who shrugged, so he continued. "With all the things happening, I'm sure the police will want to look more into this. I'll let them know about what happened in Hawaii and here. Someone is after us, that's clear. And Sasha, I'd feel better if you stayed with us at the hotel tonight, especially with a baby involved. Until we get this all sorted out."

"It isn't Eddie. I'd stake my life on it," Sasha repeated. "But I can see it might be safer if we stay together until we figure out what's happening. And if you're wondering if I'm really pregnant, I have the paperwork from the doctor in my car."

Rachael could plainly see that Tony still thought it was Eddie; so did she. She wondered if they needed to fear for Sasha and the baby. Would he try to hurt her too? Rachael really hoped they weren't misreading this and she wasn't helping him. She shuddered, and Tony put a protective arm around her. They couldn't take a chance with an innocent baby.

"We...no, you don't need to get it," Rachael said, but Sasha was already up and rushing to her car.

"You trust her?" Rachael whispered to Tony.

"I think so. Seems like she really believes Eddie is innocent, and she wants us to believe her. She's getting proof of her pregnancy. There is our future grandchild to consider. We'll keep a watchful eye on her, agreed?" Tony said as Sasha walked back with several papers in her hand.

"Agreed," Rachael carefully said with a fake smile.

"It shows the tests, my due date, and a doctor's note. They wanted me to take a week off work because of my stress levels. I have an ultrasound scheduled in three days. I think it's a girl." Sasha smiled as she handed the papers to Rachael.

Rachael carefully looked them over and handed them to Tony. They were real.

"You didn't have to provide proof like this."

"Yes, I did. I want you to believe me. I need you to," she said, as tears started to flow again.

Rachael pulled the thin girl into her arms while Tony held the papers with a frown. Would her son abandon his pregnant girlfriend? Rachael realized she didn't know the answer to that. That unnerved her.

"Well, we do believe you, Sasha. Now it's settled. You'll come with us." Rachael's tone sounded like they were going on a family vacation instead of running away from her out-of-control son. "We have a suite at the new hotel by the freeway. We can stay together. I know Kelly and Stevie would like to get to know you better."

Tony handed the papers back to Sasha and said, "We have some good plans in place. If you two wouldn't mind, let Stevie and Kelly know we're leaving soon and get them ready to go. I already packed their stuff. I'll head to the police station before we leave and get the ball rolling with that. I think it's important they know what's going on and where we'll be. Shouldn't take long. When I get back, we'll go eat and head to the hotel. I'm sure whoever is doing this won't attack us there," Tony finished with a frown.

Rachael knew he was worried about leaving them alone. It wasn't a good sign. He wanted the police to know where they were going. Maybe he didn't trust Sasha as much as Rachael did, or perhaps he knew what Eddie was capable of.

"You should go inside and lock the doors until we leave. You don't think we should involve your mom, do you?" Tony asked.

"My mom? You don't think—no, she hasn't said anything. Maybe we should leave the puppy with her, though, or take him with us, like we planned. I don't want to worry her." Rachael hugged herself.

Was her mother in danger too? This was beginning to feel like they were in a bad movie. Should she be concerned that they were separating? That was never a smart thing to do. It was surreal to think her son wanted to hurt them.

"I don't know what to think, but I want to check on her before we go. It seems centered on us and the kids, but..." Tony shrugged his shoulders. "Leo would be better off with her instead of in a hotel room. I'll be back soon. If something seems wrong, leave—don't wait for me. Sasha can drive you guys out of here, right?" Tony asked her.

"Yes, of course," Sasha replied.

"I love you," Tony said, kissing Rachael, and whispered, "Get the puppy and meet me at the car."

"Be right back, Sasha."

As soon as she got to the car, cradling a sleepy puppy, Rachael quietly asked, "You don't believe her?"

"Not sure. It was strange that she insisted on showing us her paperwork for her pregnancy, but maybe it wasn't, either. I don't know. But, more importantly, now there seems to be a baby involved, and I want it safe, so that includes her. It could be part of Eddie's plan, or she may be completely clueless. Either way, watch yourself around her, understand? Call 911 if you feel you're in any kind of danger."

"Yes, I will. Please be careful, Tony."

"I will. You watch over our kids until I get back. It's going to be okay. We'll figure this all out. And honestly, I'm being careful with the girl."

"With everything that has happened..." Rachael left her sentence unfinished.

"Right, exactly. Right now, I think, as they say, keep your enemies close—just in case. I'm going to change the hotel we're staying at—I'll text you that information. I don't want her to know where our reservations are ahead of time. If we don't bring Leo, we have many more options. If anything comes up, leave immediately. Keep in contact by text, and if you can't text, how about we meet at the college by my office, if we lose contact or cell signal? If you must call a taxi, do so. Promise?"

"I promise. You be careful, too. I love you." Rachael handed the puppy over to Tony.

"I love you, Rachael." He waved and drove off.

Rachael felt alone and unsure after Tony left. She headed back to the porch and Sasha.

"I'm glad you believe me. You'll see I'm right about Eddie," Sasha said. "I'll help you pack and load up my car," she offered and added, "in case we have to leave before Tony gets back."

"Yes, maybe we should. Whoever is doing this, we aren't safe. I'm worried we might be followed. The fact that it happened here and in Hawaii really concerns me. I'm trying to keep an open mind. I'll follow the facts, though." Rachael suddenly wondered if they should have sent Sasha home. Nothing had happened to her. Could she be trusted? Her head was going to explode, the way her emotions kept going back and forth.

"Yes, I agree. The truth will come out. Well, we have to do something. What are you going to tell Kelly and Stevie? I mean, they've had a really bad day, too," Sasha said.

"How about we tell them it was due to the fire? I don't want to worry them yet. But we do need to explain why you're here."

"What if we tell them part of the truth? Eddie is in rehab, getting cleaned up. I came by to tell you, and I'm helping. Then I should probably go home. It wouldn't make sense, me staying at the hotel with you." Sasha rubbed her hands together.

An alarm went off in Rachael's head. Why wasn't she staying with them now? Wouldn't that be perfect, to go to their hotel room and then let Eddie know where they were after she left? No, she had to be very careful, no matter how much she wanted to trust the girl.

"They understand their brother has issues. But I don't want them to know all the other things that happened. They have been through too much today; you're right about that. You're staying with us because you're lonely. I don't like not being honest with my kids."

"Right, but, like you said, with Stevie crashing today and Kelly breaking her foot on a fall, and the fire in the house, that's enough for them. They'll know the story later, but maybe wait until you know more. Are you sure you want me to stay with you?" Sasha asked. "I get the feeling you don't."

"Yes. We want you and the baby safe. You can understand, though, if we think it's Eddie doing this and you suddenly show up, how that can look, right? I mean, you can understand how confused I am right now, at least. All that said, we still want you with us, Sasha, until we figure this out."

"We disagree on Eddie, but I'd never hurt your family. All I want is to find Eddie and figure out who is doing these things to you. Would it help if I gave you my cellphone? That way, you won't think I'm trying to contact Eddie. All I want is your trust. I promise it isn't me who wants you hurt. I've felt a real evil presence since I arrived here. It scares me. It's something in this house. I'm not sure it's human, either." Sasha shuddered.

"You and Kelly will really get along. She believes the same thing, Sasha. What's coming after us is very real, I believe, and very human. Would you mind shutting off your cellphone? That would make me feel better right now, I admit. Let's go inside and prepare them to leave."

"We should load my car, for now, so we're ready to go," Sasha insisted, looking around and frowning.

"Okay," Rachael agreed.

"This house really spooks me."

Rachael didn't comment on the house remark as they headed inside. She knew it wasn't haunted. Rachael wasn't going to tell Stevie and Kelly about her belief that their brother stalked them on their honeymoon and tampered with the car and house wiring until she had to. As for Sasha, she really hoped she was what she seemed, because if not, she'd brought the enemy into their house.

* * *

YOU CAN TRUST SASHA, *Rachael,* Ed thought. He sighed as he watched Tony drive off. He wished they hadn't separated. They needed to stay together so Ed could try to protect them. There was nothing the police could do against an evildwel, unless—

He had an idea.

"You stay here and keep an eye on things. Try to keep that thing away from them. Don't let it get to you, Eddie. I'll be right back."

"What? Why are you leaving too? It isn't following Tony," Eddie said.

"I know. But I have a feeling—and I need to check it out. I'm hoping it will lead to the local police checking into what happened in Hawaii. A way to ID you. That way, they'll know it wasn't you doing this part of it, and they'll know where you are. I wish your mother understood what was going on. There's no way to convince her that a ghost is trying to harm them, or that her dead ex-husband, son, and an angel are trying to help. Kelly and Sasha seem open to the idea. That might help. You do know that leaving and going to a hotel isn't going to stop this thing?"

"I know it won't. I'll keep trying to get through to Mom. If nothing else, I'll try Kelly and Sasha." Eddie rubbed his temples.

"Good. I have another feeling that there's more to learn. The hospital and police station are pulling me, so I better get going. I have a lot to do—unless you have a better suggestion, Zelina?"

Still nothing, which Ed took as a green light.

"We know enough about Wayne Battaglia. He tried to kill his family. I'm not sure what you can do at the hospital."

"I'm not sure, either," Ed admitted. "But I have to trust what I'm feeling, or at least see if what I'm feeling means anything. This is all new to me, Eddie. I'll be right back. Don't leave their side. If you need help, ask Zelina to come help you. Although, with her, you never know if she'll show up or not."

"I'm not feeling good about this idea, Dad. We should stay together," Eddie protested.

"Noted." Ed zoomed off with Eddie watching.

* * *

"I HOPE we can do this, Dad," Eddie said quietly to himself when he was alone with the evildwel.

He knew that if it came down to it, he would gladly sacrifice himself for his family. He would go inside that thing and kill what was there, but he also knew it would probably kill him, too.

"Yes, Eddie, you may have to do that," Zelina said from behind him, startling him.

"What? Are you Zelina?"

"Of course I am, Eddie. You have as much to atone for as your father. If you survive, you will not remember all of this, naturally, so I will speak plainly to you. My hope is that the change you effect here will bleed into your life. It is much more likely that you will have to die in order to save them. It is worth fighting for, you understand, but you might even end up in that darkness—honestly, I am not sure. A steep price to pay for your loved ones. I would feel bad, but you have done so many bad things in your life thus far. Like your father, this is your last chance, too. If you cannot fix this, you will not survive the coma. You could also end up like your father, watching your life on replay and seeing all the harm you did without being able to change it. That is what your father has been doing since he died. It took him time to turn around that part of him." Zelina paused and studied Eddie for a moment.

"I want to change."

"That is important," Zelina said and then added, "You should know that no one has ever survived trying to separate these things, especially something this strong. Your father is the first to do what he did for you. This one here is stronger than yours was, stronger than any I have come across before. Know, Eddie, that love is stronger. You and your dad must use that together and, yes, go in and fight together. He knows that, even though he keeps trying to find ways around it. I have done what I can. A fax will make its way to this police department once they find a receipt your dad managed to locate on a hunch. He placed it for the nurse to find. Luckily, it was when you got gas by your house and used a charge card. They know your name now and your hometown. Yes, Eddie, if your mom survives the night, she will come to you and forgive you." Zelina looked him straight in the eyes and opened her wings, making him feel very small.

Eddie was speechless, gazing at the beautiful angel in front of him. All he could think of to say was, "My mother won't hate me?"

"No, Eddie, she will not. You will understand when your little girl is born."

"Wow," Eddie managed to say.

"Eddie, besides your baby, you must protect your mom. Her baby is special—and the top priority. Of course, keeping your sister, brother, and stepfather safe are important, too. You have a lot to do, and I cannot help you with that." Zelina flapped her colorful wings while she pushed a stray black hair behind her ear.

"My mother is having a baby? What's so special about that?" Eddie quickly regretted his sarcastic tone.

Zelina frowned at him. "That is none of your concern, Eddie. You have enough to worry about, I would say. Yes, you should be worried about the tone of voice you use with me. I am the one who has been fighting for you. I do not have to."

"I'm sorry. I'm confused." Eddie felt small, much like a mouse would feel under a hawk.

"I accept your apology, Eddie. There are others who would like to hear that from you too. I hope you remember at least that. Know, Eddie, that you must win this battle. There is no other way. Soon Tony will find out about his own father. It will be unpleasant, but that cannot stop you. Maybe this will work. I cannot see the outcome. I wish you luck, Eddie. One piece of advice I hope you consider: You *might* be able to get through to the evil man inside with love, but if not, be willing to kill him and get out before you are lost too. Do not hesitate, Eddie. So much depends on you." Zelina was gone in a bright flash before he could respond.

Eddie had no idea what to do with that information. Kill someone?

Well, he was almost dead already, but still. He watched his family pack, and he knew he would die for these people, gladly.

* * *

Ed's first stop was the hospital on Maui. The nurse had quickly found the ATM receipt on the ground by his son's bagged clothes. Name and city—that was all she needed to jump into action. Ed wasn't sure how he knew it was stuffed deeply into Eddie's shorts, but he did. He watched the nurse send a picture and name to their local police department. Unfortunately, the picture and note sat unattended at the police station.

Ed caught up to Tony right after he left Mae's house. He saw her waving goodbye, holding the small puppy. He followed Tony into the police station.

He listened as Tony told his story. They seemed skeptical, until one of them found the picture and note from the hospital in Maui. Quickly, Tony confirmed who it was. *That changes everything.* He knew that only explained half of Tony's story. It confused the problems at home, and the blame would fall on Sasha.

"We will be looking into this, Mr. Battaglia. We have all your information. We'll be talking to Sasha, of course. If you don't mind waiting a few minutes, I have a couple of papers I'd like you to sign before you go," the young police officer named Dani assured Tony. He nodded, so she added, "Just let me go print them out."

Tony stood awkwardly, looking around. Ed saw the glances he was getting from Dani. "Only a few more minutes, Mr. Battaglia," she called him over with a smile. "Can I get you some coffee or water?"

"No, thank you." Tony sat down.

Dani nodded to the police chief, who'd been watching all of this with obvious interest since he heard Tony's name. *Strange*, Ed thought. Finally, the papers were signed, and Tony quickly exited.

Ed didn't follow him. Something was up with the police chief. Ed watched the police chief make a phone call. At the same time, Dani hurried to use the bathroom, and her counterpart decided to go on a smoke break. This left the office unattended as Tony reentered. He glanced around, confused, until he heard his name come from the police chief's office. He froze.

"Hank? It's Cal. I'm calling about Tony Battaglia, who came into the station. Right. Yes. I know. He explained. Yes, it's been a while. I wondered. Maybe Tony took after the father, ya know? I'm glad you had a chance to observe him, but more has happened here. No, there was a fire set in their house, the brakes on his truck failed, and the son crashed but luckily was okay, and the daughter had a fall hiking and broke her foot. That, plus what happened there—it seems strange to me, too. I hope he isn't crazy like his father. What that man did still haunts me at night, sometimes."

Ed carefully watched Tony. He was pale and barely breathing. *Why did he come back in?* Ed wondered. Tony looked like he was going to leave, until the police chief started talking again.

"Part of the job, though. I know, Hank. Yes, yes. I know you think Tony's okay—after all, you saved him. I just wonder... Yes, of course. I mean, his father not only killed his pregnant mistress—which to this day still bothers me that we couldn't prove—but the psycho tied up his wife and held her hostage with their son in the next room. What that poor woman went through. I can still hear her telling me, in that gentle voice of hers, that her husband threatened to cut his own son's throat in front of her. They may have been lucky he left on a booze run, but the family he killed wasn't. I know you know all this—sometimes I just need to talk about it. Made me leave the city and move here. I still can't believe they moved here, too. Right, but we can't forget what a monster that man was. Sometimes the apple doesn't fall far from the tree, you know? Tony Battaglia's father was pure evil. Hank, you gotta at least wonder about the son, right? I will, Hank. I understand that Eddie kid might be to blame for what happened over there, but here? Something else is going on. Maybe an accomplice? Could be the girlfriend. Yes, I will consider it, but I'm going to keep an eye on Tony, too. I will. Thanks, and good to hear your voice. Let's keep in touch. Yes, the family is doing great, thanks. Four grandkids now. You? Great.

Heard your hotel was doing good. Yes, I'll personally keep you posted. Okay, bye, Hank."

Tony looked around the office, grabbed the cellphone he'd left behind, and almost ran out the door right as Dani exited the bathroom and hurried back to her desk. Ed decided it would be better to return to the house rather than stay with Tony. He knew Sasha would be Tony's main suspect. He suspected Tony was texting Rachael with that information at that very moment.

* * *

"Do you mind locking the house up for me, Stevie? I'll make sure there is extra food for Tootie. You need anything, Kelly?" Rachael asked.

"I'm fine, Mom," Kelly replied.

"I'll sit with her, Rachael," Sasha offered.

"Yeah, we have a lot to talk about." Kelly smiled.

"Well, okay. Call if you need anything." Rachael wished she didn't have a knot in her stomach, leaving her daughter with her son's girlfriend, but she did.

"Tootie!" Rachael called. She wasn't surprised that her fickle cat didn't come running. She quickly hurried upstairs to check under her bed. She saw eyes glowing back at her. "There you are. We must go. I'll leave you extra food and will have your favorite aunt check on you." The cat stared back at Rachael. Not so much as a meow of thanks. *Fine*, Rachael thought. She quickly dialed Ava's number. No answer, so she left a message.

"Hi, Ava. Tony is taking the family on an overnight trip because some odd things have been going on both in Hawaii and here. I know I should have told you when we got back, but I had hoped it was behind us. I don't have much time, but it started the day of the wedding with a snow globe, like the one Ed got me. Came all wrapped up, with a note that said 'Remember.' On our honeymoon someone broke into our room and cut up all our clothes—again, just like Ed did to me. I know you remember that. Then our tires were all cut up on a day trip in Maui, and then nothing, until today. Stevie's brakes failed and he crashed, but he's okay. Kelly slipped and broke her foot on a hike, and then we came home to a kitchen fire. Some metal was jammed into the outlet. So, we are getting out of here until we can figure it out. We think Eddie is behind this and aren't sure about Sasha, who claims Eddie has been missing since our wedding. Tony is at the police station, letting them know. And Ava, the puppy is with my mom. I know you'd say to come to your house, but I don't want to bring you into this. Sorry for the long message. I'll update more. If you wouldn't mind checking on Tootie—I'll be leaving her lots of food and water. Please bring Tim with you, just to be safe. I love you and will update you more soon." *Beep.* End of message.

Rachael went into the bathroom. Did she need to bring anything? Her toothbrush and brush were gone. She grabbed a sweater and headed downstairs. As soon as she hit the bottom step, a crash came from the living room where Sasha and Kelly were, and then the kitchen where Stevie was.

"Is everyone okay?" Rachael shouted.

"Fine, Mom," Stevie called from the kitchen.

"Fine in here, too," Kelly replied.

A picture was on the ground by the front door. Their wedding picture, again. Rachael hurried into the living room.

"What happened?" she asked, seeing the girls sitting next to each other on the couch.

"That picture fell off the mantel again," Kelly said and added, "It's a ghost."

"There are no such things as ghosts. Maybe it was a small earthquake."

"No earthquake. I agree with Kelly. There's something in this house with us. I'll be glad to get out of here." Sasha's eyes were wide as she held a pale hand to her throat. "I'll clean it up for you, don't worry."

"Thank you, Sasha. There's a picture down in the entry, too. Just like an earthquake would do," Rachael insisted.

"No earthquake. I'm checking," Kelly said.

"Well, they just don't know about it yet. I'm going to check on Stevie now. Don't get cut cleaning it up, Sasha."

"I won't."

Rachael almost ran into the kitchen. She found her son cleaning up a broken wine glass and the bottle of wine that had been next to it.

"What happened?" Rachael asked.

"No idea. I was locking the back door and heard the crash. Guess it was on the edge of the counter or something. An earthquake?" Stevie carefully swept the damage in the dustpan.

"Had to be. A picture fell in the entry, and another in the living room. It was a small one, I guess. You know California. Be careful cleaning it up. Thanks. I'll clean up the other mess and check upstairs. Then, we better go."

Rachael didn't bother to rehang their wedding picture. Luckily, there was no glass to clean up, but the frame was beyond repair this time. She carefully set it aside and hurried upstairs. Everything looked okay. *Strange,* she thought.

"Stevie?" Rachael called. "Could you help me with the suitcases?"

"Coming, Mom!"

"Need any help?" Sasha asked.

"No, we got it. Why don't you take Kelly outside? We'll meet you on the porch."

"Okay!"

Rachael loaded up the cat dish with dry food until it overflowed and added more water to her bowl. The cat box was still clean. She hoped that didn't mean Tootie was using someplace else for that. She sighed and checked the back door one more time and shut off the lights. She grabbed their stuff, her cellphone, and her purse and headed outside.

* * *

TONY LEFT the police station with his head reeling. He sat in the car without starting it. If he hadn't forgotten his cellphone and Dani hadn't left the room, and the guy at the desk hadn't stepped out for a smoke, he never would have heard that conversation between the police chief and Hank. Besides the fact that his stepson was lying in a hospital bed in a coma and was responsible for the clothes and tires, Tony had also learned about his father—who was evil. Tony couldn't process that information now. He had to get to his family.

He quickly texted Rachael.

"Sweetheart, I wish I wasn't telling you this by text, but you need to know. Eddie is in a coma in Maui after a car accident. He was the one who cut up our clothes and cut our tires. That leaves the question of who's doing things to us here. It must be Sasha. Please send her away and get out of there. Take a taxi. I'll check the house and then will head to the meeting place. I love you."

He couldn't tell her what he'd overheard about his father just yet. It was too much. Why didn't his mom tell him? The man was a monster, and he was the son of that monster. What were the chances that the police chief used to be an officer in his hometown, along with Hank?

Tony understood that he was a suspect now too, along with Sasha. The fact that Hank was a cop back in the day and hadn't mentioned it worried Tony. Yes, they thought it was him. He wondered if he was insane, or a killer. *No, that isn't right,* he thought. He wasn't losing his mind. It had never been clearer, and he knew it was Eddie and Sasha. He was more his mother than his murdering father. Tony shook his head. All of this was making him doubt himself, but he knew the truth. He would prove to the police it wasn't him, but first he had a family to save. He started Rachael's old SUV, thinking he would get her a new car soon, and started home.

* * *

ED FOUND RACHAEL, Stevie, and Kelly in Sasha's car. It was loaded and ready to go, but it wouldn't start.

"I don't understand. It was running fine," Sasha said.

He saw Rachael's expression as she stared at her cellphone, sitting in the back seat. She knew.

Ed noted the evildwel circling the car. He had no idea what it had in mind, but it clearly didn't want Sasha to leave with them. Ed hurried to Eddie, who was by the car watching the dark mist. He quickly updated Eddie about Tony and the hospital.

* * *

"WE SHOULD CALL A TAXI!" Sasha exclaimed. "Don't you feel the evil?"

"We need to get out of here." Rachael felt evil around them too—but it was Sasha, not a ghost. Tony had confirmed that. "Kids, get out and wait by the curb. We're going to take a taxi. I'll grab the luggage."

"Mom, why can't we wait for Dad?" Kelly asked as Stevie helped her out of the dead car.

"I want to get there and get the room ready for your dad, is all. Don't worry." Rachael smiled as she stepped out of the car.

"I'll help your mother, don't worry," Sasha added.

"I'm worried," Kelly exclaimed. "There was no earthquake reported. I checked again. Yet things flew off the walls in three rooms. We're lucky nothing hit us."

"Yeah," Stevie added. "Something isn't right. I get in a car accident, Kelly falls and breaks her foot, and we come back to a house fire. What aren't you telling us?"

"Ghosts," Kelly insisted.

"It isn't ghosts. Your dad will tell us more when he gets to us. In the meantime, we'll do what he asked and get out of here. Please, Stevie. We need to leave. Just do as I ask, please. Take your sister to the curb and call a taxi." Rachael wanted to get away from Sasha.

This was getting out of hand. Stevie walked off, shaking his head. She wasn't going to be able to keep this from them for much longer. She turned to Sasha as she pulled their luggage out of the trunk. "I talked to Tony. I hate to say this, but you're our number one suspect. Eddie was in Maui and was a part of this. I need you to go. Your car breaking down here seems too planned to me."

"I—you can't—" Sasha cried. "I would never do anything to hurt your family. I'm sorry you don't know that about me—and Eddie, he's in Maui?" Sasha asked hopefully as she wiped tears away.

"Yes," Rachael said in a lower voice. "He's in the hospital in a coma after a car accident. That's why your partner in crime hasn't contacted you."

Sasha looked like she was going to faint. Rachael wasn't going to buy into her act anymore.

"He's alive."

"He is. Now please leave us alone."

Rachael had to wonder how Sasha had managed to knock their pictures down and then try to blame it on ghosts. *Just another way to scare us,* Rachael thought. She would figure out the "hows" later. Right now, she had to get them to safety. At least she was sure who her enemies were. Boy, had she been dumb. She'd even bought into the "Gee, I'm having his baby" story. The papers were probably fake. She watched Sasha stand there with her mouth open as she slunk back into her car, which suddenly started. That made her look even more guilty.

"You are wrong about this, Rachael. You'll see," Sasha called from the car. And she quickly drove off. Rachael didn't have time to worry about her feelings—if she had any.

"Mom," Stevie called out. "The taxi will be here in ten minutes. And why did Sasha leave? I thought she was coming with us. Does this have something to do with Eddie? What'd he do?"

Rachael wasn't sure how to answer, and Kelly spoke. "Mom, I know Eddie has problems. I know he drinks too much and has anger issues. Eddie may even want to make you unhappy. Sometimes I'm even a bit afraid of his temper. Still, he'd never really hurt us. But Sasha—she's like us. I know she isn't bad. Why'd you send her away, Mom? She was going to take us."

Kelly looked so frail, standing with her crutches, but Rachael saw strength in her she had never seen before.

"I—well, it's Eddie. He did some things to us on our honeymoon. Cut up our clothes and tires. But then it all stopped until we came home. What Dad found out was that Eddie got into a car accident when he was on Maui. He's in a coma. I'm sorry, kids. I think he's behind this, and Sasha is in on it. All I know is we need to get out of here and get to safety." Rachael felt oddly numb.

"Will Eddie live?" Kelly quietly asked.

"I don't know. All we can do is pray for Eddie right now."

"He may have done some stupid things, but he doesn't deserve to die," Stevie grimly stated.

"No, he doesn't," Rachael agreed, as the taxi pulled up. They quickly loaded their stuff and directed the driver, who looked like he hadn't slept in days, to go to the college where they would meet Tony. Rachael finally felt safe.

* * *

EDDIE STOOD next to his father, listening to his mother. Tears poured down his face as he listened to his family and watched Sasha drive off. He wanted to chase after Sasha and comfort her, but he couldn't leave his family. Sweet Sasha was paying for his sins. To hear his family was afraid of him did not bring him the joy he had thought it would. They knew he was in a coma and believed Sasha was doing all these bad things to them now. He wondered how it could get any worse, yet he knew it would, with an evildwel following his mother, brother, and sister.

* * *

TONY WAS ALMOST HOME. His heart felt like it was going to come out of his chest. He met up with Sasha at a stop sign. She was crying and didn't notice him. She turned left. He checked his cellphone. No response, but Rachael and the kids not being with her showed that Rachael had gotten his message. Tony pulled over and dialed Rachael's cellphone. Rachael's phone rang and rang from the back seat of Sasha's car, where no one answered it.

Tony knew he couldn't count on the police to help them, so he rushed home first. He pulled into the driveway, only to find an empty house. He called Stevie's cell and then Kelly's. No one was answering.

They had to be at the meeting place. He quickly checked the house. Everything looked okay, and the suitcases were gone. He ran to the car and headed for the college. He drove right past a yellow taxi that had gone off the road and rammed into a tree. He was too busy checking his phone for messages from Rachael to notice. He found nothing on his phone and set it down. He needed to focus on driving. He had to get to his family. They had to be at the meeting place, but he didn't find them there. He was beginning to panic.

* * *

"Are you guys okay?" Rachael asked.

"Yeah, bumpy ride," Stevie tried to joke. "Kelly?"

"Fine. What about the driver? He isn't moving."

"I'll check him. You guys get away from the car in case—well, you know, it blows or something," Rachael warned. She smelled gas.

"Our stuff?" Stevie asked.

"Just see if you can flag down some help," Rachael said.

"Yeah, I never heard of anyone being in two car accidents in one day," Stevie mumbled as he helped his sister to the road.

Rachael didn't hear what Kelly said to him. She was too intent on checking the man in the taxi. She saw both kids' phones on the seat. One of them was ringing. *It will have to wait,* she thought. She approached the driver, whose ID said he was named Stan.

"Stan? Are you okay?" she asked.

His head was bleeding badly. He wasn't moving or responding. She felt a slight pulse in his neck. She wasn't sure if she should move him, but the gas smell was stronger, and smoke was pouring from under the car. She made the quick decision to pull him out of the car. He wasn't as heavy as he looked. He didn't wake up when she moved him. They had to get him help.

As soon as she got him away from the car, she went back for her purse, the kids' cellphones, and the overnight bag she had packed. As she was dialing 911, a police car pulled over. She quickly hung up, grabbed their suitcases from the popped trunk, and then gestured toward Stan.

"Over here!" she yelled, just as the flames shot from the car. She set their things down and quickly pulled the driver farther away right as the car caught fire. She couldn't believe what she was seeing.

"Are you okay, ma'am?" the short, mustached officer asked, running up.

"Yes, but he's bleeding badly and isn't conscious."

"What happened?" he asked, checking the man and beginning CPR.

"I think we got a flat tire. He lost control, and we hit this tree. I was just able to get the kids to the road, him out of the car, and our stuff out before it blew." Rachael started to shake.

"There's the ambulance. Let them check you out, ma'am. You must be in shock. Hurry!" he yelled to the man and woman in white. "He isn't responding. I can't find a pulse," the officer said.

They went to work on him for what seemed like forever, but they finally stopped.

The officer quietly led Rachael away to her kids.

"I got a hold of Dad," Kelly said. "He's on his way. He passed us but didn't see the accident."

"I'd like to get you checked out at the hospital," the young officer (Rachael never did catch his name) repeated.

"I'm okay," Rachael insisted. "Is the driver—"

"He didn't make it. I'm sorry. If I could get some information from you—"

Rachael numbly gave him all he wanted just as Tony drove up.

* * *

"WHAT HAPPENED?" Tony asked.

"We got a flat, and he lost control," Rachael said.

"Is everyone okay?" Tony looked more afraid than Rachael had ever seen him. That scared her more than the crash.

"We're fine, Dad," Stevie said.

"Yeah, we're okay, but the driver isn't," Kelly added as they wheeled his covered body past them and loaded it into the back of the ambulance.

The mustached officer with the freshly shaved head and no name tag walked up. "Yes, your family was very lucky here. I suggest you get them checked out. I got all the information I need right now, except why your family was in a taxi and you were driving."

"We were down to one car, officer. We were meeting up, is all. I can't believe this happened. Do you think the driver was drinking?" Tony asked.

"We aren't sure, sir. Take your family to the hospital. We'll be in touch with you. Don't forget your stuff," the officer added, studying Tony.

Tony thought the cop didn't trust him. Did he think his wife and kids were trying to get away from him?

"Thank you, officer. I'll make sure they get checked out."

The officer nodded in response as he wrote something down.

Tony loaded his family and their stuff into the car as the fire department pulled in to deal with the flaming taxi. He glanced back before pulling out. The officer was still watching him. He shuddered. He couldn't blame this one on Sasha. Something else was going on. And he was determined to figure it out. He planned to put some distance between him, Sasha, and whoever else was involved in this. He made the call and got the perfect place for them to stay.

"That was lucky, and I already know where the spare key is. There's usually someone staying at the cabin this time of year. You guys will love it there. I promise," Tony said.

"Yes, that was very lucky. I guess we're going on a minivacation." Rachael forced a huge smile.

"Lucky," Kelly agreed in a flat tone. Stevie nodded, but continued looking out the window.

The rest of the ride was unusually quiet. No one wanted to talk about what had happened. Tony didn't blame them for their silence. He didn't want to push them. Someone had died in front of them. He turned onto the main highway and headed to the mountains where he used to fish. They wouldn't be fishing this time. They would be surviving.

He would let Mae know where they were tomorrow. He felt bad lying to her that they were taking a quick family vacation, but he didn't want her to worry. *If she only knew,* he thought, but at least she was safe. Or at least he hoped so. Sasha was still around.

Tony shook his head. On second thought, he would call her once they got settled and update her. Then he would insist that she join them. Yes, that was his plan, and it was a good one. Everyone had fallen asleep by the time they hit the two-lane highway. He ran into a small store and picked up a few supplies. No one stirred while he was gone. He hoped he'd left the bad behind them, but knew better. At least there was a hunting rifle and bow and arrows at the cabin. He would use them to protect his family against whoever or whatever came at them, he grimly promised himself.

CHAPTER 11

The father and son stayed inside the car, unseen by the sleeping family. They watched the evildwel grow bigger and bolder as it circled the car. Ed was against them taking off to a secluded cabin. It was kind of cliché, like a bad horror movie. But since they were unaware of what their danger was, Ed guessed it didn't matter where they tried to hide. Wherever they went, the evildwel would follow.

Ed had learned he could push the evildwel away if he focused on his loving emotions for his kids. Sounded corny, but it worked. *There will be no accident on the way to the cabin, like there was with the taxi,* he thought. He didn't like that he was learning on the job and the people who paid for his lack of knowledge were his kids. His son remained quiet. He was obviously preoccupied, thinking of Sasha and his baby. Eddie was lucky Tony and Rachael suspected Sasha. It was keeping her safe, for now. He hoped Mae stayed safely away from all of this, too.

"We gotta focus, Eddie."

"I am, Dad. That thing isn't going to hurt them with me around."

Ed smiled but didn't respond. *I hope so, son,* he thought as they turned left off the main highway onto a two-lane, redwood-lined road. Finally, they went down a dark dirt road. It was long, with sharp turns and a few potholes that Tony narrowly missed. Ed turned his gaze to the evildwel. It was smiling at him as it kept circling.

The redwoods opened into a circular driveway. There was a small log cabin with a huge deck on the side of it that was surrounded by several large, ancient redwoods and other flora Ed didn't recognize in the dark.

"This is a place I would have loved to have taken you when you were a kid."

"Better late than never, Dad." Eddie grinned.

"Sometimes," Ed responded. The evildwel bumped against the car as Tony parked it.

The car shuddered off. Ed had let his guard down for only a few seconds by taking in the scenery and thinking about what he should have done in the past and forgotten about the present. The evildwel took advantage of it. The dark mist poured out from under the car hood like a bad fifties horror movie. Wayne's face was smiling smugly. Ed knew the evildwel had rendered the car undriveable. They were trapped here.

Ed glanced at Tony. His face confirmed that thought as he jiggled the key and tried to restart the car. Nothing. Tony frowned deeply, sighed, and pasted a fake smile on his face to wake up his family. At least they weren't alarmed, just groggy. How long would that last?

"You aren't going to win," Ed said to the evildwel, trying to sound more confident than he felt.

"We got this, Dad."

The evildwel didn't respond. Wayne's face was gone again, and those red eyes replaced it, which unnerved Ed more than Wayne's face. It studied Ed. He held its gaze in an act of what he hoped looked like bravery. No response. Then it headed into the cabin as the family unloaded the car. That said it all to Ed. It believed it had already won.

"Come on, Eddie. We aren't going to let that thing intimidate us like that. We're going to make our final stand and win." Ed followed it.

"We got this, whatever it takes," Eddie confirmed.

"Yes, Eddie. Whatever it takes. We owe them that. I will show you how to push this thing away. I used it on the ride here but couldn't tell you about it, or I would have lost my concentration," Ed said and added, "Eddie, Sasha is safer away from this."

"I know, Dad, but I can't help worrying about her. You know how it is." Eddie shrugged. "Yeah, show me. Anything to stop this creepy smoke man."

Ed quickly showed him, and then they headed into the dark cabin, where the evildwel was waiting.

* * *

ZELINA WAS glad Ed had figured out how to push back the evildwel on the drive to the cabin. She was not happy that she could not save the taxi driver. She wished Ed had figured it out sooner, but she was letting him learn as he went, as instructed. Stan had been only a few hours away from dying of a massive heart attack. Maybe this was the better way to go, but she did not like anyone to lose even a few extra hours if they did not need to. Stan was a good man. He was at peace now, and his family would grieve. They would be looked after, but that never made things like this any easier.

Although Stan was not one of her assignments, this family was, and she took that very seriously. She had grown fond of them. Hard not to do, no matter how many times she was told it was best not to get involved. That was the reason for her past success—she cared. *No one could argue with that,* she thought with a smile.

She watched the evildwel render the car nonoperational. Now it was in the cabin waiting, along with Ed and his son. The family slowly unloaded the car, Stevie with their luggage and Tony with the groceries, while Rachael and Kelly carefully made it up the stairs of the deck to the front door, with the crickets chirping in the background. Could be the scene of a pleasant family getaway, but it was not. At least the room they would be staying in was on the ground level.

That might come in handy, she thought.

Tony quickly found the key tucked away under a lighted toadstool by the front door. Soon they were in the quaint cabin. Tony sat everyone down before they settled in.

"Let's talk about the accident," Tony said.

Kelly wanted to check on Stan's family when they got back home, and Stevie quickly agreed. Kelly was so pure and open—Zelina sent her some love. That was why it had happened this way. Zelina did not always see the outcome of things, but now she did. Stan's family would need help because the mother was sick, and the teenage son, Brent, would struggle taking care of her the rest of his high school years. Brent would lose his mother the same month he graduated high school. Tony and Rachael would be a strong influence in his life, including college—if they survived. They had to survive. Brent depended on it, too. Zelina shook her head. So much depended on them. Brent would either succumb to drugs or go to college and become a teacher. *No pressure, Ed,* she thought.

"And about Eddie—" Tony stood in front of his family.

"He got into an accident and is in a coma," Kelly stated.

"So you guys know?" Tony asked.

"Yes, Dad, we found out after Sasha left. We know they might be responsible for doing some things, but he'll be okay, right?" Kelly adjusted her foot.

"Of course, and we have to go see him. He just needs a good butt kickin'," Stevie added.

Rachael glanced firmly at her son, but all she got out of him was a shrug. Tony continued as if Stevie hadn't spoken. "They're taking good care of him in Hawaii. As soon as this gets sorted out and we are safe, we'll go see him. You understand he's done some bad things, though?" Tony looked at Stevie.

"Yeah, but he only cut up some clothes and stuff, nothing to really hurt us. He wasn't the one who cut my brakes or tried to set the house on fire—that was someone else." Stevie crossed his arms.

"You're right about that," Rachael agreed.

"I know. He comes to my games—I'm the only one who sees him." Stevie frowned.

"He does?" Rachael's eyes widened.

"Yeah."

"You never mentioned that." Rachael caught Tony's glance. He shrugged.

"I saw him at the games, too. He does love us, no matter how stupid or even scary he's been acting," Kelly interrupted. She smiled stubbornly at her mom. "I still say it isn't Sasha—it's something else."

Tony held his hand up. "Whatever and whoever it is, well, we should let the police sort it out now. I'll call them in the morning. Right now, we are safe." He held his arms out for a family hug.

Stevie helped Kelly off the couch. Kelly shook her head but fell into the embrace. Rachael wiped away a tear. Zelina knew they were still in a state of shock, with all that had happened. Kelly was the closest to an answer, but Zelina knew they were not listening to her. At least Zelina could nudge the family here. She found a memory in Tony's mind and got him to remember this cabin. Luckily, it was available.

Prying eyes would not have helped, and someone might have gotten hurt trying to help them. They would soon realize that Sasha had nothing to do with it, but she was safe, and so was Mae, for now. It was hard for humans, except for the exceptional ones like Kelly, to realize there was something more than they could see. This family had to embrace that, or they would lose the battle here.

Zelina remained hopeful as she watched the family settle into normal roles. That would bring them a little bit of peace before the showdown. Their shock would be worse when they realized what they were dealing with. Zelina sighed.

Tony started a fire while Rachael unloaded the groceries and began dinner. The kids were instructed to rest, so Kelly quickly picked a true-life ghost story from the bookshelf once she found out they had no cell signal. *She has no idea how accurate her reading material is,* Zelina thought grimly.

Stevie was unusually quiet and appeared to be intrigued with the fire, but he was really rereading the reply from Cassie telling him no problem, she would see him when they got back from their trip, and have fun. There was no way for him to respond to that text, and he certainly was not going to have any fun tonight. Zelina knew the kids would be more open to what was going to happen than Tony or Rachael. Tony was checking the shotgun. It was loaded. The bow and arrows were on the wall upstairs. Weapons were not what was needed.

The evildwel circled Kelly and Stevie, but it stayed a comfortable distance from them as Ed and his son kept pushing it back. Other than making the evildwel keep its distance, the father and son were not making much headway with it. The battle had just begun. *May the good side win,* Zelina thought. She sent love again. It was all she could do—or was it? Zelina smiled. It would not hurt anything if their eyes were opened to the danger just a little bit. *That would not really be breaking the rules.*

* * *

"I THINK everything is going to be okay now, Rach." Tony kissed her cheek while she added some ground beef to the sizzling pan.

"I hope so. It's been quite the day. Next time, we need to bring Leo with us." Rachael added some salt and garlic that she'd found in the cabinet. She was moving and talking, but completely dead inside. *Shock?* she wondered.

Tonight was spaghetti and salad. For tomorrow they had eggs and bacon for breakfast, chicken for dinner, plus all the snacks and canned food Tony had gotten at the store. They were set until they could go home—or go to Eddie. No matter what he had done, he was still her son. Finally, feelings were starting to surface, but, she needed to remain calm for her family. She quietly sighed.

"Yes, a lot has happened. I would love to come back here for a real vacation, Leo and all, Rach, but this isn't a vacation—it's survival. I think it's pretty clear it's been Eddie and Sasha who are causing our problems. The police will sort it out, I'm sure. I'll call them in the morning, but there is one more thing I need to tell you." Tony glanced over at the kids and signaled Rachael over to the pantry.

Rachael's chest tightened. *There's more?* "What is it?" Rachael turned the meat down so it wouldn't burn and followed Tony to the pantry, which was loaded with salt, pepper, garlic, and some canned vegetables, fruit, beans, and chili. Someone could survive here for a lengthy period of time, although she would prefer that they not have to.

"You remember that accident we saw on the Hana drive?"

"Yes," Rachael replied, with a sudden chill rushing through her. How had she not made the connection before?

"I'm convinced that was Eddie," Tony gently said to her.

"I guess I always knew. I tried to find information about it, but I couldn't. But...and it was him trying to hurt us...I have to—oh, Tony —" Rachael fell into his arms but was unable to cry.

"I'm sorry, Rachael. We haven't had a moment alone to talk about this, and I'm sorry you had to see it happen. It's been one emergency after the next. My only thought has been to get you all to safety. I mean, with Sasha, it seemed obvious, but I started to wonder—what if there's someone else? I'm heartbroken about all of this, Rachael. I've done a lot of things wrong lately, including suggesting that Sasha come with us. I guess I bought into her story at first, but we can't trust her or anyone else until we figure this out. I know we can't make calls from here, but we can always drive to the store and check on Eddie's condition and see if the police have found anything new. I didn't want to do that with the kids in the car, especially after the shock of the accident. I figured we were on the same page. Then you all slept, and we don't have a cell signal to check now. But for tonight, I just want us safe, okay? You understand, right?" Tony asked.

"I understand your reasoning. I know all you want is what's best for this family. I wish we had called and at least checked, but I don't want to do it in front of them either, in case we get bad news. It's been so much at once, and that's why I didn't tell them about a possible baby. I honestly haven't thought straight since the accident. And Tony, thanks for getting us here," Rachael replied as she studied him. There was no relief in her response to him. All she saw was pain in his eyes. Something else was going on. Carefully she asked, "That isn't what you wanted to talk about, was it?"

Tony sighed and quietly said, "No. I went back into the police station after making the report to get my cellphone and—well, I overheard a conversation." He quickly filled her in on the details.

"Oh, Tony! I'm so sorry! You're nothing like that man, I promise you. They're crazy if they think you had anything to do with this. And Hank was the one who found you? Why didn't he say something to you? I'm not sure how this all fits together, but maybe there's more than one bad person coming after us." Rachael grasped his hand and squeezed it.

"That's what I'm afraid of, Rach." Tears filled his eyes that he quickly wiped them away and hugged Rachael before exiting the pantry.

"Smells good." Stevie was stirring the meat.

Tony flinched but recovered quickly and pasted a phony smile on his face. "It does. Why don't you help me set the table while your mom finishes dinner?"

"Mom?" Kelly slowly hopped into the kitchen on her crutches.

"Yes?" Rachael poured the noodles into the boiling water.

Rachael quickly went back to her functioning but numb state, like she used to do when she was with Ed.

"I still don't think Sasha had anything to do with this. Eddie, yes; her, no. The book I was reading talked about situations like ours. We should be thinking about a supernatural explanation." Kelly tossed the contents of a ready-made bag of salad into a large yellow bowl.

"Eddie is very human, and so is Sasha." Rachael turned the burner off and removed the meat from the stove.

"Sasha isn't involved. I know Eddie has done a lot of bad things, but I think he can change. Don't you?" Kelly asked.

"We can't take any chances, which is why we're here. Stevie could have been killed in that crash, and we believe the brakes were tampered with. The house could have burned down. And you falling, Kelly—I'm sure it was just an accident, but the timing, along with the taxi crashing—well, there must be another person involved besides Eddie. The coincidence of Sasha's car breaking down and having to call a taxi—well, who knows how deep their plan really went?"

Rachael stumbled through her words and added, "Your brother will need support to heal both physically and mentally. Maybe this crash will knock some sense into him, and he'll change. I hope so; but first he must pay for his crimes, though." Rachael pulled her family into another group hug.

"I'm right about Sasha and the ghost," Kelly stubbornly mumbled.

"Or not." Stevie tugged back from the hug first.

Kelly continued as if Stevie hadn't spoken. "We will fight this together as a family. I'll keep reading. Maybe I'll find something to help us."

"Ghosts don't tamper with cars and start fires." Stevie rolled his eyes.

"As a matter of fact, they do." Kelly flounced off on her crutches.

"The Battaglia family can survive anything," Tony quickly said, defusing an argument between Kelly and Stevie.

"Yes, we can. You go hang out with the kids while I finish our meal. Don't worry, the dishes are yours," Rachael said.

"Deal, Mrs. Battaglia." Tony gave her a quick kiss and sat between the kids. It made her happy to see them sitting together now, all of them reading. Maybe it was going to be okay here. No one knew where they were. She quickly stirred in pesto sauce to the meat. She felt bad for Tony and couldn't believe his mother had never told him, but she knew her husband was no monster. She was shocked he doubted himself, even for a moment, because she didn't.

Dinner went by peacefully. After cleaning up, they all sat around the crackling fire. In that moment Rachael could pretend they were on a vacation, not hiding away from danger. Maybe everything would work out; they could go back home, and Eddie would be fine. Yes, she would make the best of this cozy evening. Put everything out of her mind for now. Too bad they didn't get marshmallows to roast. Rachael cuddled with Tony and watched the fire dwindle. Everyone had fallen asleep next to her. Good. It had been a long day, and tomorrow everything would look better.

She picked up Kelly's discarded ghost book and set it on the coffee table. She saw something move out of the corner of her eye and hoped there weren't mice at the cabin. She carefully studied the shadows. Nothing was moving now, but she felt a strong sensation of being watched. She shivered and pulled the wool blanket over her. Tony and the kids were sleeping soundly. She hated to wake them up to move them to beds, but figured she had better at least get Kelly to lie down. It was better for her broken bone.

Rachael was nudging her sleeping daughter when she saw it again. It was more like a shadow, and she swore she saw red eyes staring back at her. She shook her head and knew it was time to go to bed. She was so tired, she was seeing things. Tomorrow she would make that call about Eddie, check on his condition, and see if the police had any new information. The clock said it was 10:00 p.m.—past their bedtime tonight.

"Kelly, honey. Come on, let's get you into a bed and get that foot elevated," Rachael quietly said.

"What? Huh? Oh, okay, Mom." Kelly grabbed her crutches without waking up Stevie or Tony.

There were two bedrooms in the cabin, one upstairs and one downstairs. The downstairs one had two double bunkbeds, which Kelly and Stevie would sleep on. The other room upstairs had another bunk bed and a double, where Rachael and Tony would sleep. There was one bathroom off the small kitchen that had a shower, sink, and toilet. It was all they would need. Although it was small, it had a large main room for everyone to be in. It was perfect.

Rachael and Kelly found sheets in the closet next to the downstairs bedroom. Rachael silently put them on the two lower bunks and added an extra blanket. Even though it was June, it was cold as soon as the sun went down in the Santa Cruz Mountains. Rachael thought that if she had her choice of living anyplace in the world, this was where she would live: in the mountains, but right next to the ocean with the redwoods. Maybe tomorrow they could ride the train from Felton to the boardwalk in Santa Cruz. Well, maybe not tomorrow, with all that was going on, but soon.

Then the entire family could ride the wooden Giant Dipper roller coaster (the fifth-longest-running roller coaster in the United States, built in 1924—she already knew Tony would tell them this), and then they would lounge on the beach with some saltwater taffy and maybe check out a band playing later that night, or play some video games, or do more rides. She enjoyed trying to grab the brass ring on the carousel. It was going to be a great summer—if Eddie recovered. She sighed. She couldn't keep reality from her thoughts, as much as she kept trying. She helped Kelly into bed without bothering with her PJs. She added a pillow under her foot.

"Good night, Kelly." Rachael kissed her on the forehead.

"Night, Mom." Kelly shut her eyes.

Rachael turned off the light, and then she heard a crash.

Kelly shot up. "What was that, Mom?"

"No idea," she said and added in a louder voice, "Are you guys okay out there?"

"We are, but this picture fell off the wall," Tony yelled back.

"Mom, this is more than someone playing tricks on us or even rigging the car to crash. Pictures falling off the walls here *and* at home? I felt like I was pushed, Mom, but no one was there. I told you that, and you said it was just an accident. What if it wasn't? You can't ignore the facts. It might be something like a ghost. It can't all be Eddie and Sasha." Kelly sat up and gathered the red plaid blanket around her.

Rachael frowned. "Kelly, there is a logical explanation for what's going on. There are no ghosts or otherworldly beings. That's just stuff in movies and books. We'll figure this out. We probably ran into the picture earlier, and it fell," Rachael explained as those red eyes appeared in the doorway and then disappeared.

"I suppose you didn't see that either, Mom?"

"No, I saw it. Probably a reflection from the fire. You stay here. I'm going to check on the boys."

"Oh, no. You aren't leaving me here alone with red eyes around." Kelly grabbed her crutches.

They rushed into the main room, where Tony and Stevie were trying to pick up all the broken glass.

"Darn thing fell off the wall. No wonder—look at the cheap nail holding up such a heavy gun display case. Good thing I took out the rifle earlier. Might have got damaged in the fall," Tony said.

"Be careful you don't cut yourself," Rachael warned. "Let me see if I can find a vacuum."

"I found it!" Stevie said. "I got this."

"Well, okay. I got your room ready, Stevie. I'll go fix up our room." Rachael started up the stairs.

"Could we—would it be okay if we all slept together tonight?" Kelly asked. "Like we're camping?"

"I...well, why not?" Tony said. "That's a good idea, after the crazy day we've had. Sure."

"We'll finish getting the room ready if you boys have this under control." Rachael came back down the stairs smiling.

"Yeah, with that red-eyed thing watching us, I think it's better we all stay together." A frown crossed Kelly's face.

"Red-eyed thing?" Stevie asked. Tony looked over at Rachael. She shook her head.

Kelly nodded. "Yes. Mom saw it, too."

"Well, I saw something. Could've been a reflection off the fire. It's been a long day; let's get some sleep," Rachael said firmly, to convince herself, too.

"I know what I saw, Mom. I wish I had some sage to burn to ward off evil. I'm going to look for some salt and put it around the room to protect us. We'd better figure this out, though. I don't think it's going away." Kelly hobbled off, her crutches clicking loudly on the hardwood floor.

Stevie sighed and shook his head.

"She doesn't want to believe her brother is involved, is all," Tony said.

"I know. She'd rather believe a ghost is haunting us over her own brother. I'd rather believe that too, but ghosts aren't real." Rachael glanced at her retreating daughter. Following close behind her was a dark mist, and it turned to look at Rachael. It had red eyes, but there was also a face. It was a man with a beard, and it was sneering at her. "What the hell is that? Did anyone see what I saw behind Kelly?"

"Strange reflection," Tony said, not looking convinced, as Kelly (and her black mist stalker) took the salt she found and went into the bedroom.

"It was more than a reflection—it had a face." Stevie was visibly pale.

"No more talk about ghosts. We're seeing things. Let's get some sleep," Tony insisted.

"I hope you're right, Tony. Because I'm usually not one to see things. There might be something to what Ke—" Rachael hadn't finished when Kelly screamed.

"Kelly!" Tony ran toward her.

They found her on the ground. She looked like she had fallen and wasn't moving.

"Kelly! What happened?" Rachael screamed.

Her eyes opened just as Tony and Rachael got to her.

"I...what? Oh, it happened again. I was pushed *again*." Kelly sat up slowly moving her legs and arms.

"You probably tripped over this old throw rug with your crutches, Kelly. I'll move it, and it won't happen again," Tony said.

"You okay?" Stevie pushed by and helped his sister up.

"I don't feel like I hurt anything, but I know what happened. It wasn't an accident." Kelly looked around the room. "I don't think we'll be able to outrun whatever this is, either. We better figure out how to fight this ghost, or whatever it is."

"There are no such things as ghosts, Kelly," Tony insisted as he folded up the rug in the corner, but he didn't sound as convinced as he had before.

"There is, Dad," Kelly insisted.

"Come on, let's get some sleep. Things will look different in the morning," Rachael said and added, "I'm glad you're okay, Kelly."

"I'm okay for now. It sure seemed like it didn't want me to put down the salt. I don't care how crazy you think I am. I'm going to do it." Kelly took the big, round, warehouse-sized saltshaker she'd found in the kitchen and had carried in a bag around her neck. *No wonder she tripped.* Rachael watched her daughter spread the salt around the bunk beds.

"I'll take a top bunk," Stevie offered.

"Yeah, me, too," Tony said. "Come on, Kel, let's get some sleep. I have a loaded shotgun next to me if anyone tries to hurt us. Don't worry."

Kelly nodded but continued spreading salt to the bedroom door. "I don't think the gun will help, Dad. I think what—" She didn't finish as a huge crash came from the main room. "Just another coincidence?"

* * *

ED CIRCLED THE EVILDWEL. He was sick of it. No evildwel was going to hurt his kids. The evildwel threw a pan from the kitchen into the fireplace. At least Ed was getting a reaction from it. That must be good. He pushed at it, and it pushed back. He was getting to Wayne Battaglia, the murderer, and whatever else was in there with him. Eddie was behind him. Another pan flew toward them, and it hit the fireplace loudly as Tony rushed into the room. Ed knew Tony had to have seen that. Then a chair came flying at them.

"Please understand what you are fighting, Tony! You know your dad is evil. He is a part of this monster. Come on, figure it out!" Ed yelled.

Rachael was right behind him. She'd seen the chair fly across the room. Her eyes widened in fear.

"Rachael! Listen to Kelly. She might know something that can help," Ed said.

"You aren't hurting my family, you evil piece of shit!" Eddie yelled. "Come on, Wayne, come at me! Or are you afraid of grown men?"

Another chair flew at them as Tony rushed Rachael back into the bedroom. They heard the door lock, not that it would help if the evildwel wanted them. Unfortunately, it had made its presence known to them. They were next.

"You not only beat on women and kids, but you killed them too! Proud of yourself, huh? Killing that poor woman who was pregnant with your child? Then that family you crashed into and killed. Boy, you're a real man, huh? Who knows who else you killed—a few mistresses? No one was going to leave you, huh? Big man. Left your wife tied up at home with your son sleeping in the next room. Yeah, a real badass you are. What's wrong, don't want your son to be nice? Or happy? You make me sick. I'm ashamed I was like you in any form. We end this right now. You aren't hurting my family again! Bring it on, serial killer!" Ed yelled at the evildwel.

It wasn't smiling now. It looked enraged as more furniture flew at them. If it was distracted by them, it was leaving Tony, Rachael, and his kids alone.

"Yeah, I may be in a coma, but at least I can wake up and have another chance. You're screwed. You are pure evil and must live with what you did, if there's anything left that's you in there. We aren't going to let you hurt one more person. Got that, you slimy, dark marshmallow?" A knife flew past Eddie and landed in the wall. "You missed, and you might have noticed—there's no *body* to hurt."

"Big macho murderer. Can't do much to real men, can you?" Ed added.

Suddenly the flying objects stopped. The face broke into a smile. It slowly turned and headed to the room where their family was locked in. Ed and Eddie looked at each other.

"Damn it. I shouldn't have pointed out that it can't hurt us," Eddie said.

"It knew. It's just messing with us. Now it's time we mess with it. We must get inside it. That's how I got you out. Come on, Eddie."

"Let's do this."

They both ran at the dark mist and were pushed back. Ed grabbed Eddie's hand. "Remember to do this out of love, and I love you!"

"Right! I love you back."

They tried again—and this time they landed hard inside the dark mist. *It's terrifying, like landing in the middle of one's worst nightmare,* Ed thought. Everything outside the evildwel looked hazy, like it was in a thick, dark fog. Time moved more slowly as they moved toward the door that was supposed to protect Rachael, Kelly, Stevie, and Tony (it wouldn't). The evildwel was beyond wicked, and it wanted Ed, too. It would take every ounce of his being to fight for himself and his son.

Giving in was not an option, but it would have been the easiest thing for him to do. Let the numbness take over. So simple and safe.

Ed clung to his son's hand. He knew Eddie was fighting the same battle. It was them against the evildwel. The mist made the man inside, Wayne, seem tame. Ed could sense the presence of decades—even centuries—of evil. Adolf Hitler was once in this thing, along with Jack the Ripper and Vlad Dracula. He could feel them and wondered how many more of those monsters were in this thing. Were they still watching? He was sure part of them was. It was the purest form of evil Ed had ever been exposed to. It was horrifying, and he had to battle it.

Together. Ed focused on and moved toward what used to be Tony's father. The evildwel easily pushed them through the door. They faced the terrified group. It was up to him and his son to save them. Ed and Eddie kept moving forward. Each step felt like they would sink into an icy eternity.

ZELINA STOOD next to the new family. She hoped that what Ed and Eddie were doing would work, because she had no way to control this evil. She knew her presence might buy this family some time, but that would not last. The evildwel had rammed straight through the bedroom door with Ed and Eddie inside. It hovered in front of the petrified family. All of them saw it. Tony put himself in front of them. It was smiling again. She tried to send her strength to Ed and Eddie, but she could not. It bounced off the evildwel. She was afraid.

CHAPTER 12

Rachael, Kelly, and Stevie huddled behind Tony. Rachael felt a fear she'd never felt before. All her nightmares had been caused by humans in the past. What stood before her wasn't human. Kelly had been right all along. *How did Eddie fit into all of this?* Rachael racked her brain, thinking of an appropriate response. She had none. *How do you fight a dark mist with a face peering out of it?* she wondered. She was glad it wasn't moving toward them, but why not?

"What is it?" Rachael whispered and pulled her children closer.

"No idea. A ghost? Any suggestions, Kelly?" Tony asked, sounding a lot calmer than Rachael knew he was. She could see that every muscle in his body was tense and on alert.

"I'm not sure if it's a ghost; it might be. Looks like nothing I've seen before in stuff I've watched or read about them." Kelly shifted on her crutches. She was sweating in the icy chill of the room. "I already put the salt around the beds—maybe we should get inside the salt barrier."

"Worth a try." Tony helped Kelly step inside it.

"Be careful not to move the salt. It needs to be a solid line around us," Kelly warned.

After the family was inside the salt circle, Tony added more salt to any parts they'd disturbed. It was a short-lived hope that it would work. A dresser drawer flew at them, just missing Rachael.

"It can still throw things with the salt around us? Maybe we need to find some shelter from this misty menace," Stevie finally spoke up. He was trying to sound as confident as Tony, but Rachael could hear the fear in her son's voice.

"It's not a ghost. Not sure what it is," Kelly admitted in a muted tone. "Try throwing some salt at it. See what it does."

"Okay." Tony smiled at his family.

He poured some salt into his hand and tossed it into the dark mist. It fell harmlessly to the ground like Rachael knew it would. Another drawer came at them, which Tony blocked. Rachael saw that it had cut his arm, but there was no time to stop the bleeding now. They were trapped, and this thing meant to hurt them. Rachael felt the red eyes piercing through her soul. The thing was grinning. It was playing with them. For a split second she could have sworn she saw the image of two men in there, but she couldn't see their faces. What *was* this thing?

"Use the bed as a barrier!" Tony yelled.

Stevie helped his sister sit as Rachael and Tony pulled the bunk bed out and used the mattress to block more incoming drawers. If they hadn't seen it come through a closed door, Rachael might have had some hope that they stood a chance.

"I still have the gun." Tony held it up.

"You saw salt pass through it. There's nothing to shoot." Rachael pointed to the salt on the ground.

"Holy water might work." Kelly flinched as another drawer bounced off the mattress.

"Yes, I have some in my pocket," Stevie replied.

"If it comes at us, I'll shoot it, and you guys make a getaway. Can't hurt to try." Tony squeezed Rachael's hand.

"We stay together," Rachael firmly told him.

Tony shook his head. "Maybe I can communicate with it. Haven't tried that yet. See what it wants."

"It obviously wants to hurt us," Rachael replied. "I wonder if this is what has been causing all our problems."

"Not all of them." Tony let go of her hand.

"There's a window over there. Maybe we could get out of here. Get away from this smoky blob," Stevie suggested.

"Good idea, Stevie. We'll move this bed over to the window. You must help your sister out, but get your mom out first so she can help Kelly. Once all of you get out, I'll follow. I promise. I'll distract this thing if I can." Tony waved the gun in the direction of the monster.

"I want us to stay together," Rachael repeated. "I don't like this idea."

"I agree with Mom." Kelly peeked around the mattress.

"It's all I have. Unless anyone has a better idea?" Tony asked as something else hit the mattress.

"No." Rachael sighed loudly.

"Good. Let's do this." Tony hugged his family.

Rachael could have sworn she saw the mist move slightly away from them during their hug. Interesting. She kept this information to herself for the moment. She had no idea what it heard and understood, but thought that might be useful. They slowly moved the bed toward the window. The mist stayed where it was but kept a steady pace of throwing objects at them.

When they were at the window, Stevie opened it. The air was cool, but it was warmer than the chill the creature had created in the room. Rachael watched her husband step from behind the barrier. The red eyes were watching Tony. It grinned at him and nodded. Was it mouthing his name? She shook her head as she carefully climbed out, ready to help her daughter. Rachael tried to make the landing as gentle as possible but heard Kelly's cry of pain. She quickly got her to her feet and supported on her crutches.

Rachael couldn't shake the feeling that this was personal and it had something to do with her husband. Stevie landed next to Rachael with a thump. Rachael and her two children stood at the window, waiting. She peeked in and saw her husband standing there with his mouth open.

"Tony, come on!" Rachael hissed.

He looked shocked but replied, "Head to the car. I've got the keys."

Stevie picked up his sister and carried her like she was a small child, and for once she didn't complain. Soon they were at the car, with Tony closely following. *Maybe we're going to make it,* Rachael thought. *Leave this haunted house.* That feeling of joy lasted only a few seconds as the family piled into the car. The engine wouldn't turn over. They were trapped.

"I forgot! It sounded weird when we stopped, and wouldn't start. Let me check the engine really quick. Might be a loose connection at the battery." Tony hopped out of the car.

"You can fix that?" Rachael asked, watching the night for that thing.

"I could, if it was that. It's not the battery. All the wires and hoses are shredded," Tony grimly informed his family.

"Now what?" Rachael glanced back at the house.

"We run." Tony pointed.

They saw the red-eyed mist slowly coming toward them. Stevie grabbed his sister again out of the back of the car and took off, carrying her. Rachael and Tony followed them into the dark night, with the evildwel right behind them.

* * *

HANK STOOD next to the boy in the hospital bed who was hooked up to all the wires and tubes. This was Eddie Jackson, Rachael's son, the kid who stole and crashed his spare car. He wasn't planning on pressing charges, but this kid would require some help. Following his mom and stepdad on their honeymoon to ruin it—he had some issues to resolve. Hank wanted to help him, but he was more worried about what was going on in California. Was he wrong about Tony? Was he crazy like his father was? Hank was usually a good judge of people, and Tony certainly seemed like one of the good ones to him. He would trust his cop instinct. If it was Eddie's girlfriend causing the rest of the issues, then why didn't she know something was wrong instead of searching for her missing boyfriend? It could be an act, but no—something didn't add up.

"Hang in there, Eddie," Hank said to him. "You've got a wonderful family waiting for you. All you must do is ask their forgiveness. Grow up and be a man. All that anger almost got you killed. I know about that. I was once like you, too. Cost me my family. Spent my whole life trying to make up for it. Helping you is my penance, if you're wondering why I'm so involved," Hank said and sat down, watching Eddie's chest rise and fall in perfect rhythm.

"You see, Eddie, it's time you knew the truth. When Tony Battaglia was a baby, his father went crazy. Or maybe he was always crazy. He was more than an abusive husband to his wife; he killed his mistress and their baby and who knows how many others. You know, the night I met Tony, I had to untie his mother and tell her that Wayne had died in a car accident—and had taken a young family with him. Looking her in the eye, I told her she and her son were lucky to be alive.

"It was in that moment that everything changed for me. I couldn't be that angry man who took it out on his family after drinking all night. I changed, son, and so can you. It's hard work, with a lot of meetings and therapy, but it can be done. It was too late for my marriage, but you know what? She forgave me years later. I was a part of my kids' lives from that point on. I made up for it, but they never completely trusted me again. It's hard when you lose someone's trust like that. At least my ex-wife found a good man who made her happy. They raised my two sons into fine men.

"So know, Eddie, that I know men like you. Tony told me his suspicions about you. If you got that girl of yours to help you, well, I hope you didn't take anyone else down with you. Not likely—you wouldn't trust her enough to help you. You probably think you are her king and she is lucky to obey your commands, even in your darkest moments. Yes, there were times those thoughts crossed my mind too, Eddie. I'm ashamed to admit it.

"But I'll stay with you until your family can get here. I'm praying for the recovery of both your body and mind. Praying hard, Eddie. Hang in there," Hank said as a tear fell down his cheek.

All Hank's memories came rushing back at him. His stressful job and his drinking were excuses for what he became. He lived with that. He was almost proud of the man he had become now, with years of hard work. He always helped when he could, and he would help Tony and his family. He had to. He thought they might call the hospital tonight. Maybe they were already on the plane.

His cellphone beeped. He received a text from his old partner Cal.

"The family has gone missing. No one is answering their cellphones. They aren't at the house. The girlfriend was picked up, but was released. Her alibi was solid. It wasn't her. She claims the family was headed to a hotel. So far, we've had no luck in finding them. The only thing that makes any sense is Tony. So far, you would think he was a saint from talking to his colleagues. One interesting thing: The wife and kids were in an accident in a taxi. The driver didn't make it. Tony picked them up, and they haven't been heard from since. You see my concern. Will keep you posted. Let us know if you hear from them or if the son wakes up."

Hank sighed. He refused to believe Tony would hurt his family. There had to be another explanation. He almost booked the next flight off the island, but he realized it would be too late by the time he got there. Besides, someone had to stay here. His only hope was that they were on their way here. He quickly replied to his friend.

"I'm sure they caught the next flight here to be with Eddie. Did you check the flights out of Oakland and San Francisco? Maybe even San Jose or Sacramento? You never know."

The response came quickly. "Yes, of course we thought of that. Nothing."

Hank didn't respond. He wasn't going to be able to change Cal's mind. If only Eddie would wake up, then they might find out who was working with him. He was afraid for the Battaglia family. Whoever meant them harm wasn't playing around anymore. He decided it was time to go to the chapel. This was out of his hands now.

As soon as he got into the chapel, he turned his phone off. He missed the next text telling him they had a lead. They thought the family might be at a friend's cabin. They were sending police to check on them. Cal would update him soon.

* * *

ED HELPLESSLY WATCHED Stevie carry Kelly. Tony and Rachael were following behind as they ran deeper into the woods. Ed clung tightly to Eddie. He wasn't going to let him go, but Ed was barely able to fight off the evildwel. He did all he could to keep upright. The evil was weighing him down. It was like walking through a sandstorm barefoot, blind, and naked, while bees stung you. He could see Wayne Battaglia in the center of this dark storm. He knew he was waiting for them to join him and all the past evil. He didn't want to look any closer to see what he would find. Wayne kept smiling at them. He looked like a kind young Santa Claus. Off to his left, Hitler, Dracula, and the Ripper fellow (who was much younger than Ed thought he would be, and from a wealthy family, he could tell) were sitting by a cozy fire. Were they having tea? He could join them. His pain would be gone. Yes. The room was full. Who was that next to Hitler? She looked familiar. Just a few more steps, and they could join them and find out. It would all be over soon. Walking became easier, until he saw Zelina next to Rachael. That snapped him out of the evil trance. He would have to be careful from now on. He shook Eddie, who was dazed.

"Eddie. Look at me. It's trying to take control over us. Don't let it. Look at your family. Think of Zelina." Ed found moving harder again. That was a good thing inside this evildwel.

"What? Huh? I thought...This thing is powerful, Dad. I saw Adolf Hitler and a bunch of people I didn't know having tea," Eddie said, shaking his head.

"I saw the same thing, Eddie. This thing is old. And who knows how many people it's taken inside? Be careful," Ed warned.

"I'm trying, Dad, really. All those people and evil. I can't. But Dad, there's another voice talking to me. Not here but somewhere else. He said he would help me and stay with me. What was his name? Herman, Howard..."

"Was it Hank? Back in Hawaii? Hank?" Ed repeated.

"Hawaii? Yeah, right. I think that's the name. Where my body is. I can hear someone talking to my body. Weird. Who is he?"

"He was the guy who Charlie tried to kill, remember? We've talked about him; he's the detective who found Tony when he was a baby. Hank's a good one, but he didn't always used to be. He's changed, like you're going to do. You'll see. But I'm glad he's watching over you. Maybe he won't press charges against you for stealing his car."

"Oh yeah, Hank. How did I forget about him? He's the guy trying to help me? You're kidding me! The guy I stole from—an ex-cop, no less—is helping me? Does Zelina have something to do with this?"

"I have a feeling she has a lot to do with a lot of things. I feel like we're her personal project or she's trying to prove something with us. But I don't want to let her down. Come on. We have a few things to say to Mr. Battaglia," Ed said and slowly walked through the heavy stench.

He could see his family running into the dark forest. They weren't going to be able to outrun this thing.

"Don't you find it weird that we're fighting a man who's like what we were, or are?" Eddie asked.

"I'm learning 'weird' is the norm with an angel around. Always trying to teach us something, and frankly, I'm ready to learn. Aren't you? Time for you to be happy. And what would make me happy is stopping this evildwel—or at least stopping Wayne." Ed flinched as bullets flew harmlessly by them. Tony was shooting at them. They needed to act fast before this evildwel finished with them.

They were both sweating and breathless when they got to Wayne. Who knew ghosts could sweat or lose their breath?

"Welcome," said a deep voice.

"You have to stop this," Ed spoke first.

"Yes, leave my family alone," Eddie said.

"I have to do nothing but what I want," the evildwel replied.

"We know who you are, Wayne Battaglia," Ed said.

"Do you, now? I'm much more than him. You realize that? I'm a place of peace for people like you. So unhappy in your lives, but you're safe in me. All I do is collect sad and unhappy people like Mr. Battaglia, and I'm sure you've seen some of my other guests. They would love to get to know you. As for Mr. Battaglia, here, well, he isn't in control like he thinks he is. He has no idea I'm even talking to you. I don't usually, but you two are so intriguing. No one has done what you've accomplished here.

"You see, Mr. Battaglia's kind of evil feeds me. I have hungers to fill that keep me going, like you did as a human for your evildwel, Ed. Sorry, Eddie, you're still one of those humans. I've been with Wayne, here, for years. I only acted on what he wanted, keeping him happy. I'm a wonderful host, you'll find. Keeping men from his wife. And his son—well, I've kept more than one woman away from Tony, as you've found out. It's been fun. This woman, Rachael, was different, though —thanks to you, Ed. I could have some fun with her first because of all her old fears," the evildwel replied with an eerie red smile that matched its eyes.

"I paid for that, and you will too. Let us talk to Wayne." Ed demanded.

"I can't do that. He's happy here inside of me right now. He needs me and soon will join that peaceful tea party you saw. You'll like it. Too bad I can't live off you two, but I have another appointment soon. I'm going back into politics. Been many years. I have a lot of fun with that, too. So what do you say we do this the easy way? Join me, and I'll leave that sorry group alone. Move on. I've had my fun."

"Not happening," Ed shook his head.

"No? Too bad you want to fight me. You won't win, and then I'll kill those sorry souls to spite you."

"Like we can trust you! We'll win. We know your weakness," Eddie said.

"True—you're a smart boy not to trust me. But weakness? I have none, sorry. Now let's get this over with. First, I would like to introduce myself. I'm called Aten. I'm the oldest of my kind. We've always been here, and humans have always provided for us—well, not always, but then, we won't get into that. Just know that we are old, and I'm the oldest surviving one from ancient times. So, save yourselves the bother. There are more of us here than ever before in history. There's no beating us. Trust me. Join me and be at peace, instead," Aten the evildwel said and smiled, adding, "Too bad you lost your evildwel, Eddie. He was a young one, though. He'll learn, or will cease to exist."

"I'm not going back," Eddie replied.

"Oh, but you are," Aten said.

"No, I respectfully disagree on that point." Ed arched an eyebrow.

"Oh, please don't try to talk. I know it's hard. Watch how I finish this for Wayne. How happy he'll be. It will be wonderful. Imagine how powerful you can now be. Then, we will find another person to live in, in Washington, D.C. It'll be exciting and a good life for you. Come closer. Join us," Aten encouraged with a huge smile.

Ed couldn't believe what he was hearing. A creature that lived off human misery and evil? Ed knew that to stop this, he had to get Wayne away from it. Wayne would have to pay dearly for what he did, but at least this creature couldn't keep using him to do his bad deeds and then hang onto him in that surreal tea party. It certainly wasn't going to get him and Eddie. He had no intention of hanging out with Hitler, Dracula, or that Ripper fellow and whoever else was in there. He wouldn't allow that. He formed the only plan he had left and moved closer.

RACHAEL GRASPED that there was no way to outrun this red-eyed monster. It had followed them deep into the forest. It was getting harder to see as the moon went behind the clouds. Stevie was panting and sweating as he carried his sister. Tony grabbed her from him and carried on. Rachael heard the gentle burble of a stream up ahead. Maybe the thing would be afraid of water. Or maybe this would be the end of her family. She turned to see how close it was. The red eyes were gone. Where was it?

"I don't see it," Kelly said. "It's gone. Set me down, please."

"I don't think we should stop." Tony studied the dark trees.

"She's right. I don't see it, either." Rachael drew in a deep breath.

"Well, maybe we lost it. We could rest for a bit, but we need to hike to town." Tony rolled his shoulders.

"No one will believe that a misty creature with red eyes was trying to kill us," Stevie said.

"I know, Stevie," Tony said. "But *we* know."

"It wasn't Sasha." Kelly rubbed her leg above her splint.

"No, this has nothing to do with Sasha. We owe her an apology once we get out of this." Tony set his daughter down on the grassy bank of the stream.

"I still don't see it." Stevie's eyes widened and his head swiveled around like an owl.

"Wait, there it is," Rachael said grimly.

Its red eyes stared at them, but it didn't come any closer. Its mist was lighter, and there were two other forms inside it. They weren't smiling.

"It looks different." Kelly tried to get up. Tony reached down and helped her to her feet.

"The two men inside—they look like they're hugging." Stevie moved to his sister's side.

"Hugging," Rachael said. "Right. When we hugged inside, it seemed to back off. I think love pushes it away. Come on, group hug. I love all of you." They stayed still, hanging on to each other, watching. Rachael caught a glimpse of one of the faces in the mist. She couldn't believe it. "Is anyone else seeing what I'm seeing?"

"Eddie?" Kelly said.

"How is he inside this thing? Isn't that Dad, too?" Stevie asked.

"I see them both. There's one more person in there—my father. I recognized him from pictures, when we were back in the bedroom. I thought I was losing my mind." Tony moved protectively in from of his family.

"Why are they all in there?" Kelly asked.

"Not sure," Rachael answered. She didn't have time to explain about Tony's dad, and she had no clue as to why they'd see Eddie and Ed.

"We should keep moving. This thing looks busy now. Maybe it's projecting faces in our lives back at us. Come on." Tony pulled away from them and sighed. He went to pick Kelly up, but Stevie stepped in and grabbed her.

They hurried away, and the red-eyed thing didn't follow them. *Maybe the hug helped,* Rachael thought. They could hear a car zoom by with a loud bass rumbling as they stepped out of the woods onto the side of the two-lane highway that they had driven on a few hours ago.

"All we have to do is wait for another car to drive by and try to flag it down," Tony said, more calmly than his haunted expression showed.

"What if that thing follows us?" Kelly quickly asked.

No one had an answer for that.

CHAPTER 13

*E*d watched Stevie pick up his sister and move away from them. He hoped they could distract Aten the evildwel long enough so that Rachael, Tony, Stevie, and Kelly could escape. The family headed in the same direction that he had heard a car passing with loud music blasting only a few moments ago. Ed's hope was that they could quickly find a ride to town. No matter where they went, though, the only way they would truly be safe was if he finished this. *I can do it,* he tried to reassure himself. He glanced at Eddie, who nodded to him. They were in control now, right?

"Wayne?" Ed called. "I know you're in there. You need to come with me. To see your son. He's a fine young man."

"Really?" Aten asked. "You think you are powerful enough to get him away from me?"

"As a matter of fact, creepy creature thing, we do. Bet you haven't had to deal with someone coming in to take your victims away from you, have you?" Eddie asked.

Ed inched closer. He was more than creeped out that Aten used Wayne's face when it allowed people to see him. Now they'd finally got to the real man trapped inside the evildwel. The resemblance between father and son was stunning. All you needed to do was put a beard on Tony, and he would look like his father. Wayne's mouth was open like he was screaming—yet there was only silence vibrating out from him. His red eyes were empty and unaware. Wayne was right in the middle of anyone's worst nightmare. Of course, Ed and his son joined him in this heavy place. Ed could almost feel sorry for the man —almost. All he had to do was think of any of the number of things Wayne had done while he was alive. It only continued in the afterlife.

Besides, not knowing what would happen to an already-dead Wayne (even if they did get him out of this evildwel), Ed's main concern was what would happen to his son. He was the only one of them still alive, and Ed needed Eddie's help in getting Wayne out. It was the only way to remove this evil that called itself Aten surrounding his kids and ex-wife. They would do what they had to do to stop this thing and protect their family. Ed would gladly give himself up for this cause, but he didn't want his son to lose his chance at a good life. But that part was out of Ed's hands now.

Let Wayne pay for what he did. That's what happens when you live the type of life he did. Ed knew that all too well and hoped he could give his son that chance he'd never had in life. He pulled Eddie into a hug. *I'm going to make this work for everyone,* he promised himself.

Love is what will beat this thing, Ed remembered Zelina telling him. The love between Rachael and Tony forced it away. He was pretty sure Rachael had noticed that expressing love repelled the creature. So if that was the only thing that worked against this Wayne-evildwel named Aten, then that was what he would do.

Ed hugged his son harder. "I love you, Eddie. I'm very proud of you. I know you will do the right thing from now on."

Eddie looked surprised, but responded, "I love you too, Dad. I'm going to try to be the man I should be and a good father to my daughter, if I'm allowed to."

They kept hugging. The red-eyed creature tried to pull away from them, but it had no place to go inside itself. Ed smiled and winked at Eddie.

"I love you too, Wayne. Thank you for the amazing son you gave the world. He's a wonderful father to my children and husband to my ex-wife." Ed nodded to Eddie and whispered to him, "Keep up the love."

Eddie whispered back, "Got it," and then, louder, he said, "Yes, thank you, Wayne. Now I have a wonderful father and a grandfather for my baby. He'll show me what kind of man I should be."

Soon tears fell from Wayne's eyes, but he wouldn't look at them. The air lightened around them for a moment. The red was gone from his eyes and was now in the mist next to him.

* * *

HE'S A WEASEL, Eddie thought. *A weak version of Tony. No!* Eddie shook his head as he and his father were pushed back. The mist darkened again. *Love, keep it in there.*

He thought of Sasha and how she'd stood by him. He didn't deserve her and was going to show her how wonderful she was, if she would let him. That was a first for him—to realize he had no control over whether she stayed with him. No anger welled up at her. He realized he would need to act better toward her for that to happen. He had to treat her as well as she had been treating him, to act like the man Tony was. Eddie had thought it was weakness all this time, but it turned out that Tony was one of the strongest men he knew.

Eddie was the weasel, like this man in front of him, when he treated Sasha badly. He had to show Wayne love so he could show himself the same thing. Eddie smiled; he finally got it. He could get closer now to Wayne, with his father clinging to him.

Aten sneered at them with its red eyes and mouth. "No. You will not win."

But everything around them was getting brighter.

Ed raised his eyebrows at his son and replied, "I disagree, Aten. My son and I will win. It's time for you to move on, although the world certainly doesn't need you anymore. It's love you're afraid of, isn't it, Aten? In a world so full of hate, I can see how you've been thriving, but you must have run into love, too. You're done here, Aten. You'll hurt no one else using Wayne. We aren't afraid of you anymore. In fact, we're sorry for you." Ed grabbed on to Wayne.

Wayne's brown eyes grew aware for a slight moment, while the red eyes flashed brightly but kept their distance on the other side of him.

The red-eyed evildwel spoke out of the mist. "I'm too strong for you. You know that. I'll soon end these silly lives, and you'll have no choice but to stay with me. You'll like it." The evildwel tried again. A red mouth formed and smiled at them.

Ed shook his head. "You underestimate love. You always have, I guess. Come with us, Wayne. It's time to go see your son. You'll be so proud of him."

Wayne looked at Eddie and his dad for the first time. He looked confused and angry.

"Yes, he's a teacher, father, and husband. His family isn't going to leave him, either. He's safe and loved." Eddie tugged on Wayne's arm. Wayne weakly tried to pull away.

He made eye contact with Eddie. His obvious rage was fading quickly to fear. He looked around as the mist started to clear. Ed and Eddie latched tightly on to him. Wayne struggled harder than Eddie had when his father pulled him out of his evildwel. Time stopped, and everything grew silent. Eddie kept pulling on the man, who was heavy and anchored down with all the weight of the world's hate. Eddie was drenched in sweat, and his face was scrunched up in concentration.

They pulled and pulled, yet never got anywhere. *Are we strong enough to do this?* The red eyes were further away and not as bright. Maybe they were.

"Come on, Wayne. It's time to leave your dark nest," Eddie insisted.

Eddie felt a slight give, which moved Wayne a small amount toward them. He felt renewed hope and smiled encouragingly at his dad. Wayne looked like he was falling asleep. How long this went on, Eddie had no idea, in this vacuum, but he wasn't giving up, no matter how long it took—even forever. If it kept his family safe, he was all for it.

"I grow weary of this standoff," the evildwel named Aten said.

"This world is full of Waynes just waiting for me. I've had my fun. He's all yours. Good riddance."

* * *

THE MIST SUDDENLY CLEARED. Ed heard the nearby creek trickling again. The moon was shining brightly on them. The forest was dark, but the darkness was gone. Ed and Eddie held on tightly to Wayne's arm, afraid he might bolt if given the chance. Ed pitied him. What he was about to endure, when his mind cleared out of this mist and confusion—well, it wouldn't be pleasant. That was if he was lucky enough to get that option. Whatever happened to him, Ed was sure it would be horrible, as horrible as what he had done. Wayne had made the choice to step into all that hate and anger, and what was most important to this man, Ed realized, was control. Wayne would have none of those things soon—only regret. *Good,* Ed thought, as he watched the pale, bearded man try to take in his surroundings.

"Good riddance, evildwel. Hello, Wayne," Ed said, smiling hugely to Eddie. He grinned back—they had done it!

"Who do you think you are? Why did you remove me from where I was happy?" Wayne demanded.

"I'm Ed, and this is my son Eddie. Your brain didn't stop working inside the evildwel, just your free will. The other evildwel had my son, but I got him out of that one, too. You're here because we brought you here. You can thank me later."

"I know who you are. My statement was referring not to who you are, but to who you think you are, doing what you did? And if you expect me to thank you, you'll have a very long wait. You pulled me from my revenge. You'll pay for this. I will get my friend back; we were a great team. You'll see." Wayne's eyes narrowed as he scanned the darkness for his buddy.

"The evildwel has moved on, Wayne. If we're lucky, it will die. Now you'll pay for all the things you've done." A knowing shudder passed through Ed.

"Pay? I did pay, when I died in that car accident. They ran into me, you know. People were always getting in my way, never leaving me alone when I required it—and that night I required it. A simple trip to the store was all I needed. Then I could have finished off the other obstacles in my life. It's amazing how many people in this world make a point of ruining any chance for a man to find his peace. I don't like it when that happens, you understand. I always made a point of showing my displeasure. I like to think I was quite talented at that. I could really make a person suffer for wrecking my day. You know what I'm talking about, Ed. You were like me." Wayne smiled confidently at him.

He could have been gently talking to a small child about his manners, but Ed understood what he was saying. He trembled but didn't let go of Wayne.

"I may have treated my wife poorly—no, badly. I paid for that, as you will. But I never killed anyone. That is a line I never crossed. I'm not sure what will happen to you now, Wayne. I don't envy you."

"You have become weak, Ed. I don't envy a weak man. You let people use you. You are a man; act like one. Show them who is the boss. These women are here for us. What kind of example are you setting for your fine son? Did you forget you were a man?" Wayne puffed up importantly.

Ed thought Wayne was trying to goad him into letting him go. He doubted he could escape Zelina.

"No, Wayne. I now know what it is to be a man," Ed replied.

Wayne sneered at him. Ed ignored his taunt and nodded at his son, who frowned back at his father.

Eddie sighed. "My father isn't weak anymore, but you are. Your son is the real man. If I'm lucky enough to wake up from my coma, I'm going to follow his example. Tony is lucky he never knew you. His mother raised a great man despite who his father was. I'm sorry for you," Eddie added as he shifted his feet.

Wayne shook his head and tried to pull away, with no luck. He shrugged. "You made your son weak, Ed. He needs to discipline his house when they get out of line. I was king. I will stay king. You're both weak, pathetic excuses for men. Well, you can't hold me here forever. When you let go, I'll find my evildwel. Then you and my son will pay for this." Wayne smiled. "I have nothing but time."

"I don't think that's the case." Ed looked over at the white light reflecting on the creek.

"Is that—" Eddie's mouth dropped open.

"Yup. Just in time," Ed said as the light's intensity grew stronger. Eddie smiled at Wayne. "We have a visitor."

"I have no time for that." Wayne pulled harder. He tried kicking and head butting, but they did not let go. He was like a wild animal desperate to escape its trap. He screamed in frustration as they tackled him to the ground.

"If you let me go, I will do anything for you. I promise. Keep that thing away from me," Wayne begged.

Ed smiled. "You aren't going anywhere, Wayne. You have a lot to answer for, and Zelina is the angel to do it."

"I demand you let go of me!" Wayne struggled harder until tears began to flow. He stopped fighting and pleaded, "Just let me go. I won't do anything. I promise. I'll change. I will be like you. No, wait, please. Keep her away from me. She means me harm. Haven't you changed? Help me!" he begged as Zelina stood before them. Ed and Eddie pulled Wayne to his feet to face her. Wayne's body slumped in defeat.

"It is too late, Wayne Battaglia," Zelina's voice boomed. "You have a lot to pay for. You should thank these men for making sure your payment is not worse than it is. You will have a lot to answer for, Mr. Battaglia." She added, "Thank you, Ed and Eddie. You both did what was said to be impossible. Ed, you have been redeemed. I have a job to offer you now, if you are interested, but you also have the option of enjoying some peace. Eddie, you have a body that awaits you." Zelina smiled as she relieved them of Wayne. Ed was positive Wayne was going to faint. He was so terrified of her. *Serves him right,* he thought.

Zelina grinned at Ed. He grinned back at her. Yeah, she knew what he was thinking. He didn't mind this time.

"Thank you, Zelina." Ed smiled proudly. "I'm not sure what I want to do right now, if that's okay?"

"Of course," Zelina said.

Eddie asked, "I'm gonna live?"

"You are, Eddie. You are very lucky to have your dad and that this all worked out so well."

"That thing named Aten—what happened to it?" Eddie asked.

"Ah, you found out its name. That will be useful. It is a name I have heard of. It is the oldest evildwel in existence, I believe. Unfortunately, it lived and is carrying on a plan only it knows."

"It said it wants to get back into politics in Washington. Wanted to bring us along, but we had better things to do." Ed grinned.

"That is good to know. We will keep an eye on that. We will talk more later, Ed. It might be important to hear everything it had to say to you. Of course, we all know these creatures are not known for being honest, either." Zelina shrugged making her green wings flutter. Ed nodded.

"What about my family?" Eddie cut in. "The police are involved. What will they think happened to them? I mean, don't they think Tony is responsible now?"

"Yes. I have that all figured out. As luck would have it, Mr. Battaglia has a brother, right, Wayne?"

"Mario? Yeah, he's in prison. He was dumb enough to get caught, you know. I never did." Wayne stood a little taller, although he still looked small next to Zelina, who quietly waited for him to finish. "I haven't had any contact with him after he got sent away for his crimes. It was his idea, you know, because then they would think I wasn't like him. It worked, too. They never suspected me when I had to remove those girls who insisted on bothering me. People never learn," Wayne smiled proudly. "Mario taught me all I know."

"Yes, well, he will pay for that detail, too, Mr. Battaglia," Zelina said as another light hovered over the river and then came toward them.

A male angel with brown, flowing hair and a rearranging white gown like Zelina's suddenly appeared. His smile almost lit up the whole forest, but his voice was soft and gentle as a warm summer breeze. "I hear you are to be congratulated, Zelina. I thought it would be best if I personally escorted Mr. Battaglia to where he cannot hurt anyone else, or himself. Well done, Ed, and you as well, Eddie."

Ed had never seen him before, but his very presence made him feel completely tranquil.

"Thank you, sir," Zelina beamed proudly.

"Uh, yes, thank you, sir," Ed replied to the new angel.

Eddie's head was bobbing up and down in agreement, and his mouth hung open.

"You are quite welcome. I hope you take Zelina up on her offer, Ed. We would be pleased to have you working with us. I cannot stay, sorry." he seized Wayne, and they were gone in a flash of light.

"I did not expect him to show up," Zelina said. "This worked out better than I thought it would. Thank you both for your part in this. He is a very important angel; that is all you need to know. Someday I will properly introduce you, Ed."

"I look forward to meeting him again."

"Of course you do," Zelina quickly agreed.

Ed shook off the calm and asked, "What's next, and what happens to Wayne? What about my ex-wife and kids? You said there was a plan?"

"I am honestly not sure what they will deem fit for Wayne. It is not my call. I assume they will start with him watching his life over and over. Unless they do not, and then I prefer not to talk about the other option. As for your family, like I was saying, Wayne had a brother who had been in prison for killing several young girls. He recently got paroled. It all worked out perfectly, except for the two other lives he took before I got to him.

"After that, he was easy to lure here with a young girl. I promise she was not injured, but the other two..." Zelina sighed and paused for a moment, frowning, and then pushed her wings out and continued. "Well, there was nothing I could do about that. The best thing to happen now does not involve the truth. I want you to note that I am not a fan of that, but it must be done. The story the humans will hear is that Rachael and Tony had an unknown stalker who turned out to be Tony's uncle. This pathetic man wanted them dead—which would not be too far from the truth if he ran across them. The police will find he tampered with the truck so the brakes failed, set the fire at the house, and then tried to kill them at the cabin.

"This was not easy to pull off this time, but it is something I can do, and no one will remember what really happened. So I will do what angels do and remove the memories they do not need right now. What they will recall is the story I told you. Too bad the uncle died in an unfortunate car accident. All the evidence found on him will clarify to the police what he has been doing since he was out of prison and his plans for his nephew and family. Tony will not take the blame. That was very important, along with forgetting how bad his father was."

"You really can do all of that?" Eddie asked.

"Of course I can. I do not like to. Ed, it is time to take Eddie back to his body and say your goodbyes. You can wait for me there at the hospital. And Eddie, you are very lucky. You really have no idea. You may not remember me, but you might feel me around you. Do not go back to any bad habits. Understand? I will be watching, and so will your father," Zelina warned. Her deep brown eyes demanded an answer from him.

"I understand, and I promise." Eddie made an X over his heart with his index finger. "Thank you."

"Do not break your promise to me. You will not like it," Zelina threatened. She smiled and added, "You are welcome. Now, scoot, as the humans say."

Before he could respond, Zelina was gone.

"She's one scary angel. The other one wasn't." Eddie shook his head.

"This one is a bit of a hard-ass. Trust me, you don't want to cross her. I've never seen the other angel before, but he looked familiar. Well, we better get you back," Ed said.

"I'm really going to wake up and get another chance?"

"Yes, Eddie. We both did," Ed said quietly and then added, "Let's get you back."

* * *

RACHAEL HAD an arm around her husband as they walked down the side of the road toward town. She felt safe but didn't trust that feeling. Her husband had been quiet since they'd gotten here. He was clearly in shock. He shook as he began to speak.

"Why was my father in that thing? And Eddie?" Tony burst into tears.

Rachael pulled him into a hug as Kelly and Stevie looked away, watching the road. It was an uncomfortable few moments as they all tried to make sense out of what happened.

"I don't know, Tony. The thing was pure evil, that was for sure," Rachael said.

"What's that?" Kelly pointed.

"It's back," Rachael whispered, but found herself unable to move.

A light glowed in the forest next to the empty road. It came closer. Tony moved next to Kelly. Rachael could see he wanted to run again but was frozen in place, like she was. They watched the thing get closer. The light brightened everything around it. Finally, Rachael could make out what the light was—the most beautiful creature she had ever seen, with wild black hair and beautiful, caring brown eyes. She had on a silver gown that flowed like water around her. She spread out her colorful wings and smiled.

"An angel," Kelly whispered in awe. "She won't hurt us."

"An angel?" Tony repeated.

"Yes, I am an angel. My name is Zelina. I think a bit of an explanation is in order. I have been working with Ed and Eddie to defeat an ancient creature called Aten. An *evildwel* is what we call those things. They feed on human misery. The evildwel absorbs souls that are already bad and then feeds on them. That evildwel was the worst one I have ever seen. It gave its tenant what it wanted—revenge. I honestly was not sure it could be done, but Ed has redeemed himself through a tough battle, Rachael. Be happy knowing he has changed. He has earned a bit of peace now. Eddie too. When Eddie wakes up, you will see in him what you have always wanted to see—a kind young man.

All you must do is show him some love, and he will respond. Of course, he will always have to work on himself, but I know he will. Oh, this has been a successful assignment. I think we will be doing it again, now that we know it works like I thought it would." Zelina grinned broadly.

"Are you saying Ed and my son were really in that thing?" Rachael asked.

"Yes, they were, at the end. They were the only ones who could fight it, and they pulled out Tony's dad, who was inside it," Zelina said.

"I saw him, and I overheard what he was, at the police station," Tony confirmed.

"I know you did. He did a lot of bad things in his life," Zelina said.

"There's more?" Tony asked, as Kelly and Stevie looked at each other and shrugged.

"You all need to hear the whole truth before it is gone. Tony, your father was cruel and a killer. He murdered more than one mistress when he tired of them. He had managed to avoid getting caught, but he was on the police's radar. The last one, as you know, was pregnant." Zelina shuddered while folding her wings behind her, making her look smaller, but not any less impressive.

She continued, with their full attention. "On a deeper level, kids, I want you to always understand what you encountered, even if you will not remember it. Now, Wayne Battaglia was not only abusive, like Ed, but he was going to do the unthinkable that last night when he died. Of course, he was drinking heavily, but he found out that Tony's mother was planning on leaving him. He stopped her and tied her up and planned on killing their son in front of her. Luckily, he ran out of booze. He left the baby, Tony, sleeping in the other room, with his wife still tied to a chair, and fled. Before he got to the store, he had a car accident and killed an innocent family. Everyone died instantly." Zelina paused for a moment and put her hand on Tony's shoulder. Rachael's heart went out to her husband. Kelly grabbed her mother's hand, and Stevie's eyes were pinned on Zelina.

Zelina smiled at Tony and gently continued. "Your father, Tony, is responsible for keeping men away from your mother, which I am sure you realize now. He also kept you from having relationships, including your girlfriend who broke up with you. It was deemed a boating accident, but it was no accident. He wanted to prevent you from getting back together with her. He loved playing with people like that. Then, when you found your soulmate, Rachael, he saw his chance to play his sick games with you. He used Eddie for his own ends, and I have never seen two evildwels work together. That was troubling. Fortunately, Ed ejected Eddie from his evildwel, the first time that has *ever* been done. Just know that the evildwel Aten was feeding on all of this and encouraging all that anger inside of Mr. Battaglia, like Eddie's did to him." Zelina paused, opened a wing, and gently wrapped it around Tony's back.

He was speechless, but the wing had a calming effect on him. For the first time, he looked at Rachael, who smiled encouragingly at her husband.

Zelina smiled at the stunned family and continued. "So, this is what was responsible for all the strange events around you, down to the falling pictures and Kelly's accident. Ed used to have an evildwel in him when he was alive. Luckily, the evildwel left him when he died, so I got him. I gave him a chance to do good by helping his family. First, he worked alone, watching over you until he rescued his son. Yes, Rachael, he was there with his son during the accident. Together, they won against something evil, ancient, and strong and pulled Wayne out of his evildwel, making it the second time that has ever happened. Now Wayne will get what he deserves. It bears repeating: Ed has repented. He is a new man, Rachael, and so is Eddie," Zelina said, looking at Rachael.

"I don't think I understand any of this," Rachael admitted.

"I know," Zelina said.

"My father was worse than I thought." Tony sucked in a deep breath and let it out loudly. He wiped his eyes and frowned deeply. "Why wouldn't my mother tell me this? She told me he'd been wonderful. I believed her, until today. He wanted me and my family dead, after haunting my mother and me for years? I must ask: Was he behind my mother's death, too?"

Zelina withdrew her wing and faced Tony. "Yes. I am sorry, Tony. You are nothing like him, though. Take comfort in that. And, I am sorry to say, he found a way to kill your mother. He literally scared her to death the night she was going to talk to you, but she is okay now and could not be prouder of you. She sends her love."

"What? You talk to her?" Tony said.

"Of course I do. She is a lovely woman. She feels bad that you did not know, but at the same time was glad. It is hard to be a parent. You will soon find out, Tony."

"Yes, I have a family now, but I couldn't imagine lying to them like that." Tony frowned.

"Well, yes, I can understand that, Tony. I am not a fan of untruths. Do you honestly think you would have believed your dead father was causing all your grief? I think that if you look inside, you will find the answer is no. Your mother, on the other hand, always knew. She has told me many times that you were the one good thing in her life, Tony. Do not hold any of this against her."

Tony shrugged and grabbed Rachael's hand. Kelly stood close to her new father, and Stevie looked confused. It was a lot to take in, Rachael thought, even after what they'd just seen.

Zelina continued. "Okay, I can respect you not having an answer, but I can see in your heart you have already forgiven her. Well, it is almost time for me to leave. I have a lot to do, but here is what you will remember. The issues with the police have been neatly resolved. They are on their way to you now. They found out about this cabin and will soon find you. Your part is to tell them about a man named Mario with thick, gray-and-black hair and a white beard who claimed to be the older brother of your father and who was the one terrorizing you."

"You want us to lie to the police?" Tony asked.

"Yes, Tony. I am afraid it is necessary. The story you will be telling the authorities is simple, and you will believe it is the truth. To sum it up again, you have an uncle you did not know about. He tried to kill you and is responsible for all the bad things that have happened since you have been home. Kelly, of course, was just an odd accident, as well as that taxi ride. Eddie will be taking responsibility for what happened in Hawaii."

"Eddie is going to wake up?" Kelly asked quietly.

"Yes, Kelly, like I said earlier, and he will be different. You will see. Soon you will get that call." Zelina gently stroked Kelly's cheek. Kelly looked at Zelina in awe and smiled. There was a connection between them. This explained Kelly's fascination with the unseen all these years. She knew.

Rachael felt tears running down her face as Tony hugged her. "Thank you," she choked out.

"No need to thank me. The work that needed to be done is done. Now listen, you need to hear the rest of this and remember, because it is time for me to go. The police will not find Mario here, but there will be enough evidence in a car accident happening right as we speak. He was drinking and driving, exactly like his brother. I know it is unusual to have serial killer siblings, but here, it happened.

"The truth is that Mario was the one who introduced Wayne to killing, but Mario did not bother to look up his family when he got out. He went right back to killing young college women. It took a lot to get him to leave his hunting grounds in Southern California. For the legal part of this, all the dots will be connected, as humans say, and this case and those murders will be closed. Otherwise, I would have had to find another explanation, and I would have had to be creative. I wish I could have prevented his last two victims. I assure you again— Wayne and Mario will answer for all they have done." Zelina's eyes narrowed.

"My father and uncle were both monsters? What does that make me?" Tony looked at his family with slumped shoulders.

"Whatever went wrong with those two did not go wrong with you is the simple answer, Tony. I can see good and evil. You are good. Remember that." Zelina gently placed a hand on his shoulder.

"I knew that," Rachael added with a half-smile.

"Yes, of course your wife and family know this already. Unfortunately for you, none of you will remember what happened—only the story you need to tell. There will be enough evidence to convince the police of this story; I made sure of that" Zelina pulled her hand away and fluttered her wings.

"What? How can we forget what we just went through? I will never forget that." Stevie shook his head.

"It is something angels need to do sometimes, Stevie. We need to keep ourselves hidden; otherwise, we couldn't help humans like we do, right, Kelly?" Zelina winked at her.

"Right," Kelly agreed quickly.

Zelina continued. "As time goes forward, after I leave, you will not remember how the events really played out today. You will not forget the story about Mario. Tony, you will forget what you know about your father, besides how he died drinking and driving. I am sure the police will not share their suspicions about your father with you, either. I had to plant some thoughts to cover that. Know that none of this is going to trial, so it will not need to come out. The most important thing you will not forget, though, is love. You all have a wonderful life ahead of you.

"Oh, Rachael, your dad is happy, as well. He is proud of how you and Patrick have taken care of your mother. And he loves his grandchildren. I believe I covered everything. I must go. Take care of each other, and go pack for Hawaii, because Hank is sending you a gift. You have a son who needs you." Zelina winked.

"Tell my mom I love her and understand," Tony said.

"I will," Zelina replied with a huge smile.

"My dad…tell him…" Rachael said.

"Yes. I will. I have to go. The story will evolve naturally. Do not worry, and be loving."

"But wait!" Kelly called, but Zelina winked at her again and was gone.

The memory of Zelina and the evildwel was fading fast. All that was left was the suggestion of Wayne Battaglia's brother, Mario. The police pulled up. Tony and Rachael began their tale, and the memories completely vanished.

* * *

SOON ED and his son were back at Eddie's body, with Hank sleeping in his chair next to him. Ed hugged his son.

"I'm proud of you, Eddie."

"Thank you," Eddie replied as his face reddened.

"I hope you can remember how much I love you, even if you forget everything else." Ed smiled.

"I love you too, Dad." Eddie hugged his dad.

Ed didn't want to let go of his son, but he knew it was time Eddie got back to his life. He gently pushed him at the sleeping body. Eddie smiled and waved as he disappeared into his body. He would miss his son.

He watched him breathe and waited. There was nothing different on any of the machines monitoring him. *Why isn't this working?* Ed wondered. Zelina had said he would wake up. Was there something else?

"Come on, Eddie," Ed encouraged. "Wake up!"

He watched. Nothing. Eddie's chest went up and down in a soothing rhythm. Hank slept soundly in the chair. He would be stiff when he woke up, Ed numbly thought. Was this all for nothing?

Something moved. Eddie's hand. Then his eyes fluttered. Ed proudly watched his son open his eyes. It was like watching him being born all over again.

Ed knew his son wouldn't remember what happened to him, but he also knew Eddie was changed. He hoped Zelina would let him watch over Eddie, or at least check on him occasionally. He kissed his son's cheek, with no reaction from Eddie, who seemed to be trying to take in where he was. He loved seeing those eyes look around the room. Ed bumped against Hank's chair hard enough to wake him up —he thought. Hank kept on snoring. Ed knocked over Eddie's tray.

Bang!

Hank awoke and quickly tended to Eddie. Now the work would begin for him. He could handle it—after all, they'd just taken on an evildwel and won.

Zelina appeared next to him and smiled.

"We have to go," Zelina quietly informed him.

"I know," he said to her, but then he added to Eddie: "I love you." The room disappeared, and they were on their way to wherever Zelina decided they needed to go. Ed didn't mind, though, and planned on telling her he would accept the job, whatever it was. He wasn't ready for all that peace just yet.

* * *

EDDIE WAS wide awake and in a hospital bed. Memories flooded him of how he'd gotten there. He felt ashamed. Next to him was a man he didn't recognize, or maybe he did. He couldn't place where he had seen him before. Perhaps he was the police. Maybe he could escape. But the man suddenly woke up. Eddie realized at that moment that, no, he wasn't going to run anymore. For the first time in his life, he decided he would have to pay for all the things he did. He watched the man smile at him.

"Hi, Eddie. I'm Hank. You've been in a coma. I've been sitting with you until your family arrives. Can I get you anything?"

"My family? How long have I been in this coma?"

"Over a week, Eddie. The doctors weren't sure you'd wake up, but I knew you would," Hank said and added, "Yes, Eddie—your family."

"Um, who are you? Are you the police?"

"I used to be, but right now I own a hotel. Your mother and stepfather stayed there. I helped them with the room break-in," Hank said, looking at Eddie.

"I—well—you see, I was stupid. I had a guy help me get into the room and cut up all their clothes." Eddie wondered if he should be saying this and why it was coming out of his mouth.

"I know, Eddie, but I'm glad you're admitting your mistakes. That gives me hope. Unfortunately, the young man who helped you, Charlie, didn't see the error of his ways. He tried to kill me and ended up in jail. I always feel bad when I can't save a young life. It'll be different with you, though. I've been keeping your family updated, and they have a flight scheduled. They learned about your accident after they got home, which is why I'm here and not them. Do you remember your accident?" Hank asked as a nurse rushed in and took Eddie's vitals.

"Charlie's in jail?" Eddie asked, like he hadn't heard Hank's question.

Hank nodded as the nurse introduced herself and began with her inquiry. "Are you comfortable, Mr. Jackson? Any pain?"

"I'm fine, no pain."

"You remember how you got here?" Nurse Blanche asked.

"I was driving on Hana Highway and lost control of the car. No one else was hurt, were they?" Eddie asked.

Blanche looked at Hank and smiled at Eddie before leaving.

Hank replied, "No, Eddie. No one else was hurt, thankfully. You were drinking, you know."

"I admit I was. It was stupid," Eddie said, not believing the stuff coming out of his mouth. He had never been this honest in his life. Maybe because he was going to be a dad? *Sasha*, he thought. He felt pain now, remembering how he'd treated her. Would she forgive him? He had a lot to make up to her. Maybe he'd hit his head hard enough to knock some sense into himself. He smiled.

"You were. You must face the penalty. I think rehab would be in order, and some therapy," Hank said.

"But there was a car. I stole it." Eddie felt bad about that. He knew it had to be totaled.

"Yes, you did. It was my car. Even though it was my backup car, you'll help me fix it. It will be a couple of months before you can get back home. I'm sorry for that, Eddie, but you see, I already talked to the judge, and this is the deal I got for you—if you woke up. And Eddie, I did this before I knew who you were."

"You're helping me?" Eddie asked.

"Yes, that's what I do," Hank said. "We'll get to know each other really well over the next few months. Then you'll be ready to go back home, if you want to."

"I want to. I have a girlfriend and a baby on the way," Eddie said.

"Well, congratulations. Then I think we should begin our work together as soon as we can."

"Okay. But why are you doing this, Hank?" Eddie asked, puzzled.

"I have a lot to make up for, myself. Like I said, we can get acquainted over the next several weeks. Then, at the end of that, if I think you are a changed man, I'll let the judge know, and you can go on with your life. Deal?" Hank asked.

"Sure, but you said you used to be a police officer. Is that why you have so much pull around here?"

Hank laughed. "Like I said, I help people, and people help me. You'll see. It's a wonderful way to live."

Just then, the doctor walked in to check Eddie and proclaimed that he was fit and should be released after some tests in the next day or two. As soon as the doctor left, Sasha burst into the room.

"Eddie! You're okay! I've been so worried. And all the stuff your family told me. And then they believed I was helping you," she blurted out. She looked at him with her hands on her hips like she was ready for a fight. Eddie couldn't blame her. That was what she had come to expect from him.

"I'm okay, and I'm so sorry for everything I've put you through. I was stupid. I'm a different man now, and I plan to prove that to you. Is my family with you? I owe them an apology too," Eddie said.

Hank quietly slipped out of the room to give them privacy when he saw how Eddie reacted to her. *That's a good sign,* he thought and grinned. It was a good day.

CHAPTER 14

The Battaglia family arrived back at their house as the sun was rising after a long night of questioning. Rachael couldn't believe that Tony's uncle wanted to hurt her family. The serial killer blamed Tony for his father's death, a screaming brat who pushed his father to "drink and drive" (as quoted in an old letter found on him). Tony had been surprised to learn that was how his father died, but more surprised that he had an uncle, Mario, who had been responsible for so many deaths. Why did they let him out? he had asked. "Good behavior" was the dismal response.

They learned that Uncle Mario had pictures of their family on him when he died. The police concluded that Mario had a couple of good prison buddies who were released and who owed him—they watched Tony for years and then reported back to Mario. When he got out, the first thing he did was to go after his nephew and family while adding a couple more kills to his count. The man was heartless. He spent his life taking away people's innocence. His next goal had been to take everything away from Tony, who Mario believed was responsible for Wayne's death. It didn't make sense to Rachael, but then, a murderer's mind wasn't something she understood.

At least the nightmare was over for Rachael and her family, after

Mario had tampered with their car brakes and almost killed Stevie and messed with their outlet and almost burned the house down. *Almost,* she kept reminding herself. Then the psychopath followed them to the mountain cabin. They barely got away. She usually didn't wish death on people, but him dying in a horrible car crash—well, it was a relief. Rachael shivered. Her image of him included a beard and red eyes. The police officer looked at her strangely when she mentioned that, but she would never be able to get those eyes out of her memories.

It was a night Rachael and her family wouldn't soon forget. They had not only survived someone trying to kill them, but Hank let them know Eddie had woken up from his coma. Eddie would be required to stay in Hawaii for the next few months. He would be living with Hank and working off his charges, thanks to Hank getting Eddie probation if he worked with him. She couldn't believe their good luck in staying at a hotel that Hank owned and that he wanted to help their son, who had stolen his car. Rachael wondered if they'd used up all their pink luck, as her mother called it, in the last couple of weeks. Even her old SUV would be fixed later today, but most important, they were safe now.

The only thing left to resolve involved a trip back to Hawaii and seeing Eddie. Hard to believe her son had been doing things against them at the same time as Tony's uncle. What a way to start a marriage! Hopefully, all that was behind them, and Eddie would see the errors of his actions, with a baby on the way. Rachael felt bad about how they had treated Sasha. She'd had nothing to do with any of this. Rachael would call her after she booked their flight to Hawaii.

Someone was at the door. Now what?

"Just sign here," the FedEx driver said.

"Okay, thanks."

"Have a good day," she said and left.

I plan to, Rachael thought, looking at the padded manila envelope. It was addressed to the Battaglia family. She quickly opened it up and couldn't believe what she was seeing. It was four plane tickets to Hawaii, with a typed note.

"Here is my wedding present to you. Come see your son. Your room is still available at the hotel. I left the date open, so call and schedule. Look forward to seeing you and meeting the rest of your family. Hank"

Rachael got on the phone and booked a flight for later that day. Perfect!

"Tony!" Rachael called.

"I'm in here. Did you get the flight booked?" Tony asked.

"I did, but…" Rachael said, but Tony continued.

"I just spoke to Ava. I had a lot of explaining to do, but she'll watch the house and the cat. Your mom will oversee Leo. They both let me know they weren't happy that we didn't tell them what was going on," Tony said with a small smile.

"I'm sure they weren't. Thank you for taking care of that, Tony. Look what just came." Rachael thrust the tickets into Tony's hands.

Tony looked at the plane tickets in disbelief. "This is amazing. What a gift, and what an incredible man we met in Hawaii. He's doing so much for Eddie."

"I know. We're so lucky," Rachael said.

"Right, Mrs. Battaglia, I agree, but I'm sorry our marriage started off so rocky. First Eddie pulls some pranks, and then my father's brother, and all the accidents, too. It doesn't sound real, no matter how many times I say it. But I promise you, that won't be the case from now on. Got all our bad stuff out of the way, as they say. I believe Hank can turn Eddie around, too. He's still young and has a baby on the way. What more incentive does one need?" Tony pulled Rachael into his arms.

Even with all they had been through that night, Rachael still felt wonderful crushed against Tony. "Yes, I feel good about Eddie, and the rest—well, it's over. We need to call Sasha and apologize to her for the way we treated her. I wonder if she will forgive us."

"I'm ahead of you. I already tried calling her. No answer. Hank texted me a little bit ago and told me she was there. Apparently, she sold her car to get to Eddie and paid off some of his debts. I'm hopeful that Eddie wants to apologize to us." Tony smiled.

"You believe he can change, right?" Rachael asked. "And that Sasha will forgive us?"

"I think anything is possible. Look at what we survived in our short time as a family," Tony finished, tapping his chest.

Rachael felt tears form in her eyes. How did she get so lucky to have such a wonderful man? She gazed deep into Tony's brown eyes. She gently touched his lips with hers. Soon they were lost in a kiss.

"Mom?" Kelly asked, entering the kitchen loudly and breaking the newlyweds apart. "Are we going to see Eddie?"

"We are. I was able to get a flight out today," Rachael confirmed, holding the tickets up.

"You are amazing, Mrs. Battaglia," Tony said.

Rachael smiled at her husband and added to her daughter, "The man who is going to help Eddie sent us the tickets."

"Cool. What time do we leave?" Kelly asked with a grin.

"Six forty p.m., but we will get there at 9:10 p.m. with the time change—or just in time to go to bed again." Rachael chuckled.

"I think we should all try to get some sleep. We should leave around two to be safe with traffic. Do you need help with anything, Kelly?" Tony asked.

"No, I'm fine. Stevie is already sleeping. I think I'll try, too, after I make a sandwich." Kelly pulled the bread out.

"I can do that for you, Kelly—" Rachael said.

"Mom, I broke my foot, not my arms," Kelly protested.

"Well, okay. But can you make it up the stairs by yourself?" Rachael asked.

"Yes, I've done it many times since we got back, no problem." Kelly grabbed the peanut butter from the fridge.

"I saw her do it. She'll be fine." Tony grasped Rachael's hand.

"Mom," Kelly paused as Rachael turned around. "Sasha will forgive you, and Eddie will be a new person. The pretty woman told us, remember?"

"The pretty woman?" Rachael asked.

"Yeah, the angel. You already forgot, too? So did Stevie!" Kelly frowned.

"The angel?" Tony repeated.

"Oh, never mind. It was just a dream. But everything will be okay. We can go upstairs together now." Kelly stuffed her sandwich into her pocket. She followed Tony and Rachael up the stairs. Rachael was ready to grab her stubborn, and sometimes strange, daughter if she needed help, but she didn't.

"Night!" Kelly called out and shut her bedroom door.

"Night, Kelly," Rachael called.

"Night." Tony then said, in a lower tone, "Kelly's right. I know it's going to be okay."

"I know it is," Rachael responded, hoping they were all right, as they entered their bedroom. Rachael already missed their new puppy. She was sure Leo would be completely spoiled by the time they got back from Hawaii. She was suddenly exhausted and collapsed onto their new bed, with Tony right next to her.

"You know Kelly has always had an active imagination. I've been meaning to talk to her about it, but maybe right now all she needs is some sleep."

"It has been a long twenty-four hours, and the kids have a lot to process. I'm not worried about her. She is strong, like her mom. I don't think it's a bad thing if she believes in angels," Tony stated.

"First she believes in ghosts, and now angels? Well, it kind of does feel like an angel has been watching over us. As someone said to me, 'At least we are all okay'." Rachael smiled at Tony.

He drew her into another deep kiss. They didn't hear Tootie jump off their dresser and head under the bed.

"I think a nice shower before we sleep is a good idea," Tony suggested.

"I think you're right," Rachael responded, not feeling exhausted anymore.

Tony gathered Rachael into his arms and headed for their shower. They were going to get less sleep than the kids. That was okay with them.

The alarm went off at one, and it was like they had started a race. Soon they crossed the finish line as they got seated on the plane, in first class so Kelly would be comfortable, at Hank's insistence. Rachael was asleep, after taking another pill, by the time they were airborne. Before she knew it, and a half hour ahead of schedule, their plane was landing on Maui. They collected their hastily packed luggage and made their way to the hospital. They were assured by Hank, when they let him know they had arrived safely, that visiting hours wouldn't apply to them.

* * *

EDDIE WAS HOPING to be discharged. Maybe they weren't going to release him until morning. He'd spent most of the day talking things over with Sasha. He told her he would prove himself and earn her trust again. The accident made him see things differently. He saw in her eyes that she still believed in him. That gave him hope. Hank gave him hope, too.

"I only need this one chance, Sasha," Eddie told her. "If I ever do another thing to hurt you again, I want you to leave and take our child with you. I wouldn't deserve to be a husband or father if I hurt you again."

"Are you asking me to marry you?" Sasha asked and blushed.

"Yes, I am. But not until I've done my time and repaid the damage I've done. And I plan on buying you another car. I can't believe you sold yours to get to me and pay off my debts. I promise to repay you for all you've done for me, for the rest of our lives. I have some therapy and rehab to go through, and then I'll be whole for you. Knowing you're there for me will make it all easier to do. All I ask is that you think about it. When I'm done, then answer me if you want to spend your life with me."

"I will agree to that, but if you ever raise a hand to me again or lie to me, I'll leave you. This is your final chance," Sasha warned and put her hands on her hips.

Eddie bit back a smile. He loved her so much. She didn't know how adorable she looked, but it would only make her madder at him if he said that right now. So, he answered her truthfully. "That's all I can

221

ask from you. Even though I don't deserve this, our child does. I'll do right by both of you. I'll work hard and honor and love you like I always should have. I'm not my dad; I realize that. Tony is my new father and a man I can look up to and hope to be like."

"I'm glad to hear you say that. Although I understand why they treated me like they did, it still hurt me," Sasha said as a tear ran down her face and dropped on the cold hospital floor.

"I know they must feel bad, Sasha. It's my fault, not theirs. They'll grow to love you as much as I do. Please keep an open mind about them. They're really good people, even if I was too stupid to see that," Eddie said, right as his family walked through the door.

"Eddie," Rachael said through tears as she gathered her son into a hug. "I'm so glad you're okay. And Sasha, can you forgive us? We didn't know. So many bad things were happening. It turned out to be Tony's uncle, who he didn't even know he had. He was just released from prison and came after us. Like my son just said to you, we were stupid too." Rachael reached out to Sasha.

Sasha stood silently for a moment, studying Eddie and then Rachael before she replied. "Yes, I can forgive all of you, but I don't ever want to feel like that again." Sasha hugged Rachael and then the rest of the family.

"Lookin' good, bro," Stevie said.

"Yeah, I'm glad you're okay," Kelly said, sinking into the chair.

"You have no idea how happy I am to see you," Eddie said. "I'm sorry for the way I treated you, too."

"It's okay," Kelly kissed his cheek.

"Yeah, no prob," Stevie patted his brother's arm.

"I'm not sure how I got so lucky, but I'm going to take advantage of it," Eddie smiled and added, "Do you mind if I call you Dad?"

"Mind? I would be proud if you did." Tony offered his hand, but Eddie reached out for a hug. "Thank you, Eddie."

Rachael caught Hank at the door and hurried to hug him.

"Isn't this amazing?" she asked. "He's okay and ready to make changes. It's a miracle."

"Good thing I believe in miracles." Hank winked at Rachael.

"I do now, too." Rachael smiled.

"You have the room for the week. Sasha can stay with Eddie. They can make their plans before he finishes working on himself," Hank said.

"Tony and all of us are lucky you came into our lives, Hank. Kelly believes in ghosts—and now angels. If there are angels, then you are surely one," Rachael said.

"I'm far from an angel, but I agree with Kelly; they're around us." Hank winked at her.

"Well, all you have done for us—you must let us return the favor someday. I insist you come to visit us," Rachael said.

"I might take you up on that. I usually visit my kids in Southern California as much as they will let me, but this year they're taking a trip to Europe for the holidays. So, I'm open to coming anytime, really. Northern California is one of my favorite places to visit, and it's been a while. I'll let you know," Hank said.

"Well, if you're free at Christmas, I insist you visit us then. And before, if you can make it," Rachael said. "And we might have a grandchild by then. It's due right around Christmas."

"A what?" Kelly asked, looking at Sasha.

"Yeah, Eddie and I are expecting a baby," she confirmed.

"Hey, congrats, bro," Stevie said, while Kelly pulled Sasha into a hug.

They were going to make a great aunt and uncle, Rachael concluded. "I insist, Hank."

"First, let's get Eddie right, and then I will answer you with a date," Hank said.

"You have a deal, and Hank, thank you for all you're doing for our family, including first-class tickets," Rachael said.

"You're welcome." Hank smiled.

The nurse came in to check Eddie, interrupting their reunion. They wanted to keep him one more night. He'd be discharged in the morning. They all left him to get some rest. The next morning, Eddie headed to Hank's house with Sasha. Rachael still wasn't completely sure how Hank pulled off getting Eddie out of jail time, but she was grateful he had pull in the local courts.

The week rolled by quickly as they snorkeled, swam, and just hung out together as a family, with Hank keeping a watchful eye on Eddie when he joined them. Eddie bore bruises from the accident but no other damage. Kelly was content sitting on the beach with Sasha, who kept her company, since she couldn't swim with her broken foot. They were becoming fast friends. Rachael had never felt happier to have them all together. It didn't matter what they did, which was hang around the hotel, except for the amazing day they went to the aquarium and had dinner at the Hard Rock Café.

Soon they were saying goodbye to Eddie and Sasha, with the promise to check on their apartment for them. Rachael intended to make sure their rent and PGE were up to date, at the least. She didn't want Eddie to have any reason to go back to his old ways.

Their plane touched down at the San Francisco airport and woke Rachael up. She would remember this trip as Honeymoon Two—the perfect family vacation. They grabbed some burgers and headed home. Even with the late hour, they were greeted by Leo, Tootie, Ava, and Mae. Rachael gushed about the trip and how well Eddie was doing.

"It's a miracle," Rachael said.

"It is! I'm happy for you." Ava hugged her friend goodbye. "But if you ever keep me out of the loop like that again, well, know I won't be happy. Tim said to tell you the same thing, but your godchild was the most upset," Ava said, grinning ear to ear.

"Godchild? You?" Rachael asked.

Ava beamed and nodded.

"Oh, Ava! Congratulations! I'm so happy for you!" Rachael pulled Ava into a hug and added, "I promise never to sneak off into the night again. The good thing is we don't have a serial killer after us anymore." Rachael pulled away and looked into her best friend's eyes, which were shining—like opals. Rachael shrugged with a sheepish grin.

"You'd better not." Ava frowned for a brief moment before her happiness broke through again and almost blinded Rachael. "I have to go. We'll get together in the next couple of days and really catch up. Besides, I think your mother wants a full update now. Love you." Ava rushed out the door.

Tony was upstairs unpacking, Stevie was visiting Cassie, and Kelly was in her room resting. She had an appointment this week with the specialist. Kelly was convinced she would get a special shoe and be walking normally again soon. Rachael hoped so. She hurried into the kitchen to spend some quality time with her mother, who had a cup of hot Earl Grey tea and Leo waiting for her.

Things got back into a calm routine over the next few weeks. Kelly was in her new shoe and getting around as though she didn't have a broken bone. Stevie got his job at the local coffee shop and was dating Cassie, who was now his number one fan when he played football—or when he sat around the house with her. Rachael had never been happier in her life with her family and Tony. She was two weeks away from starting her new job, but she kept getting sick. Had to be nerves, with her upcoming first day of teaching, she concluded.

"You'll be fine, Rachael. You'll see; they will love you as much as I do," Tony said.

The room began to spin as he was talking, and Rachael ran to the bathroom just in time. Tony sat next to her. "I can't teach school. I can't. Look at me. I'm throwing up, I'm so nervous," Rachael said, rinsing her mouth out.

"What if it's not nerves? What if it's something else?" Tony grinned. "You've been tired, haven't been eating much...I wonder..."

"You mean? You think?" Rachael asked.

Within an hour, they were looking at a plus sign. They were having a March baby. Their life was truly perfect. Rachael kissed Tony and then threw up again. It didn't bother either one of them. They made their announcement. Her grandchild would have a younger aunt or uncle. She smiled. That didn't bother her, either. She was getting her happily ever after, she hoped. Yes, she certainly had a lot of hope.

CHAPTER 15

Five Years Later

*R*achael sat contently on the front porch on Christmas Eve watching her newly turned four-year-old granddaughter, Mazie, and her three-and-a-half-year-old son Lucas playing with Leo on the front lawn on an unusually warm day. Leo loved the kids almost as much as they loved him. Although Lucas was the last child she could have, after complications, she felt blessed and lucky to have him in their lives. His best friend was little Thomas. The boys took after their moms in taste, Ava always kidded. Although Thomas was several months older, Lucas kept up with him, no problem. Rachael adored Mazie and Thomas, almost as much as their proud parents did.

She smiled as she rocked in the swing. Everything had been so perfect since they got back from Hawaii the second time. Eddie had really changed and just finished school. He got a job as a fireman at the local fire station, and he and Sasha had just closed the deal on their first house. They would soon celebrate four years of a happy marriage, but first they had another child to welcome to their family

—a boy. Rachael was waiting for the call saying that the baby was here. She hated the waiting part but was excited too.

Rachael was proud of Sasha, who worked at the college day care while Eddie was in school. She wanted to go back to school too and become a nurse when the kids got in school full-time. She was an incredible mother and wife. Rachael loved that Sasha had proved her wrong about her, and they had become as close as if she were her daughter.

Rachael was especially proud of her son Eddie. He had really made changes in his life and was a joy to be around. Not only had he provided well for his new family (working his way through college), but he'd also developed a close relationship with his siblings. He encouraged them both in college. Kelly was studying to be a marine biologist only an hour and a half away, but Stevie was in Oregon playing football and getting a degree in journalism, of all things. Cassie had broken up with him when he went off to college. He had been heartbroken and hadn't dated again until recently. Cassie, on the other hand, went through many boyfriends. She worked at a local store and still lived at home. She and Kelly barely spoke anymore. It was awkward when Rachael ran into her. She thought Cassie still felt guilty, but honestly, Rachael didn't hold a grudge. She saw that they would never work out. They were too different, but that didn't stop her son from being hurt. Now the poor girl seemed so lost; maybe she would figure it out someday and meet the right guy. Stevie had finally met a new girl, Nina. He wanted his family to meet her after Christmas. That had to be a good sign, Rachael thought.

Stevie was in his last semester and had a professional football team interested in him. Not the Oakland Raiders, but she didn't think it mattered to him. He wasn't sure if he would play professional football or go directly into journalism. Rachael wondered if Nina might have something to say about it. Rachael supported her son no matter what he chose to do, as long as he was happy.

The phone rang.

"Little Ethan is here—all nine pounds of him!" Eddie exclaimed.

"Oh my! Congratulations. I can't wait to meet him. How's Sasha?" Rachael gushed and added, "I love you."

"Sasha did so well and is doing good. I can't wait for you to meet him. He looks a lot like you, Mom. I love you too," Eddie added and hung up before Rachael could respond.

"Lucas, Mazie!" Rachael called. "It's time to go meet Ethan! He's here!"

Rachael had worked through her own pregnancy but had to take off a semester to recover from a rather rough delivery that ended the expansion of their family. Now she was working full-time again and used the day care, with Sasha, and preschool at work. Rachael loved that Lucas and Mazie were in the same class there. The kids were so close you would think they were brother and sister and not uncle and niece. When they got together with Thomas, it was a free-for-all. Rachael loved every minute of it, too.

"Baby here, Rach?" Tony called from upstairs. He'd been practicing daily on his guitar so he could play Christmas songs tomorrow for the family.

"He's here. Best Christmas present ever! Help me gather the troops to go meet him, and we'll call Stevie and Kelly on the way. They can meet us there," Rachael said.

"Be right down." Tony strummed his guitar one final time.

Mazie and Lucas ran and jumped into her lap. She pulled them into a huge hug.

* * *

ZELINA AND ED stood next to Rachael.

"You have another healthy grandchild, Ed. Congratulations," Zelina said.

"Yes, thank you for letting me check on my family, Zelina." Ed smiled at Mazie.

"Yes, well, you earned it, and keep earning it. You have made an art of taking down evildwels. I like to think we are making a difference with these creatures. Let us head over to the hospital and see that new grandson of yours before you meet the next family that needs our help. I will tell you all about it on the way over," Zelina said.

"Okay, and Zelina? You mentioned earlier that Wayne might be getting a second chance. Do you mean like me?" Ed asked.

"Not a second chance like you got. He will be getting stronger input now. He is fighting his recovery, if you can believe that. Some we can never reach, but I am not giving up yet, because where he would go next—well, I do not like to talk about it, as you know." Zelina shivered. "Come on, Grandpa. We have work to do."

"I won't ask, then, because from what I've heard, I'm very lucky. Someday you will show me?"

"Someday, perhaps. It is not my place, though. You understand?"

"It's not your job," Ed said.

"This is not really a job, but it is what I do. You have a lot more to learn first."

"Okay. I can accept that answer, but one thing that puzzles me is why Hank never told Tony about his father."

"Oh, he will not. I made sure of that. He does not want to burden him with that information, and I agree with that." Zelina smiled.

"Makes sense to me. That man...well, you know. Anyway, I have a grandson to meet," Ed replied and glanced back one more time to watch Rachael kiss the children tenderly.

"You do. Come on." Zelina left.

"Take care of them, Rachael." he followed Zelina to the hospital.

"Oh, it's getting cold out," Rachael said and shivered. "You need your coats! Come on, Grandpa/Dad. Let's go!" Rachael herded the children into the new black minivan, which seated eight.

"I'm coming, Mrs. Battaglia. I say it's about time for a date night, don't you think?" he asked and helped her get the kids into their car seats.

"I agree. Even though Mom and Hank just got back from their honeymoon and selling the hotel, the very first thing she asked me was if she could watch Lucas. Ava has also been asking to have Lucas over for a playdate, although she needs to rest more, with the twin girls coming in a couple of months. Who'd have thought? Ava is such an incredible mother. Anyway, we have two babysitting options, but I think Eddie and Sasha might need some help for the first week or so. Then we can get that date night in after the first of the year, don't you think?"

He reached over, kissed her deeply, and looked her in the eye. "I would wait forever for you, Mrs. Battaglia," he said, and she felt that tingling feeling in her stomach.

We will never tire of each other, she thought and smiled.

WATCH

I watch you and wonder:
    Do you love her as much as you love yourself
    Or do you hate her more than you hate yourself?
    Your comforts come first,
    Your contempt directed at her and never yourself.
    Her purpose in life
    Is what she can do for you.

Your purpose is to make her feel
    That she is incapable of that.
    The better question is:
    Why does she keep trying to please you—
    Is it out of love, or fear?
    Does she hate herself more than you do?
    Is she supposed to respect a person who has no respect for her?

No tenderness
    No empathy
    No love
    No feelings at all

But concern for themselves…
It's never his fault
And I wonder why she stays.

I see her side of this, too.
I know she sees how other relationships go.
She admires them openly
With a sad smile, when he is not around.
She works
She is strong
She gives all she has.

Maybe he will change if…
If only I…
He is just stressed…
I don't want to be alone…
No one else would want me…
He needs me.
Underneath, he is a good guy.

Excuses abound
In a vacuum of anger and fear
That feeds the existing darkness
Until it all seems normal.
It isn't.
Help is not welcomed;
That is, until it is—unless it is too late.

Then comes innocence—a child
The woman protects and nurtures
While he watches her,
Pointing out all she does wrong
Without lifting a finger to ease her burdens.
He is her judge and jury.
He is her reality, and now she feels trapped.

In his web spun of lies and hate
    She tries to please,
    To create this illusion of family.
    It will get better, she thinks, *if only...*
    Maybe another child—
    Maybe...
    I watch helplessly.

Any comfort is rejected by his influence.
    Right now, it's only words
    Which cut into her just like a fist would.
    Someday he will cross over from words.
    Maybe he already has.
    That wouldn't be his fault, either.
    Nothing ever is.

Once I thought she was finally free
    But she went back.
    "Can't help who you love," I was told—
    But it isn't love.
    It's hate, insecurity, fear, and above all, control.
    I hope it isn't too late for her.

For all the *hers* out there
    As they feed that bottomless pit of anger
    They are living with—
    It will never be filled
    And it will never change what it is
    But it is *not* love.
    Silence is empty, but heavy on my stomach.

I bite back all the unsaid words
    Even though I've said them before.
    I quietly wait for her to wake up.
    Come to me—

I will help you
I promise.
I do not want to hurt or judge you.

Just see you safe.
And to just see you happy,
To be loved as you are capable of loving.
I wait because you will never be alone.
I wait until you see what we all do…
Not only is he watching
But I am, too.

AUTHOR'S NOTE

This is my first adult fiction. The subject matter of abuse is serious but is told fictionally, here. I've seen many strong and amazing women, and men, after these relationships, rise up with amazing strength and hope. I have complete admiration for them. I know that not all the stories have a happy ending, but here in this world, people atone for their actions. If you are so moved, please reach out and support your local women's shelters and other organizations that help families in need.

First, I must thank my wonderfully supportive and loving husband, along with my family, as I continue my writing journey. I thank my first reader, Danielle L.M. Johnson, for all her invaluable input. My deep appreciation goes to those who made my work readable: Denise at *Artful Editor, Jessica Jesinghaus,* and Diane at *Donovan Literary Services.* The most important thank you is sent to you, the readers who take this journey with me. If you enjoyed this story, please leave a review. It is the best gift an author can receive, with much gratitude!

ABOUT THE AUTHOR

D. L. Finn is an independent California local who encourages everyone to embrace their inner child. She was born and raised in the foggy Bay Area, but in 1990 she relocated with her husband, kids, dogs, and cats to Nevada City, in the Sierra foothills. She immersed herself in reading all types of books but especially loved romance, horror, and fantasy. She always treasured creating her own reality on paper. Finally, surrounded by towering pines, oaks, and cedars, her creativity was nurtured until it bloomed. Her creations include children's books, adult fiction, a unique autobiography, and poetry. She continues on her adventure with an open invitation to all readers to join her. You can learn more about Ms. Finn at her website www.dlfinnauthor.com or email her at d.l.finn.author@gmail.com.

EXCERPT FROM THE BUTTON, ANGELS & EVILDWEL SERIES BOOK 2

Castro Valley, California, 1976

Lynn was suddenly aware of her surroundings. It was tranquil floating above her still body next to angels. She felt indifferent at seeing her pale form hooked up to wires and IVs, although the beeping machines indicated that her body was still alive.

"You have to go back—you have more to do," the female angel informed her.

Lynn met the angel's steady gaze. While she was in awe of her beauty, it was the angel's silver dress that drew her attention. It reminded her of how the water in her grandmother's pool had wrapped her in serenity when she sat at the bottom. She'd loved doing that for as long as she could hold her breath. It was one of the few times she felt safe, cocooned in water where no one could hurt her. That dress, flowing like water around the angel, affected Lynn in the same way as the pool did—it made her feel safe. The angel pushed her hair back, causing it to cascade over her peacock-green wings.

Lynn turned her attention to the male angel. His smile was mesmerizing—like a lava lamp, hot and fluid. *What a babe!* With his long brown hair, strong chiseled features, and green eyes she could get lost in, she felt she could totally spend eternity with him. He smiled broadly at her, but the smile quickly disappeared when the female angel scowled at him. *Wait a minute—do they know what I'm thinking? Not cool!* Lynn felt her face redden.

The embarrassment was quickly erased as both angels smiled at her again. Lynn wished they'd say more, but she wanted to continue to hang out with them. She was feeling a peace she'd never felt before.

She started to express her desire to stay. "I don't—" was all she got out before images of an older version of herself filled her mind all at once. Then she was thrust back—into her life and that pallid body hooked up to the beeping machines.

The angels observed the girl in the hospital bed. "Why did you show Lynn all those things about her life, Zelina? She will not remember them." Thomas shook his head.

"I know, Thomas, but she will feel them when the time comes. I had to give her hope. She has that now. I do not see her trying to kill herself again, although she will get into some very dark situations." Zelina winced.

"But what about the person who wants to kill her? And that woman sitting next to her, who did not love and protect this girl enough to prevent her from getting to this point? I will never under-stand humans." Thomas stumbled through his words. There was more, but he couldn't bring himself to say it out loud.

"Things did not go as they should have for Lynn. We cannot change the past or perfectly predict the future. It is frustrating how limited our influence is sometimes. You saw why Lynn is important— and her kids. She just needs help to get past a few bumps."

"Well, you are blind to Lynn's dark side. She could become like her mother."

Zelina raised a perfectly formed black eyebrow as she held

Thomas's gaze. "She will conquer it. With maturity comes wisdom. Remember that."

Thomas blushed and looked away. "You cannot guarantee that. I know I am young, but I was always at the top of my class and graduated early. And as for that one time—well, at least I tried."

"Yes, you did try. But you were, and are, lacking the wisdom to apply all that knowledge you so quickly acquired. I am able to apply experience to my knowledge when dealing with humans, which is why I believe Lynn can be helped."

Thomas turned his palms up and slightly bowed his head. He was not trying to be disrespectful, but he needed to understand. "How can I get the experience I need if I am only allowed to train?"

"It is possible."

Thomas held back a sigh. Always such vague answers to his questions. He tried another approach. "Can you at least tell me why you brought me to observe this specific girl? I assume there is a reason behind it."

"There is."

Thomas waited a moment. "Okay."

Zelina smiled at him but did not respond.

Thomas expressed his frustration with a sigh. He tried again. "So what about the person who plans to kill Lynn? Can he be helped?"

"You will know things when you need to. As for that man, no. I wish we could help him, but an evildwel has found him."

Thomas shivered. "Oh, I missed that. Those red-eyed black clouds certainly make it hard to help humans. Evildwels are no better than leeches, except the evildwels live off fear and anger instead of blood." Thomas paused, studying Zelina, who kept all expression from her face. "I know, trying does not explain what happened my first time out. I will not make that same mistake again, I promise, but I still believe there is a way to remove an evildwel from its human host in the same way you can a bloodsucking leech. I do not like having to watch and not be able to do anything—it makes no sense."

"Not everything has to be understood or make sense, but I do believe that someday we will be able to expel evildwels from their hosts."

"Well, right, which is why—"

Zelina held her hand up. "Patience. You cannot force things that are not meant for you."

Not meant for me? Thomas had never considered that he might not be the one to accomplish the removal of evildwels. That idea jolted him. Although he had to admit now that he had not been ready his first time out. Thomas had pushed—no, he'd used his charm and good looks—to be sent on assignment after passing all the required tests years ahead of his classmates. He did not want to be that angel who manipulated to get his way anymore. The familiar guilt washed over him, and his normal reaction was to push it inside and bury it. Unfortunately, it kept digging its way back up. He thought it might be helpful that he was now with an angel who had a reputation for being tough.

Time to be honest with Zelina and himself. "If it is not mine to do, then I will do what I can. I understand forcing my own ideas of what I think should be happening instead of what should—well, you know." Thomas paused and shrugged. Zelina didn't respond, so he continued. "I know Lynn is free of evildwels, which is good, but to do what she did to herself, she not only had to feel there was no hope, but she must have turned all her anger and fear on herself."

"Yes, honesty is always the best approach with others and oneself," Zelina said with a slight smile. Thomas turned deep red with the embarrassment of knowing he was with an angel who could peer so deeply within him. Zelina cleared her throat. "I am very glad you are looking at the why of this situation."

"I do understand why she became despondent with a family like that, and then the horrible accident took her best friend from her two years ago—Tammy was her name?"

Zelina nodded grimly. "Yes. Lynn has suffered a great deal over that loss. Tammy and her family were Lynn's safe place. Luckily, Stacy took over that role, but not to the same extent as Tammy and her family. And of course, there is the matter of the person responsible for the accident."

"Yes, he should atone for his part in that tragedy."

"What needs to happen will happen, hopefully. You know that part is very complicated."

Thomas shrugged and sighed. "Yes, I do. But Lynn, she has had many things going against her in her mere fourteen years on Earth, and she has more coming. Luckily for her, you have been with her the whole time after I—you know. So am I here with you to repair the damage my mistake caused?"

"You should know the answer to whether we can fix the past, but I will refresh your memory. We only have right now. What is needed from you is your history with this family and approach to things. What you will be given is guidance to help this particular girl." Zelina looked away while twisting her black hair and laying it over her right shoulder. She smoothed her flawless dress.

"As much as I would like to change what happened, I am not so sure I am the right angel to do this." Thomas swallowed hard and then frowned. He was glad Zelina was focused on her gown and not him. He knew feeling sorry for himself was not going to help. He had been told that more than once. "I have truly tried to accept what transpired —and the result. I have been learning and training hard, as suggested. I thought I had moved forward. Yet being here with his daughter, it all comes rushing back to me."

Zelina met his gaze with a surprisingly sympathetic expression. "Yes, I know you have been holding on to this. It really is time to let it go. Guilt has no place in an angel's heart." She smiled and added, "I promised I could get you through this, so you had better not make me a liar."

"I...you..." Thomas could not reply as he held the tears back. *That night.* He was supposed to protect Lynn's mother, Carrie. Instead, he had tried to help Leonard, her husband. Thomas had made the wrong choice.

Zelina moved closer and wrapped a wing around him to comfort him. Thomas did not trust himself to speak. The moment of silence lasted for what seemed like forever.

"This is not about me or my feelings. I should not have said that about making me into a liar." Zelina retracted her wing and smiled gently at him. "And that is the closest thing to an apology you will get out of me," she added in a lighter tone,

Thomas's dark mood vanished. "Okay, thanks."

"You are not through with Lynn and her family yet. And Thomas, I am pleased you have more clarity than you used to."

Thomas prevented a smile from forming on his lips at her compliment, but he was having a hard time knowing what to do with himself, or perhaps with his old feelings. He focused on his hands and suddenly wished angels had pockets. It was something he had seen humans do when they were uncomfortable—bury their hands in their convenient compartments that were filled with objects they could move around, like coins. He knew Zelina was waiting for a response. He didn't have one, even though he'd spent many hours rehashing his mistake since the night it happened. It would haunt him forever. But now it seemed like he was getting this second chance, so he decided he had better angel up and deal with it.

Thomas forced himself to look at Zelina. She was not smirking at him like he thought she would be; in fact, her expression indicated that she felt sorry for him, which made him more uncomfortable. "What is expected of me?"

Zelina put a hand on his shoulder and looked into his eyes with an intensity he had not seen in other angels. "Nothing you are not capable of. Remember this is not about how you feel about past actions. As angels, we do not experience regret, only possibilities. Humans are free to make their choices. You need to let their choices and your actions go and learn from them from this moment on. Understood?"

"Yes, but it is not easy. No one ever lets me forget—including me."

"I understand. I know this has been said to you before, but I hope you really listen this time. Part of your issue is you have allowed pride and self-pity to rule you. It was an evildwel that killed Lynn's father, not you. Yes, his death happened when you appeared to him as an angel, but the evildwel was in control of his actions, not you, when Leonard drove off that cliff. To be clearer, Leonard made the choices that drew the evildwel to him. Then there was Carrie. I understand you tried to get the evildwel out of her husband, hoping her life would be better, but Leonard was not a good man, even before he was an evildwel host. Carrie always made poor choices when it came to men, including Lynn's stepdad. As for Lynn, there is still hope for her, even though she chose to drink herself to death. I was right next to her through all of that. All I could do was encourage her to land on her side so she might live. She did.

"We can focus on the best possible solution for now and the future using our wisdom and judgment. We both know suicide is the darkest experience for any human." Zelina shook her head and wiped a tear away. "What I see in you is that you are willing to take chances to save humans from themselves. Now you need to go forward and do things for the right reasons. I believe when you are fully developed, you could be one of the strongest angels we have helping humans."

"You think that?" Thomas asked in disbelief.

"Yes, but do not allow your pride to absorb that statement. That is what got you into trouble before."

Thomas shook his wings out and smoothed his hair. "I will try."

"We cannot just try—this is too important. We have to work from here." Zelina put her hand on his chest.

"My heart?"

"Yes. Lynn's father is making progress, reviewing his life and reflecting on what *he*—not an angel or evildwel—could have done differently. Carrie—well, we will see. It is up to Carrie, though, not us. With all that in mind, I am to be your teacher now. I expect you to listen and watch closely. I will be showing you how to follow the rules and which rules can be bent—just a bit—without, well, you know." Zelina shrugged.

Thomas smiled. "I welcome the chance to work with you. You are known to be a hard-nosed angel."

Zelina smiled back. "Thank you. I have heard that once or twice.

Now I want you to watch Lynn's reaction when she wakes up. See how she responds to things. That will be important. But we have a few years to work on your training before everything goes sideways for her."

"I look forward to my training, although I am not looking forward to when things go sideways for Lynn."

"Neither am I." Zelina sighed.

Thomas nodded solemnly. They turned their attention to Lynn as she awakened from an eight-hour coma after her failed suicide attempt. A matronly nurse rushed into the hospital room to soothe the agitated patient; a youthful, sleep-deprived doctor followed to check her vitals.

Her mother sat immobile in her chair until the doctor declared that Lynn would be all right, then the first sign of forced compassion crossed Carrie's face. It was a shame Lynn would spend the next four years living with a woman whose feelings were so buried that she might as well have been a robot. At least Lynn had a strong rebellious side that would carry her until she could move out. After that, the same rebellious side might prove to be a problem. Thomas hoped he and Zelina would be enough to help her. Zelina touched his arm and nodded. It was going to be a long seven years.

CASTRO VALLEY, CALIFORNIA, 1983

In high school Lynn Hill had a black button with white writing that said "Fuck Off and Die." It was pinned to her worn, flower-embroidered denim purse. Lynn relocated her button to the inside of her purse when she graduated, so only she could see it. It wasn't that Lynn had suddenly changed her attitude upon accepting her diploma with 451 other people representing the first class of the new decade, either. As far as she could tell, 1980 was no different than 1979. What prompted the removal of her audacious public expression was the acquisition of a job and an apartment, or basically becoming a responsible adult. Lynn was mindful that appearing to be an upstanding citizen was necessary, an opinion confirmed by her old history teacher.

"Young women who are successful do not have swear words pinned to the outside of their purse," the teacher, who reminded Lynn of a shriveled apple doll, had informed her while handing back her essay in the final month of high school.

Lynn was fully aware that the teacher didn't like her, but she didn't care. Most teachers didn't like her, but she always got A's and didn't cause problems, so they usually left her alone. No one had ever tried to take the button away, but Lynn did get some looks, which she shrugged off.

She was convinced that more than one teacher had the same sentiment, but they had to pretend to be responsible adults, like she was doing now. Lynn only hid the button from her parents, who would have shown their displeasure in ways both physically and emotionally painful. She escaped that house the day she turned eighteen, moving into an apartment with her best friend, Stacy.

Lynn's fingers brushed across that button on the inside of her purse as she searched for her strawberry lip gloss. It wasn't that she hated everyone and wanted them to die, as her button stated; she simply didn't trust most people. Why should she? They only managed to disappoint or hurt her, but she wished for their absence, not their actual demise. Although there were a few people she felt the world would be better off without. They seemed to have no reason to exist other than to cause others pain.

Lynn applied her lip gloss, slipped it back into her purse, and pasted on a fake smile. It was her final touch before entering the rundown bar with Stacy. A blonde and a brunette together got the attention of guys at the bars, Stacy insisted. Lynn didn't bother pointing out that it was Stacy's large bust and fashion-model looks that got all that interest. She knew Stacy was aware of her effect on the opposite sex.

The young women flashed their fake IDs to the guy at the door. It was obvious that the old biker didn't care about the age of the females who entered the bar as long as they were somewhat pretty, boosted alcohol sales, and had a card, legal or not, that showed they were old enough. Lynn was immediately greeted by loud music, a local band whose name she had already forgotten. They were playing a current hit from the radio. *No big deal, just some wannabes,* Lynn thought. There wasn't even a cover to see them. How good could they be?

Stacy and Lynn squeezed between the red vinyl barstools to order their drinks. "I know you, I walked with you once upon a dream..." Why was the song from *Sleeping Beauty* in her head? She hadn't thought of it in years. It had been one of her favorite songs when she was a young girl. She used to listen to the record while following along in the book. She would sing the song loudly if no one was around and pretend she was dancing with her prince through the forest.

In those days she believed she would find her prince someday. Did she still believe in love and happily ever after? Not really. She sighed right as the bartender caught her glance. He had wavy brown hair and the most beautiful brown eyes she'd ever seen. She gulped and started to sweat. She needed a drink, and fortunately, Stacy was already ordering them.

"Can I see your identification, please?" said the bartender with those amazing eyes in a voice that was used to talking over loud music.

"We just showed them to the guy at the door," Stacy shouted in response, showing off her perfect white teeth in a big smile.

"I'm sure you did, but humor me. Show me your papers," he replied.

Stacy sighed and handed her ID to the bartender. Lynn had thrown the fake International Identification Card she'd gotten in Berkeley two years ago back into her purse. It only worked in some clubs, and this had always been one of them. Besides, she was only a few weeks away from legal drinking age. She dug out the photo ID that said her name was Andrea Louis.

"Thank you. I see your papers are in order, Andrea and Sally," the bartender said, with an engaging grin directed at Stacy.

"They are." Stacy's loud voice was almost drowned out by the band. She gave Lynn an eyeroll while the bartender made their drinks. Lynn responded with a slight grin.

He handed them their drinks with a small smile. "Sorry, I've been wanting to do that since I saw the movie *Firefox* last weekend. It's still playing at the Chabot Theater in Castro Valley. Seen it yet?"

"Uh, no, but I heard it was cool. It came out last year, right?" Stacy said, immediately sipping her drink through the narrow red straw.

"Yeah, it did. They're showing it again because Clint Eastwood has another movie coming out soon. Promotion thing." He shrugged and continued. "Well, you guys should see it before it's gone. I wouldn't mind seeing it again, if you want…"

Stacy showed her lack of interest by pretending to watch the band, so Lynn responded with one of their standby stories. "Oh, sorry. But, um, we have boyfriends, and they would mind if we went to the movies with another guy. They don't care if we dance, but going to the movies…" Lynn felt oddly disappointed. *Too bad, because he has a face I could spend my life looking at.* But he only had eyes for Stacy. *No happily ever after in real life,* she decided. She wished Stacy would brush off all her adoring fans herself. Instead, she always left that to Lynn.

"Well, if you ever find yourself unattached, you know where to find me, right? My name is Kent, by the way." He pointed to his name tag.

Lynn had done her job, so Stacy responded. "Totally, thanks, Kent. How much do we owe you?" She held up a ten-dollar bill and gave her best "I really like you—please don't make me pay for my drink" expression.

"The first one's on the house," Kent said with a wink.

"Oh, cool. Thanks, Kent," Stacy said with a practiced fake smile that Kent quickly returned.

They all fell for Stacy, no matter how she acted. Lynn thought it would be nice if, occasionally, guys fawned all over her. *Oh well, at least Stacy knows how to get free drinks.*

"Let's get a table," Stacy said. "Thanks again."

"Sure."

Stacy confidently led the way, as if she expected all eyes to be on her. And they were—even the ones belonging to men who already had a woman with them. Lynn smiled when she saw one get hit on the arm for looking.